# I AM NOT A *Vampire* (ANYMORE)

# I AM NOT A *Vampire* (ANYMORE)

DARCY MILLER

RANDOM HOUSE NEW YORK

Random House Books for Young Readers
An imprint of Random House Children's Books
A division of Penguin Random House LLC
1745 Broadway, New York, NY 10019
penguinrandomhouse.com
getunderlined.com



Editor: Elizabeth Stranahan
Cover Designer: Trisha Previte
Interior Designer: Megan Shortt
Copy Editor: Clare Perret
Managing Editor: Rebecca Vitkus
Production Manager: Liz Sutton

Library of Congress Cataloging-in-Publication Data is available upon request.
ISBN 978-0-593-90316-2 (trade)—ISBN 978-0-593-90317-9 (lib. bdg.)—
ISBN 978-0-593-90318-6 (ebook)

Palm trees by EMA/stock.adobe.com.

The text of this book is set in 11.5-point Adobe Garamond Pro.

Manufactured in the United States of America
1st Printing

The authorized representative in the EU for product safety and compliance is Penguin Random House Ireland, Morrison Chambers, 32 Nassau Street, Dublin D02 YH68, Ireland, https://eu-contact.penguin.ie.

**FOR MY LOCAL LIBRARY**

**(AND YOURS, TOO)**

# I AM NOT A *Vampire* (ANYMORE)

# CHAPTER One

IT'S EIGHTY-THREE DEGREES OUTSIDE, AND I'M wearing leg warmers.

Despite the early morning hour, the parking lot already smells like melting asphalt and salt, the humidity so thick that I may as well be swimming. With every step, I can feel my painstakingly crimped hair deflating a little more.

By the time I reach the school's main doors, I'm panting slightly with effort, and my ridiculous spandex leotard is sticky with sweat. When I step inside, the air-conditioning blasts me with frigid, subarctic air.

Awesome.

Now I'm both sweaty *and* freezing to death.

Never change, Florida!

After dumping my backpack in my locker, I fan the front of my leotard back and forth, rummaging around for my chemistry notebook.

As per usual, I'm running late, which means I have . . . exactly nineteen minutes to finish my homework.

Okay, fine.

So I have exactly nineteen minutes to *start* my homework.

*Sue me.*

I'm just wrapping my fingers around the pencil when I sense someone behind me. I feel them before I see them, their breath warm on the back of my neck.

I stiffen, my nerve endings humming suddenly to life.

Sneaking up on me is a bad idea.

Every fiber of my being tenses, telling me to attack.

I tighten my grip on my pencil.

As the unseen hand slides around my waist, I brace my right arm, jabbing it backward as hard as I can. I hear a loud grunt as my elbow sinks into my would-be attacker's stomach, but I don't pause, sweeping my leg out to hook their ankle and yanking them to the ground instead.

Whipping around, I face them, the pencil raised menacingly above my head, my teeth bared in a snarl. One wrong move and I can sink it into their heart faster than—

"Lily, what the hell!" Max cries, throwing up an arm to shield himself. "It's *me*!"

I freeze, stilling my hand above his chest.

"It's *me*!" Max says again, his voice barely audible over the thundering of blood in my ears. "It's *Max*!"

My hand goes slack, the pencil trembling in my grip.

"Max?" I ask, my voice breathless.

Not an enemy.

*Max.*

My *boyfriend.*

Whom I tried to stab with a pencil. In the middle of the hallway. While wearing leg warmers.

Max blinks up at me, his blue eyes wide with alarm.

Across the hall, I can see Eve Kha backing away from us, a hand pressed to her mouth in shock. Next to her, Olivia Andrews already has her phone out, her eyes whipping gleefully between me and her screen.

She's not the only one filming us, I notice, peering dazedly around. It feels like half the senior class has gone full paparazzi, their excited murmurs growing louder and louder as their voices overlap into a single, chaotic din.

Well.

It looks like this day just got even more awesome.

Turning back to Max, I try to force a smile.

"Hey," I say. "Sorry. You, um . . . startled me."

"No shit," Max says, still staring at the pencil in my hand. Suddenly painfully aware of the fact that I'm straddling Max in public, I shift my weight backward and scramble to my feet, guiltily tossing away the pencil and offering him a hand.

Out of sight, out of mind, am I right?

For a split second, Max hesitates.

I watch in disbelief as a nervous-looking freshman darts forward, scooping the pencil from the floor like some sort of crime scene trophy.

"Seriously?" Max asks the kid.

Flushing a mottled red, the freshman mumbles something vaguely apologetic before scurrying away toward his friends.

I can feel the panic building in my throat, the cold sweat gathering beneath my armpits.

Oh, God.

Is Max about to break up with me?

Did I just ruin my entire life *with a pencil*?

I'm already mid-spiral by the time Max grabs my hand, his fingers warm around mine.

"Call me paranoid," he says, hauling himself to his feet. "But I'm suddenly *very* glad I didn't do one of those surprise promposals."

He grins down at me and, for a second, the brightness of his smile makes me dizzy.

Max is all white teeth and glowing skin and wide shoulders; I swear, he probably came out of the womb with perfectly tousled blond hair.

Sensing the end of the show, the rest of the hallway slowly begins returning to its scheduled programming.

"Technically, I asked *you* to the dance," I point out, relief pouring through my veins.

This year's prom theme is Love Among the Stars. Which, for the record, was *also* the dance's theme in the original 1976 horror movie *Carrie.*

Apparently no one is concerned that it . . . did not end well for anyone involved.

"Are you sure you're okay?" I ask Max, eyeing him anxiously up and down. He looks worrisomely natural in his '80s-rich-kid prepster costume: a pastel pink cashmere sweater knotted casually over the shoulders of his polo shirt, and his thick blond hair feathered perfectly on the sides.

"I'm fine," he says. "Although you might have punctured my spleen with your elbow." Pointing at his side, he pretends to wince. I'm glad I didn't go with my initial instinct: slam him so hard into the lockers that he left an indent.

"Your spleen actually is on your left side," I say. Stepping forward, I rest my forehead against his chest. "But point taken."

My head fits snugly beneath his chin, right in the hollow of his throat. His sweater is scratchy against my cheek, and I can hear his heart beating against my ear.

He holds himself stiffly, at first, and I can feel myself start to spiral again. But then his arms come up, pulling me closer, his chin dropping to rest on the top of my head.

"Have I mentioned that I'm really, *really* sorry?" I ask, burying my head against his chest.

"It's fine," Max says. "I mean, that foot sweep thing?" He pulls his head back a tiny bit, looking down at me. "Badass. Seriously."

A smile tugs at the corner of my mouth. "Yeah? So, you'll still be my date to the dance?"

Logically, I know that prom is an exclusive, outdated tradition that promotes unrealistic standards of beauty, creates unnecessary financial burdens, and romanticizes the monarchy system.

But still.

I really, *really* want to go.

"Obviously," Max says. "Hey, speaking of which, you're wearing black, right?"

"Yeah," I say, thinking unenthusiastically of the floor-length satin dress currently hanging in my closet. Is it disturbingly poofy? Yes. But more importantly, it's also cheap. "Why?"

"My mom wants to order you a . . . what's it called? The

flower thing?" Max reaches out, tracing a line across the inside of my wrist to demonstrate.

"Corsage," someone says behind me, their voice flat. "It's called a corsage."

I turn to see Max's best friend, Ezra, leaning against a nearby locker, his head tipped back far enough to keep his dark curly hair from falling in his eyes.

"Oh," I say. "Hey, Ezra. I didn't, um . . . see you there."

For some reason, Ezra always manages to catch me off guard.

I step self-consciously away from Max, feeling myself flush.

Ezra runs his bloodshot gaze up and down my costume, his dark brown eyes dull with exhaustion. There's a grayish tinge to his skin, and his curls are sticking sweatily to his forehead.

He looks sick.

Or hungover.

Or possibly both.

"Nice outfit," he says at last, letting his head drop back against the locker. "Very . . . *flammable*-looking."

"Aw, thanks, Ezra," I say sweetly, adjusting the strap of my leotard. "Have I mentioned how much I value your opinion?"

Sunrise Harbor High has a full week of activities leading up to the prom, starting with today's Eighties Day and ending with a School Spirit–themed pep rally on Friday.

Because nothing says *school spirit* like mandatory attendance, am I right?

Anyway, as a member of the prom committee, I'm expected to participate in all the dress-up days. Which, up until this very moment, seemed like a great idea.

"Don't mind Ezra," Max says, sliding his hand reassuringly around my waist. "He's allergic to fun."

Raising my chin defiantly, I lean back into Max's solid warmth, giving Ezra a considering look.

"Now that you mention it, he *is* looking a little green," I observe.

"I'm fine," Ezra says, his eyes still closed. "*You're* the one who went full *John Wick* on her boyfriend, remember?"

Max lowers his head to murmur softly in my ear. "Mmm. I love those movies."

He goes to drop a kiss on my cheek, but I purposefully turn instead, slipping my hands around his neck.

Ignoring Ezra, I lean in, kissing Max squarely on the mouth.

Max's kiss is warm, and familiar, and safe.

Exactly like him.

And for a minute, at least, the rest of the world disappears: There's no Ezra, no Olivia, no hallway full of people still whispering my name . . .

There's no one but me and Max: a regular boy and a regular girl, kissing in the hall before class.

It's absolutely perfect.

Somewhere in the background, I can hear the first bell ringing. I cling more tightly to Max's shoulders until Ezra clears his throat.

"Um," he says. "You guys *do* realize that Mr. Markowitz is staring at you, right?"

Max gives a little choke, pulling abruptly away from me.

I turn to see the grizzled, middle-aged teacher watching us

from his doorway, his arms crossed against his chest in disapproval.

"Hey," Ezra says, raising his hands innocently. "Listen, if that's your thing, don't let me stop you."

Ignoring Ezra even harder, I turn back to Max, straightening the popped collar of his polo shirt. "You should go," I say. "The final bell's going to ring soon."

Unlike me, who's signed up for the absolute bare minimum of graduation requirements, Max has spent the past four years taking every AP class he can get his hands on. A bunch of Florida colleges have already offered him swimming scholarships, but he's still waiting to hear back from his dream school: Dartmouth.

Which also happens to be his mother's alma mater.

What a coincidence!

Anyway, Max's AP Bio class is all the way on the other side of the school. Where the bathrooms are actually clean, and the air-conditioning *doesn't* smell like leaking Freon.

I hear it's nice.

"Okay, yeah," Max says, dropping a final kiss on the top of my head. "I'll see you at lunch." He takes a few steps, then turns, pointing a pair of finger guns in my direction. "And watch that pencil," he says. "If I hear about you trying to stab some other dude, I'm going to be jealous."

"Ha ha," I say. "You're *hilarious.*"

Max grins as he rounds the corner. "And don't you forget it!"

As I turn back to my locker, Ezra shakes his head, looking physically pained by our interaction.

"You know what?" he asks. "Maybe I really *do* feel sick."

Ducking my chin, I rummage around in my backpack. Maybe, by some strange miracle, I can finish my homework in the next four minutes. Well, as long as I can find a new—

"Pencil?" Ezra offers innocently, holding one up for me.

Slamming my locker shut, I turn on my heel.

I can feel Ezra smirking at me all the way to class.

# CHAPTER *Two*

"QUESTION."

Sarita Peterson drops her lunch tray onto the table next to mine with a loud *thunk*, peering down at me with a stern look. "Did you or did you not try to stab your boyfriend with a pencil this morning, and, if so, *follow-up* question: Why am I hearing about it over freaking *social media* instead of from you?"

I close my eyes, suppressing a wave of panic.

"Is it everywhere?"

"Of *course* it's everywhere," Sarita says, looking at me in exasperation. "You tried to *stab your boyfriend with a pencil.*"

Gathering her costume in both hands, she climbs awkwardly over the bench to sit next to me.

I tilt my head to the side, taking in her old-fashioned blouse and voluminous, floor-length skirt. Her lace-edged collar is high enough to brush her chin, and the sleeves of her shirt billow ridiculously outward before gathering tightly at the wrist.

"Why do you look like a Victorian governess?" I ask, reaching for a French fry. "It's Eighties Day."

Sarita gives me a smug smile, slicking her short black hair away from her face.

"Nobody said we couldn't do the *1880s*," she points out. "Although I'm starting to have second thoughts." She grimaces down at her heavy black skirt, plucking the bottom of it in annoyance. "Do you know how hard it is to *walk* in this thing?"

"Oh, please," I say dismissively. "You're not even wearing a bustle."

Sarita gives me an odd look, and I hastily grab another fry. "So, what are people saying about me?" I ask. "Or do I not want to know?"

"Well," Sarita says. "The prevailing rumor is that Max cheated on you, although the idea that you're a paranoid schizophrenic is also being floated." She wrinkles her nose. "This school needs to have some serious conversations about mental health issues, by the way, because there are some *problematic* attitudes being thrown around out there."

"Great," I say, swallowing hard.

Is it my imagination, or are Shay Wilson and the rest of the tennis team all peering in my direction? And did that girl dressed as Madonna *point* at me as she walked by?

I push my plastic tray away, the smell of hot grease suddenly making me nauseous.

Plastering a bright smile on my face, I wave at Shay.

Sarita eyes me over the rim of her soda, forcing her lace-edged collar down with one hand. "So, what did Max do to piss you off?" she asks. "Do you need me to kick his ass, too? Because I'll do it," she adds warningly. "I'm wearing my Docs under this."

I give up on Shay, turning back to Sarita.

"I'm pretty sure RISD frowns on their incoming freshmen having violent criminal records," I tell Sarita, who's been accepted to the Rhode Island School of Design's Apparel Design program for *weeks*. "But thanks for the offer. Besides, it was nothing," I add. "He just surprised me."

Sarita gives me a skeptical look. "That's it? You went all Stabby McStabsALot on him because he *surprised* you?"

"First of all, I don't *love* the nickname," I say. "Secondly, I didn't get a lot of sleep last night. I guess I'm a little . . . jumpy."

Sarita leans in, absently fiddling with her necklace as she peers more closely at my face. "Now that you mention it, you *do* look tired."

Tact: not Sarita's strong point.

"It's fine," I say. "Things are busy right now, that's all. I have work, and prom committee stuff . . ."

Sarita narrows her eyes, looking unconvinced.

"Plus, I'm pretty sure I'm failing American history," I add, deliberately baiting the hook.

Sarita bites immediately.

"Did you sit by Astrid today? Did she say anything about me?" She looks down at her outfit, her forehead wrinkling in concern. "You think she'll get my costume, right? Like, she'll think it's funny in a cool way, not funny in a weird way?"

I've been in Florida for less than a year, but I can recite every detail of Sarita's crush on Astrid Olson in painful, agonizing detail. (It starts with a dramatic monologue during freshman-year theater camp and ends with, well . . . it doesn't end.)

"Astrid is dressed as Nancy Reagan," I tell Sarita. "So, yeah. I'm pretty sure she's going to think your costume is funny in a cool way."

Sarita tucks the chain of her necklace back into her frothy lace collar, preening.

"It's good, right? Ooh, and guess what?" She pauses, doing a little drumroll against the fake-wood table. "Mia's parents are out of town tonight! Which means she's having a *PAR-TY*!"

She raises her voice on the last word, throwing her arms wide like Oprah and nearly knocking my bottle of water over in the process.

"Tonight?" I ask, picking the water up for safekeeping. "But it's a Monday."

"Oh my God," Sarita says, rolling her eyes. "What are you, a hundred years old?"

I take a sip of water, rolling my eyes right back at her.

"Anyway, I'm not taking 'no' for an answer," Sarita says, her voice firm. "My mom left for her conference thing this morning, which means that for *once* in my life, I'm lacking adult supervision. Plus, Mia said that Astrid will be there. We're *going*."

"Going where?" Max asks, dropping his tray on the table. Absently, I scoot over, my thigh brushing against his as I watch Ezra lower himself gingerly onto the opposite bench. Ezra sets an unopened bottle of Gatorade down in front of him, and I glance away quickly before he can catch me looking.

"Mia's party," Sarita says. "Tonight. Be there or be square."

"What if I want to be there *and* be square?" Max asks, reaching for one of my fries. "Is that allowed?"

I slap his hand away. "Hey! I'm still eating those."

Max holds up his hands in surrender. "Whatever you say, Stabby McStabsALot."

I give Sarita a look.

"What?" she asks innocently. "It's catchy!"

Max takes advantage of my momentary distraction to pinch another fry from my tray.

Across the table, Ezra slumps forward on his elbows, resting his sweaty forehead against his hands.

"Is Ezra dying?" Sarita asks Max and me. "Because Ezra looks like he's dying."

"Ezra is *fine*," Ezra says through clenched teeth. "All I need is a couple of Advil. Or thirty."

Sarita shrugs, turning to Max. "Nice hair, by the way," she says. "You look like James Spader from *Pretty in Pink*."

"Thanks," Max says, taking an enormous bite from his cheeseburger. "My mom did it for me this morning."

Sarita opens her mouth to reply, then thinks better of it.

"I'm going to let that one pass," she says primly. "But only because I'm a *lady*." Plucking at the side of her skirt, she dips her head in an exaggerated, seated curtsy.

Max gives an oblivious shrug, turning back to me.

"So, what do you think?" he asks. "About Mia's?"

"I can't," I say. "I have work tonight."

Burger Queen may not be the most glamorous job in town, but at least it pays the rent.

Well, almost.

"You can meet us there after your shift," Sarita commands me. "Aren't you done at nine?"

"Yeah, but I'd have to stop at home to shower and change and everything . . ." I trail off, hoping that my tone of voice is enough of a discouragement.

Across the cafeteria, a table full of lacrosse kids huddled together bursts into sudden, raucous laughter. My fingers tighten around my water bottle, the flimsy plastic buckling inward, but to my relief, no one seems to notice. After a second, I realize they're cheering for an enormous tower of empty pudding cup containers that they've stacked in the middle of the table.

Your future leaders of America, ladies and gentlemen.

"I could pick you up, if you want," Max offers, stuffing another huge bite of cheeseburger in his mouth. "Maybe see the inside of your place, finally?"

I feel Ezra's eyes flick curiously in my direction.

I stare back at him, daring him to say something, but he drops his eyes, fiddling with the label of his Gatorade bottle.

I mean, sure. Is it *slightly* weird that Max and I have been dating since September and I still haven't invited him over? Maybe. But Max lives in a three-story mansion stocked with endless Costco snacks and fizzy water. And *I* live in a shitty motel across from a strip mall.

Honestly, where would *you* rather hang out?

"Isn't Mia's house right by yours?" I ask Max, hedging my response. "I'm all the way on the other side of town."

"You could come straight from work," Max says. "You don't have to go home to change. It's not like anyone cares what you're wearing."

"Do you even *hear* the words that come out of your mouth sometimes?" Sarita asks in disbelief.

"Whatever," Max says. "*You're* the one dressed like Wednesday Addams. Besides, Lily looks cute in her uniform." He leans over, dropping a kiss on my shoulder. "And you smell like French fries after work," he adds. "You *know* how I feel about French fries."

Ezra abruptly stands, pushing his unopened Gatorade across the table. Without a word, he turns and walks away.

"Now look what you've done," Sarita says in exasperation. "What did I tell you about grossing people out with public displays of affection at the lunch table?"

"I'll go check on him," Max says, shoveling the last of his burger down in two bites. With a final grin in my direction, he stands up, stealing one last French fry for the road. "See you tonight."

"*Maybe!*" I call after him. "You'll *maybe* see me tonight!"

Max turns, giving me an unironic thumbs-up. I watch as he threads his way through the cafeteria with his ridiculous feathered hair and his even more ridiculous relentless optimism.

"Now," Sarita says crisply, reaching for Ezra's unopened Gatorade. "Let's talk about what you're going to wear to Mia's. Because no matter what Max might think, khaki is *not* your color."

# CHAPTER *Three*

SOMEHOW, I MANAGE TO MAKE IT THROUGH the rest of the day without any more embarrassing displays of public humiliation. Well, aside from when a junior in my biology class gets the bright idea to play the *Psycho* music every time I look in his direction.

I laugh along with everyone else while making a mental note to destroy him in the future.

After school, Sarita and I stay to help out with the decorations for the dance. Noah Coates, the self-appointed head of the prom committee, puts me in charge of cardboard stars and then walks around the gym, periodically yelling at all of us through a *literal megaphone.*

I've said it before, and I'll say it again: power corrupts.

By the time I leave, my back is killing me, my scissors hand has cramped up into a claw, and I've inhaled approximately six pounds of glitter.

Still, things could be worse; Sarita has spent the past hour and a half trying to untangle the enormous plastic bin full of twinkle lights, which have all balled together into some sort of horrifying rat king situation.

"Take me with you," she begs as I hurry past, brushing the worst of the glitter from my backpack. *"Please."*

I flash her a sympathetic expression but don't have time to stop; thanks to Noah's exacting papercraft standards, I'm already running late.

I throw my weight against the heavy gym door, blinking against the sudden glare of late-afternoon sunlight. The parking lot is nearly empty, and my shoes are sticking to the half-baked asphalt; every step feels like ripping Velcro. Despite the heat, a small shiver of unease runs down my back. I can't help feeling exposed out here; like I'm caught on a piece of flypaper.

I hurry to my shitty Ford Fiesta and slip inside, automatically cranking the AC to the max. Taking a deep breath of stale, humid air, I head to work.

The next few hours pass in a haze of hot grease and spilled soda and *Thank you, come again!*s. By the time the dinner rush finally ends, my cheeks ache from smiling, and I've burned myself twice on the grill.

My manager, Chad, takes pity on me, sending me to the drive-thru for the rest of my shift. I take my history textbook with me, fully intending to brush up on the Salem witch trials between orders.

But instead, for the first time all day, I take out my phone.

A sick feeling runs through me as I scroll through my feed.

Oh, God.

Sarita was right; the videos of me are *everywhere.*

My hands shake as I stare down at my screen, watching myself on an endless, repeating loop.

Me, snarling down at Max, my pencil poised menacingly above his chest.

Me, gazing around the hallway, blinking in horrified realization.

Me, scrambling to my feet, my cheeks flushed the same virulent shade of pink as my costume.

Me, me, *me.*

Over and over and over again.

*All over the internet, for anyone to see.*

I can feel the panic bubbling up in my chest, fear licking at the palms of my hands.

*Breathe,* I tell myself, dropping my phone to the counter. *BREATHE.*

Closing my eyes, I lean forward, resting my forehead against the smeared glass of the pass-through window.

*In.*

*Out.*

*In.*

*Out.*

Gradually, my pulse begins to slow, the heat in my palms fading to a dull ache.

*Everything is fine. There's no need to panic.*

At least, not yet.

I jump when my headset beeps as a car runs over the loop, pulling to a stop in front of the menu board.

"Welcome to Burger Queen," I say automatically. "What can we make fresh for you this evening?"

"Uh, yeah, can I grab a spicy chicken sandwich, an order of cheesy bites, and a side of sweet, sweet lovin'?"

I turn toward the monitor, where a familiar face grins up at me through the camera.

"Hello?" Max leans forward from the passenger seat, half hanging through the open window of his bright yellow Jeep. For some reason, Ezra is driving, his expression resigned as Max clambers over him. "Anyone there?"

I take one last, deep breath, forcing myself back to the present.

"I'm sorry, sir," I say into my headset. "But I'm actually required to contact the police when someone uses the phrase 'sweet, sweet lovin'.' Legally speaking, it's a crime against humanity."

Max's grin widens. He's changed back into a regular T-shirt and shorts, his still-shower-damp hair pushed messily back from his forehead. "Why don't I pull forward, and you can make a citizen's arrest?" he asks, waggling his eyebrows suggestively.

"Seriously?" Ezra mutters from the driver's seat, shoving ineffectually at Max's solid frame. "Get *off*!"

"You *do* realize my boss monitors this line sometimes, right?" I ask Max.

"Shit," he says, dropping his eyebrows. "Really?"

I can feel a genuine smile tugging at my lips. "Pull forward already," I say to Ezra. "You're blocking traffic."

Max gives a little salute to the camera, sitting back as Ezra drives the Jeep up to my station. I wince a little as he misjudges the distance, scraping the edge of the curb with the side of his wheel.

"Sorry about this," Ezra says in greeting. "He insisted on coming."

"I require cheesy bites!" Max calls from the passenger seat. "The dinner of champions!"

There's still a grayish tint to Ezra's skin, but he doesn't seem any worse than this morning, at least. "Why are you driving?" I ask him curiously.

I don't think I've ever seen him behind the wheel of Max's Jeep before. He looks deeply uncomfortable, his back ramrod straight and his hands gripping the wheel at exactly nine and three.

It would almost be endearing if it wasn't, you know . . . Ezra.

"Max was pregaming with some of the swim team," Ezra says. "Apparently, I'm his designated driver."

Max elbows himself over Ezra again, beaming happily. "It's true," he says. "Friends don't let friends drive drunk!"

"You had *one* beer," Ezra retorts.

"One and a *half*," Max corrects him.

Ezra rolls his eyes.

Despite his size, Max's tolerance is famously nonexistent. According to Sarita, the first time they ever drank, he chugged three Mike's Hard Lemonades, vomited all over her outdoor trampoline, and passed out for the rest of night.

By the time she woke up the next morning, Max had already hosed off the trampoline, tidied up her mother's gardening shed, and biked to the nearest bakery for fresh donuts.

"Besides, *someone* had to get you both to the party," Max

says. "I *know* you were planning on ghosting me," he adds, narrowing his eyes in my direction.

I give him an innocent look.

"Who? *Me?*" I ask.

Max is right.

Even now, I can feel the siren song of a long, hot shower and a trash reality television marathon calling my name.

"I was going to text you," I say. "*Technically*, it's not ghosting someone if you text them."

"Oh, come on," he says, aiming the full force of his smile in my direction. "It'll be fun. Besides, you only live once, right?"

Right.

You only live once.

"Fine," I say, giving in. "I'll come."

Max leans across the center console, giving his eyebrows another hopeful waggle. "You'll come, *and* you'll give us free food?"

"*And* I'll give you free food." I laugh. "But we're out of cheesy bites." Grabbing a paper-wrapped sandwich from the warmer, I toss it in Max's direction. "Um, Ezra, can I get you anything?"

He flinches as Max unwraps the spicy chicken, a wave of nausea crossing his face.

"Coffee?" he asks. "Black."

I nod, turning away from the window.

I grab a large cup and fill it to the top with the brown sludge from the drip machine, remembering the tiny porcelain cups of espresso I used to drink outside the Sant'Eustachio Il Caffè in Rome, the bistro lights twinkling overhead as the music echoed through the warm summer nights.

Italy is five thousand miles away, but it might as well be a million.

"Shit," I hiss as boiling-hot Burger Queen Blend™ coffee spills over the rim of Ezra's cup, burning my fingers.

I let go of the cup, wincing, and wipe my hand dry on my polyester pants. My fingers are red, but not blistered, the pain already fading to a dull throb. Snapping the plastic lid on with more force than strictly necessary, I turn back to the window and hand the cup through to Ezra.

"Thanks."

He takes a single sip, then sets the cup down quickly in the holder. In the drive-thru behind them, a silver minivan gives a loud, impatient *beep*.

"Come on, Prince Charming," Ezra says resignedly, putting the Jeep in gear. "Let's get you to the ball."

"You won't regret this!" Max calls through the window, bracing himself against the dashboard as Ezra bumps forward. "It's going to be the best night ever!"

I look down, ruefully wiping the last of the coffee from my still-throbbing fingers.

*Sure*, I tell myself. *Best night ever.*

# CHAPTER *Four*

MIA LIVES IN ONE OF THE COZY RANCH HOUSES on the nice side of town, where actual trees line the streets and the homes have room to breathe.

It's easy to spot which one is hers; the circular driveway is already crammed full of cars, and the front door stands wide open, spilling yellowish light into the night.

I cut the engine, letting my hand rest on the keys.

*It's not too late to go home*, I think. I could still take a long shower and curl up in bed. Pull the covers over my head and sleep for the next twelve hours straight.

But according to Max, we're only young once.

Pocketing my keys, I scooch forward, flipping the visor down to check the mirror.

I fix my smudged eyeliner and add a fresh coat of lip gloss, then shake out my ponytail and run my fingers through my hair before twisting it back into a low knot. My plain black tank top is, well . . . a plain black tank top. Definitely not Sarita-approved, but the only other piece of clothing I have in my car is my Burger Queen uniform.

So . . . black tank top it is.

Before I flip the visor shut, I pause, searching my reflection for a long moment. I'm not even sure what I'm looking for. Something I've missed, maybe: a wrinkle, or a laugh line. Something that proves I'm different now. Something that proves I've *changed* since starting at Sunrise Harbor High.

But there's nothing.

Not even a freckle.

I look exactly the same as I always have.

Giving up, I smooth my hair one last time, then flip the visor shut.

I'm reaching for the door handle when a loud *thunk* sounds from the opposite side of the car. I let out an undignified shriek, jumping halfway into the back seat.

On the curb outside, Sarita laughs, drumming her hands against the top of the car. "Nervous much?" she asks, ducking to look through the window. She presses her lips together in a kiss, leaving a bright red lipstick stain against the glass.

"Do you mind?" I ask. The driver's side door sticks as I try to open it; I throw my shoulder into it, the metal hinges groaning in protest as I force it slowly open.

"Oh, I'm sorry," Sarita says. "Did I ruin the perfection of your beautiful, beautiful car?" She gestures toward my ancient Ford Fiesta with the practiced hand motion of a car-show model.

Climbing awkwardly out of the car, I kick the door shut with my foot.

"You're lucky I don't stab *you* with a pencil," I say, forcing a smile.

"Ha ha," Sarita cracks. "But seriously, you're not going to go full Stabby McStabsALot on anyone at the party, are you?"

"No promises," I say.

She grins, linking arms with me.

Despite the heat, she's wearing a fringed leather jacket over her T-shirt and shorts, a matching pair of silver cowboy boots sparkling on her feet.

"Too much?" she asks, catching sight of my glance. She twists back and forth beneath the streetlight, making the fringe on her jacket sway.

"No such thing," I say firmly, tightening my grip on her arm. "Although, how are you not dying from heatstroke right now?"

Her grin widens. "Witchcraft!" she says, her heavy silver rings flashing as she waggles her fingers dramatically. "Now, come on," she says manically, pulling me toward the house. "I have so much to tell you! Astrid already had to go home, but we talked about movies for, like, twenty minutes by the bathroom before she left. Can you believe she's never seen *Jennifer's Body*? I told her we should watch it together, *stat*. Also, Max is already drunk," she adds, rolling her eyes. "He keeps wanting to do 'feats of strength.' It's a whole thing."

"Slow down," I say, laughing, but she's already propelling me through Mia's entryway. Despite the fact it's a Monday, the den is crammed with people from school, the odor of sweat and spilled beer hanging heavy in the air. I recognize a bunch of the theater kids that Mia and Sarita know, but Sarita pushes me forward, bulldozing our way into the kitchen.

She grabs a red plastic cup from the table sitting next to the keg, shoving it in my direction. It's only three-fourths full, with almost as much foam as there is beer.

"This way!" she calls over her shoulder, her hand still gripping mine as she weaves us through the dining room. The house is even more packed than I thought, every surface already littered with empty cups or bottles. A thin layer of haze twines its way overhead, making my eyes water.

"Where are we going?" I ask, stumbling a little on the concrete steps as Sarita leads us outside.

The small, crowded backyard has been lit up with Christmas lights, the strings threaded through the lower branches of trees and draped haphazardly across the fence. A screened-in hot tub is packed *way* above capacity, and people are laughing and shouting and splashing disgusting, bacteria-filled hot tub water in every direction.

To my relief, nobody seems to be paying the slightest bit of attention to Sarita and me.

I take a swig of flat keg beer, letting the warmth and the laughter and the *normalcy* seep into my bones.

*Hello, fellow humans*, I think. *Here I am.*

"Lily!"

Max stumbles up from one of the nearby wicker couches, almost upending the glass-covered table in front of him. "You came!" I give a little yelp as he picks me up, his breath warm and beery against my cheek. He steps away from Sarita, spinning me around in the air until I'm dizzy. My cup tips dangerously in my hand, most of the beer spilling onto the concrete below us.

"Max!" I laugh. "Put me down before you drop me!"

"Never!" he yells. "I'd *never* drop you!" Still, he listens, setting me gently back on the ground. "I'm so happy you're here," he says, pressing a kiss to the top of my head. "You look beautiful. But also, smart. And capable," he adds. "Did I mention you look *capable*?"

Sarita plops down in Max's abandoned space on the couch, wedging herself between one of his swim team friends and a girl whose name I'm pretty sure is Sophie.

"Have I mentioned Max is drunk?" she asks me, taking a sip from the bottle of water she grabs from the table.

"I'm not *drunk*," Max protests. "I'm *extroverted*."

"Your *dinner* is going to be *extroverted* all over the patio if you don't slow down," Sarita warns him, reaching up to fiddle with her necklace.

Looping his arm around my neck, Max reaches for my cup. He locks eyes with Sarita, then downs the rest of the contents in a single gulp.

Sarita snorts, taking another sip of water.

"Dude!" Max yells way too loudly. He points toward the swim team guy. *Brayden? Braylon? Definitely something with a* B. "We should arm wrestle!"

*Feats of strength,* Sarita mouths, rolling her eyes at me again.

"Yeah," I say. Wriggling out from under Max's arm, I pluck my now-empty cup from his hand. "As tempting as watching you arm wrestle sounds, I'm going to go get a refill. Which I need, because *someone* drank my beer," I say pointedly, giving him a look.

"Sorry, babe." Max grins, looking not at all apologetic. "But it had to be done. Oh, hey, that reminds me," he adds, switching tracks with sudden, drunken logic. "I'm supposed to invite you for dinner on Wednesday."

I blink, momentarily forgetting about my refill.

"Dinner?" I repeat, as if I've never heard of it. "Like . . . at your house?"

Max nods. "My mom told me to tell you that she's making pot roast." His forehead furrows in sudden concern. "Wait, you *do* like pot roast, right?"

"I . . ."

I trail off, still taken aback by the offer.

Max's mom has never invited me to dinner before.

In fact, in all the months Max and I have been together, I can probably count the number of times I've spoken to her on one hand.

Not that she purposefully *avoids* me or anything.

I mean, Max's house is huge; she probably just . . . hasn't been able to find me.

Or maybe she's been avoiding me.

I force a smile, bringing myself back to the noisy, slightly chaotic heat of the party. When I reach out to grab Max's hand, it feels warm, and strong, and slightly clammy with sweat.

It feels *real.*

And so do I.

"I love pot roast," I say, my voice firm. "I'll be there."

Max grins, his forehead instantly smoothing.

"Hey, do you want me to get that beer for you?"

He half moves toward the house, but I tighten my grip on his hand, pulling him back. The words "Max" and "refill" are . . . not a good combination right now. "It's fine," I say, giving his hand another squeeze. "Stay. Arm wrestle your heart out. I'll be back in a minute."

As I head toward the house, Max turns back to the group.

"Hey, do you think Mia has Jenga?!" I hear him shout-ask. "Like . . . the *big* kind?!"

Suppressing a smile, I make my way inside, nearly tripping over Mia's uneven porch steps.

If anything, the kitchen is even louder than before, the linoleum groaning beneath the weight of our feet and the light fixture vibrating overhead. Brandishing my empty plastic cup in front of me, I push my way into the room, feeling like a salmon fighting its way upstream.

"Lily!"

Next to the keg, Ximena Morales waves me forward, grabbing my cup as I squeeze into place next to her. "It's almost tapped," she says, raising her voice to be heard over the music. Giving the keg a couple of expert pumps, she aims the faucet into my cup. "But whatever. This place is getting shut down soon, anyway!" Returning my cup, she grabs her own, lifting it into the air. "Cheers!"

"Here's mud in your eye," I agree, clanking my Solo cup against hers.

Ximena's forehead creases in confusion. "What do you mean?" She reaches hesitantly toward her cheek. "Is there something on my face?"

"Never mind," I say, shaking my head. "Thanks for the beer!"

I move back a little as a redheaded sophomore stumbles up to the keg next to me, her eyes widening with drunken realization.

"Hey," she slurs, her voice surprisingly loud for someone so tiny. "You're the pencil girl!"

My smile tightens.

"That's me," I answer, sidestepping politely around her. She pivots, wobbling a little as she turns to keep me in sight.

"You, like . . . *attacked* someone," she informs me, her voice growing even louder. "For *real.*"

*Attacked.*

I flinch at the accusation, the world tilting dizzyingly beneath my feet. A familiar image flashes through my head, one that has nothing to do with Max.

*A dark-haired girl.*

*A rooftop.*

*Blood.*

I straighten my spine, pushing the memory away.

Holding my beer closer, I step forward, trying to edge past the girl without spilling. The kitchen is growing hotter by the second, the low ceiling pressing down on me from above. "Actually," I say, "I didn't."

The girl pivots again, nearly spilling her drink all over me.

"So, what, you *faked* that whole video?" she asks, her voice thick with bleary outrage. "That's so messed up."

I clutch my beer more tightly to my chest, static flooding through my veins. I can feel the warmth of her breath on my skin, enveloping me in a cloud of stale beer fumes. I inhale, anyway, trying to anchor myself in the present.

"Move," I snap. *"Now."*

My tongue feels thick and clumsy, like I'm three glasses in instead of dead sober. The room is closing in on me, the party growing louder and louder as the kitchen begins to blur around the edges.

The girl lifts her chin. "Or what?" she demands.

People are looking at us now, turning toward us like sharks scenting blood in the water. I can feel my palms sweating as the panic sets in, the plastic cup slipping in my grip.

"Or . . ." I whisper, staring blankly at the girl. "Or . . ." Her features blur and twist into an all-too-familiar face; the same one I see in my nightmares, every night.

*It's not real*, I think. *It's not HER.*

I squeeze my eyes shut, wishing desperately that I'd stayed with Max in the backyard. I can't lose control again. I can't make another scene, not twice in one day.

A fresh wave of panic washes over me as someone steps forward, tapping my shoulder with cool fingers.

"*There* you are," Ezra says. "I've been looking all over for you."

I open my eyes, watching unsteadily as Ezra turns to the drunk girl. "Would you excuse us?" he asks politely. "I cut my foot before, and my shoe is filling with blood."

Neither of us even register what's happening as Ezra takes my elbow, steering me away from the kitchen. When I glance over my shoulder, the redheaded sophomore is still staring after us in confusion.

The girl from my nightmares is gone.

# CHAPTER *Five*

SOMEHOW, EZRA SEEMS TO KNOW EXACTLY where he's going. Ignoring the front door, he leads us down a narrow hallway and into the laundry room, where a door opens directly into the garage.

I give him a questioning look.

"Mia and I used to date," he explains, flicking on the light switch. "Back in ninth grade. Her dad was . . . not a fan of mine."

"Imagine that," I murmur to myself, stepping past him into the empty garage. The musty air is only slightly cooler than inside, and still, but the din of the party is partially muffled through the cement walls, giving me a chance to clear my head.

As Ezra shuts the door behind us, I lean back against the mostly empty workbench, feeling my adrenaline levels starting to ebb.

"Thanks," I say, exhaling slowly. "That was oddly . . . helpful."

I feel Ezra watching me closely. "What can I say?" he asks, his voice deadpan. "I'm a helpful guy."

He tosses the quip to me like a lifeline; gratefully, I cling to it. "Last week, you told me you'd rather die than help Max and me hang up posters for the dance," I point out, feeling my heart rate returning to normal. "Those were your literal words: *I'd rather die.*"

"Fine," Ezra says, shrugging. "So I'm not a helpful guy. But it seemed like you needed an out."

"Well," I say, feeling my cheeks flush. "Thanks, I guess."

I take a hurried sip of my beer, feeling suddenly self-conscious, though I'm not sure why. I cast around for a change of conversation. "I can't believe you *Romy and Michele*'d that girl," I say. "Unless you were serious about your foot, I guess. In which case, I should probably take you to the hospital."

Ezra laughs, sounding almost as self-conscious as I feel. "I'm impressed you caught the reference."

He leans against the door, crossing his arms against his chest. He's still wearing the same T-shirt from this morning, I notice, the humidity matting his sweaty curls to his forehead.

"I love that movie," I reply, my voice slightly too loud.

"My mom used to love it, too," Ezra says. "I've seen it, like, twenty times."

"It's a good one," I agree. "I like the . . . humor."

The words hang in the air like cigarette smoke, growing more embarrassing with each passing second.

I take another sip of beer, pretending to be very interested in Mia's dad's lawn care equipment. The silence grows louder and louder between us.

It's strange; Ezra and I are like two separate planets, both rotating around the warmth of Max's sun. Sure, we occasionally pass by in orbit, but our paths have never actually . . . *synced* . . . before.

Well, until now, it seems.

Who knew that Mia Chapman's slightly mildewy garage would be the site of such a rare celestial event?

"So, you and Mia really used to date?" I ask, changing the subject yet again. The more I keep talking, the more I can pretend the incident in the kitchen never even took place. "I didn't think she was your type." Even for a theater kid, Mia is extra bubbly; like someone shook up her personality before they opened it.

I once saw her *twirl* across the parking lot on the way in to school.

For no reason.

*Just to twirl.*

"You've thought about my *type*?" Ezra asks.

I feel myself flush, my palms prickling in embarrassment. "What? No!" I add quickly, looking away.

I'm lying.

To be honest, I *have* thought about Ezra's type before.

But in a strictly clinical "Hmm, I wonder what kind of person my boyfriend's best friend is attracted to" sort of way.

Obviously.

My cheeks still stained with heat, I risk another look in Ezra's direction.

His eyes have fallen shut, the shadows beneath them looking more pronounced than ever. He sags against the door, taking shallow breaths through his nose.

Oh, God.

How did I not notice before?!

I've been too wrapped up in myself to see it, but it's clear to anyone who looks at Ezra that he's sick.

And it's even *more* obvious that Ezra would rather pass out than admit it.

"Hey," I say, lowering my beer. "You don't look so good. If you want to take Max's Jeep, I can drive him—"

"Why does everyone keep acting like I'm sick?" Ezra asks, cutting me off. "I'm *fine*. All I need is some fresh air."

He lurches toward the outside door and wrenches it open with unsteady fingers. I hurriedly set my half-empty cup down on the workbench, following after him. We emerge into a narrow alley, twinkling lights and muffled bass spilling over the fence from Mia's backyard.

Ezra only makes it a few feet before he stumbles, landing hard on his knees. Bracing himself against the ground, he leans forward, his back arching as he convulses.

"Ezra?" I pause uncertainly, one hand already on the gate to the backyard. He needs help, but I don't want to leave him here alone.

A stream of dark vomit pours out of him in response, seeping wetly into the gravel beneath his fingers.

I watch, frozen with horror, as Ezra retches again, and again, and again.

It seems to go on forever, a bottomless well of vomit that no one person should be able to contain. Ezra's shoulders heave and his body shudders and his fingers dig uselessly into the rocks beneath him.

On the other side of the fence, someone shrieks with laughter, the raucous sounds of the party forming a grotesque soundtrack to Ezra's pain.

I flinch, forcing myself not to back away as Ezra chokes on another wave of endless vomit. Dark-colored bile splatters the tip of my tennis shoe, the sharp, acrid scent making me gag, as well.

The moment stretches on and on, the music thumping relentlessly in the background as Ezra convulses over and over again.

And then, suddenly, it's done.

For a moment, I'm too stunned to move.

Ezra is trembling, his T-shirt stretched tight over his back as he huddles against the ground, his fingers still curled into the gravel below.

Strands of thick, mucus-y vomit, so red they're nearly black, drip from his mouth, splattering noiselessly against the ground.

Not vomit, I realize dazedly.

*Blood.*

My fingers are numb as I unlatch the backyard gate, shoving it open with my shoulder. Music and laughter wash over me as I push myself up on my toes, frantically scanning the backyard.

Sarita sees me first, her eyes widening at my horrified expression. Grabbing Max's arm, she nods in my direction, hissing something in his ear.

Max looks up, his smile fading.

I step aside as they hurry across the yard, nodding toward the alley as discreetly as I can.

"It's Ezra," I say. "He needs help."

Sarita presses a hand to her mouth, staring at Ezra in shock, but Max is already moving. Skidding across the alley, he throws himself to the ground, heedless of the grit beneath his knees. "Ezra?" His hands hover over Ezra's shoulder blades, skimming the air above him. *"Ezra?"* Max turns, looking wildly at me over his shoulder. "Call an ambulance!"

*Too little, too late*, I think, staring at the puddle of blood seeping slowly into the gravel.

"No," Ezra chokes out, waving Max off. "I can't afford an ambulance."

Max hesitates—the thought of money probably wouldn't have even *occurred* to him at a time like this.

But not all of us are as lucky as Max.

"Keys," Sarita says, whirring suddenly to life. "I need *keys*."

Max reaches gingerly into Ezra's pocket, feeling for his keys. Wordlessly, he tosses them to Sarita. The heels of her ridiculous cowboy boots crunch loudly against the gravel as she races toward the street.

Ezra gives another shudder, wrenching away from Max as if he can't bear to be touched.

I close my eyes and brace against the wooden fence.

For a moment, I'm no longer outside Mia's house. Instead, I can feel the cobblestones beneath my knees. The rough stones shredding the delicate lace of my gloves as I scrabble to brace myself. As I heave over and over, my own blood streaming onto the filthy ground.

The air is hot and fetid around me, the alleyway stinking in the late summer heat. Flies circle above me, skimming over the widening pool of blood that seeps across the street, staining the knees of my voluminous skirt red.

And then, somewhere in the distance, a car door slams.

I open my eyes.

"It's going to be okay, dude," Max says, helping Ezra to his feet. "You're going to be fine."

Sarita turns into the alley, the Jeep's headlights momentarily illuminating the fear and adrenaline in Max's eyes.

As he helps Ezra into the car, I numbly sink to the ground.

Max is wrong.

Ezra is never going to be fine again.

# CHAPTER *Six*

THE NEXT MORNING, I LINGER OUTSIDE THE school for as long as I can, fiddling with my fake pearl necklace as I scan the parking lot for the familiar bright yellow flash of Max's Jeep. Despite everything, I'm still wearing my Spirit Week outfit, as if dressing up in a ridiculous costume can somehow hide the panic I'm feeling inside.

The heat is already unbearable, the relentless early morning sunshine sharpening the edges of my pounding headache. My eyes are grainy with exhaustion, my stomach churning from either lack of food or lack of sleep.

I barely slept last night, and when I did, I dreamed.

Well, if you could call the short, fragmented snatches of my nightmare "dreaming."

*Ezra, convulsing helplessly on the ground.*

*The dark-haired girl, lying in a slowly spreading pool of blood.*

*A pair of icy blue eyes, following me through the crowd.*

*A blinding flash of green light.*

*The sound of my own screams, echoing in my ears.*

So, you know . . . the usual.

Sarita texted around one a.m., when Ezra was finally admitted into the ER, but I haven't heard from anyone since.

All night long, a small, wishful part of me has been holding out hope that I was wrong.

That Ezra has the flu.

Or appendicitis.

Hell, right now I'd take a *smallpox* epidemic.

But as the minutes tick away with no sign of Max, I can feel my tiny bubble of hope popping.

When the final bell rings, I give up, trudging reluctantly into school.

The morning passes in a blur. I smile, and talk, and laugh at jokes I don't really hear. I compliment Noah on his *A Clockwork Orange* costume and dodge Mia's questions about why we all disappeared last night. Ironically, I fail my history test. I check my phone so many times that Mr. Li threatens to confiscate it.

By the time fourth period rolls around, I'm about to crawl out of my skin.

I catch Sarita at her locker in between classes. She was late enough to school this morning that we didn't have time to talk, and she looks as tired as I feel, the dark circles under her eyes still visible beneath her concealer. She's skipped the elaborate *Beetlejuice* costume she had planned for today's Spirit Day, though I notice she's still wearing a **VOTE FOR PEDRO** T-shirt.

Sarita will be cold and dead in the ground before she misses out on a theme.

Or maybe, like me, she's trying to pretend that everything's okay.

"Any word from Max?" she asks, sliding her lit studies book back onto the shelf. The door to her locker is covered with magnetic poetry, the words forming slightly warped versions of famous movie quotes. I run my finger over her latest masterpiece: "Life is like a box of Soylent Green."

"His mom texted that he went back to the hospital to see Ezra this morning," Sarita goes on. "But I haven't heard from him."

Of course Max's mom has Sarita's number; she and Max have been friends since grade school.

Meanwhile, I could probably go to a *hundred* dinners at Max's house and still be the "new girl" her son is dating.

Pulling out my phone, I check one last time to be sure. "I'm going to cut out early and go see Ezra," I tell Sarita, staring at my notification-free screen. Rummaging around in my backpack, I pull a crumpled sheet of paper from my binder. "Will you hand my English essay in for me?"

Sarita takes the paper, looking torn.

"I'd come with you, but my mom saw what time I got home from the hospital last night," she says. "She's already worried that whatever Ezra has might be *catching*; if she hears I ditched school today, she'll probably send a SWAT team to check on me." She pauses, shaking her head in exasperation. "You're so lucky you're emancipated. Will you let Ezra know that I'll stop by and visit him tonight?"

I bite my tongue, trying not to remind her how lucky she is to even *have* a family that cares about her. Sometimes Sarita's obliviousness can be . . . *a lot*.

Instead, I give her a quick hug, breathing in the familiar scent of her homemade lavender and angelica perfume, then step back, adjusting the hem of my short black dress.

"Of course I will," I say, lying through my teeth.

If I have anything to say about it, Ezra will be long gone by then.

Our history teacher, Mr. Li, likes to talk about how much hospitals have changed over the years.

Back in the day, they were miserable. Dark and dirty, crawling with disease, and stinking of rot and filth. They were places of *death*, not healing; a last resort that only the least fortunate would chance.

Now, hospitals are all gleaming white hallways and cozy nooks with televisions; they have vending machines on every floor and a Starbucks in the lobby. They smell of Lysol and vanilla lattes, not rotting flesh and maggots, and the gift shops sell custom-embroidered robes.

Honestly, we don't appreciate how good we've got it these days. Having an appendectomy is like taking a spa vacation.

"Lily Morris. I'm here to see Ezra Cruz," I say, pausing in front of the main desk. A bowl of untouched candy sits on the counter, hard discs of sugar-free butterscotch wrapped in crinkling plastic. "He was admitted last night?"

The nurse on duty glances up at me, his eyes narrowing slightly as he registers my Spirit Day costume. I pull my hoodie more closely around my chest, shrugging deeper into the fabric.

"Second floor," the nurse says, his eyes flicking back to his computer. "Check in at the desk."

"Thanks," I say, but he's already forgotten me, his fingers flying across his keyboard like lightning.

I sling my backpack firmly over my shoulder and head for the elevator, walking straight past the gift shop. A GET WELL SOON! balloon isn't exactly going to cut it in Ezra's situation.

I give my name at another desk on the second floor, and they point me toward Ezra's room at the end of the hall. The door is half closed, and I raise my hand to knock, but it swings open from the inside before I get the chance.

Max blinks at me in surprise on the other side of the door, a giant stuffed panda tucked beneath his arm. He looks spent, his hair flat on one side where he must have been leaning up against a chair. "Hey," he says, breaking into a tired grin. "What are you doing here?" He steps forward, enveloping me in a hug, the panda bear smooshing us into a throuple.

"What are you *still* doing here?" I ask, disentangling myself from the panda's grabby arms and stepping back. "I can't believe your mom let you skip school."

"Yeah," Max says. "She wasn't exactly happy about it, but we couldn't get ahold of Ezra's stepdad. No surprise there," he adds, an unfamiliar note of bitterness in his voice.

I crane my gaze over Max's shoulder, trying to get a glimpse of Ezra, but I can only see the foot of his bed behind Max. The small room is dim, the lights low and the shades firmly drawn against the midafternoon sun.

I can feel claustrophobia creeping in, the shadows playing tricks on my brain. I resist the urge to stride across the room and snap the shade wide open, to let the sun stream through the windows.

Instead, I force myself to stand still, jamming my hands into the pockets of my hoodie and squeezing them tight. The vent kicks on above us, a blast of arctic air shooting over our heads.

"How's Ezra doing?" I ask, even though I already know the answer.

"I don't know," Max admits. "They've been doing tests all day, but they're still not really sure what's wrong. The nurses keep talking about his pulse, for some reason. At first, they thought it was some sort of internal bleeding, but I guess they ruled that out? He fell asleep a little while ago." He hoists the panda up, grabbing it more securely around the middle. "Anyway, they want to keep him overnight again for observation," he adds, dutifully repeating what he's heard. "They're still trying to get more fluids into him."

I shift my backpack on my shoulder, feeling the water bottle inside slosh back and forth.

It doesn't matter how much saline they're pumping into Ezra's veins; it's not going to help.

"Actually, I was going to run to his house and grab him some stuff," Max says. "Like, overnight stuff?" he adds. "That'd be good, right?"

"Oh," I say. "Yeah. That would be . . ." Good? Nice? About as helpful as that giant panda? I change tack midsentence. "Why don't I stay with him? While you're gone?"

*"Really?"* The surprise in Max's voice is palpable. "You'd do that?"

Okay.

Fine. Maybe I don't go around volunteering for Meals on Wheels and helping defenseless kittens out of trees, like Max does. But that doesn't mean I'm not a nice person.

I'm *here*, aren't I?

I'm visiting Ezra in the hospital!

And, sure, it's under false pretenses, but still.

*Max* doesn't know that.

At the look on my face, he quickly backtracks. "Sorry. But I know you and Ezra don't really, er . . . hang out . . . that much."

"Think of it this way," I say. "It's down to me or the panda to keep him company."

Max blinks down at the giant stuffed animal, as if he's surprised to be holding it.

"Right," he says. "Sorry. That'd be great, thanks."

"You're welcome." I reach up on tiptoes, steadying myself against his chest and kissing him. "Do you know you taste like Fritos?"

He grins, kissing me back. "Vending machine lunch of champions."

The giant stuffed animal leers knowingly at me as I drop back down on my heels. "And you decided to go with the panda because . . . ?"

"Flowers seemed weird," Max says with a shrug.

"Right," I say gravely. "*Flowers* seemed weird."

Max drops another kiss on my forehead. "Thanks again. I won't be long." He sets the panda in the corner, giving it a final pat before heading through the door.

"Nice costume, by the way," Max says over his shoulder. "Very, um . . . French?"

"You have *no* idea who I'm dressed as, do you?" I call back.

Max grins in answer.

I smile fixedly back at him, standing rigidly by the door as he makes his way down the hallway. The corridor seems to grow longer with every step he takes, my heartbeat throbbing louder and louder in my throat with every passing second.

The wait for the elevator almost kills me.

I clutch the sides of the doorframe, my fingers aching with the effort of standing still.

Just when I think I can't stand it any longer, the elevator doors slide open with a quiet *ding*.

There's another excruciating pause as Max steps inside, scanning for the Lobby button. But at last, the doors slide closed, Max disappearing behind them.

And I whirl into motion. I shove Ezra's door shut with a loud *click*. I drag a pastel blue visitor's chair across the room and wedge it beneath the door handle, testing the back to make sure it holds.

For a second, I worry that the slam of the door—or my pulse pounding against my wrists—will draw attention, but when I turn to Ezra, he's still asleep.

In the gloom of the tightly drawn window shades, he looks even paler than yesterday, curls of dark hair clinging damply to his forehead. Beneath the thin, white hospital blankets piled on top of him, I can see the slow rise and fall of his chest, his lungs hitching a little at the top of each breath.

Even in sleep, his face is drawn in pain, his dark eyelashes fluttering uneasily against his cheekbones. An IV runs to the small of his wrist, the clear fluid inside the plastic bag dripping steadily through the tube. There's a white patch taped to the crook of his elbow, his heartbeat jumping erratically on the monitor next to him.

I remember the dreams, the nightmares that scratched and clawed at me over and over again in the darkness.

Sometimes, I still wake up in a panic, my heart pounding and the sheets twisted beneath my fingers.

I take another step forward. The whiteboard next to Ezra's bed reads **EZRA REGINALD CRUZ**, along with a bunch of scribbled notes from each nurse.

*Reginald.*

Huh.

I reach out and gently turn his chin to the side. His skin is cool to the touch, almost cold, and clammy with sweat. It feels like a violation, touching him in his sleep, but I need to know for sure what I'm dealing with.

His chest hitches again, his eyelashes fluttering faster, but he doesn't wake.

I lean over him, inhaling the chemical smell of hospital soap. Lingering beneath, so faint I can barely smell it, is the sharp, metallic scent of blood.

Holding my breath, I trace my fingers over his neck, searching until I find what I'm looking for: two slight but unmistakable indentations in his skin, right above his collarbone.

Bite marks.

*"Fuck."*

The word comes out louder than I intend it to, although I'd scream it from the rooftop if I could.

Below me, Ezra's eyes flutter open.

I snatch my fingers away from his neck, stepping backward. My legs collide with the chair Max has pulled to the head of the bed.

"Li . . . Lily?" Ezra asks in confusion, his voice a rough-edged whisper. "What are you doing here? Where's Max?" He glances around the room, looking more confused by the second. "Is that . . . a *panda*?"

I sit down in the chair, trying to compose myself.

It . . . does not go well.

Across from me, Ezra is also struggling. He sits up, his forehead dampening with the effort of raising himself to his elbows. "What's going on?" he asks. "Why are you dressed like Holly Golightly?"

I pull my hoodie more tightly around my *Breakfast at Tiffany's* costume, ignoring the question.

"Who was it?" I ask, crossing my arms against my chest. "Who *bit* you?"

Ezra's eyes widen. "What?"

*"Who bit you?"* I demand, leaning forward, my backpack straps digging into my shoulders.

He flinches. "I don't know what you're talking about."

We don't have time for him not to understand. "Your neck," I say impatiently. "You've obviously been bitten. *Who was it?*"

"No one," he rasps. "You can't . . . It was . . . It wasn't . . . It was a dream. It had to be a *dream*."

I grab his hand, the one without the IV needle, and thrust it roughly toward his neck, his fingers cool beneath mine as I guide them to the puncture marks. I watch his eyes grow wide in realization. "It wasn't a dream," I say, letting go of him.

He looks up at me, fighting back panic as his fingertips brush the holes in his neck. "It had to be," he says. "It's not *possible.*"

I slump back in my chair, suddenly exhausted.

"Listen," I say. "There's no easy way to do this, so I'm just going to say it." I pause, letting him cling to these last few precious seconds of his old life.

And then, in one fell swoop, I rip off the Band-Aid.

"I'm sorry, Ezra. But you're a *vampire.*"

# CHAPTER *Seven*

FOR A LONG MOMENT, EZRA DOESN'T MOVE.

And then, in a rush, he jerks to sit up straighter, wincing as he moves too fast and tugs at the needle in his wrist. "Okay, I get that you're Max's girlfriend and everything, but I don't even know what you're doing here," he says, clearly in pain. "You're . . . having an episode or something. Vampires aren't even . . . They're not . . . You need to *leave*," he says firmly. "*Now.* Before I buzz the nurse."

He goes for the call button nestled at the side of the bed, but I'm faster, snatching the white plastic remote and holding it out of his reach.

I'm not going to lie; it doesn't feel like much of a victory.

"I'm sorry," I say again, my fingers tightening around the remote. "Believe me, I really am. But I need to know what they looked like."

I swallow hard, trying to dampen the edge of fear in my voice.

"It's important," I say. "Please. I *need* to know who turned you."

"Nobody *turned* me," Ezra splutters. "Are you even hearing yourself? *Vampires aren't real.*"

I squeeze my eyes shut, trying not to snap at him.

We really, *really* need to fast-forward through this part.

Obviously, the whole "vampire" thing is a lot to take in, and believe me, no one sympathizes with him more than I do, but I don't have time to sit around holding Ezra's hand right now. At least not until I'm sure about who sired him, that is.

Keeping the call button out of reach, I slip off my backpack, unzip it with one hand, and pull out the water bottle inside.

"What are you doing?" Ezra demands, a thin sheen of sweat covering his face and neck. With his free hand, he impatiently brushes the damp curls away from his eyes. "What's in that? Are you going to *drug* me or something?"

I ignore him. Bracing the water bottle between my knees, I awkwardly untwist the top, then slam the open container down on the tray at the side of his bed.

The contents slosh over the edge a little, coating the rim with thick red liquid.

Ezra stiffens.

His pupils shrink to pinpoints as he stares at the bottle, his entire existence suddenly narrowing into one razor-sharp emotion: *hunger.*

For a moment, I'm almost envious of his clarity. Of the strength of his single-minded *need.*

Ezra inhales slowly, then exhales, his dark eyes never leaving the water bottle.

"What is that?" he whispers at last, his voice so soft I have to strain to hear it.

"You already know," I say simply.

The coppery scent floods the room, cloying and unmistakable. I can feel my stomach twist in response, either from nausea or . . . something else.

Ezra's hands are twisted around the hospital blankets, his fists gripping the soft material so tightly that his knuckles are white.

He shakes his head, a nearly imperceptible motion.

"I don't want that," he whispers.

"It's *all* you want," I say matter-of-factly.

He grits his teeth, his hands gripping the blanket even tighter.

A shudder runs through his body, violent enough to make the bed rattle. One of the machines he's hooked to begins to beep, an ominous, hollow sound that echoes through the small, high-ceilinged room.

He licks his dry lips, already chapped with thirst.

"You're not sick, Ezra," I say. You're *dying.* Okay? Your heart is already shutting down. In a few hours, you won't even have a pulse."

He shudders again, his teeth chattering.

"That fire you're feeling, racing through your veins? The pounding behind your eyes? Those are your arteries shriveling."

Ezra tears his gaze away from the water bottle to look at me.

"Vampires aren't alive, Ezra. Their hearts don't beat. They don't need food, or water, or air. All they need is *blood.*" He flinches at the word, like I've hit him. "*You* need blood, Ezra. And, right now, this is the only way to get it." I push the bottle closer to him.

He inhales sharply but doesn't move. His hands are shaking with the effort of not reaching for it.

"No," he says again. "*No.* This isn't real . . . You're . . . This is some sort of . . ." He trails off, the words dying on his cracked lips.

"Let me guess," I say. "It happened a few days ago. You blacked out and woke up with a headache. It felt like your skull was caving in every time you blinked. You were thirstier than you've ever been in your life," I go on, pushing away the memories threatening to float to the surface. "The kind of thirst that wouldn't go away, no matter how much water you drank."

I remember water spilling down my chin, soaking the high-necked collar of my nightdress. My hands trembling and my fingers clumsy with need as I grabbed the glass from the nurse, tipping it greedily upward.

When the water ran out, I begged for more, but the pitcher was empty. The nurse soaked her handkerchief in the washbasin and pressed it to my lips, to my forehead, to my neck, trying to cool the fever that raged beneath my skin.

It didn't work.

*Nothing* worked.

Until . . .

"You can't know that," Ezra says, interrupting my thoughts. His voice has dropped to a hoarse whisper, barely audible over the soft *beep*ing of his hospital machines. "How can you *know* that?"

"Everything was too bright," I go on. "Too loud. Too sharp. Too *everything.* Like you stepped into a fun house and couldn't find your way out."

The uneven rasp of Ezra's breath is coming faster now.

"You never noticed how loud other people's heartbeats were before. You could hear their pulse, thudding through their veins. Their *blood*, calling to you."

The hospital ward was packed to the gills, some of the beds stuffed double. The stench of infection was everywhere, open wounds festering and putrefying with sickness; it made my head spin and my stomach churn.

But beneath it all, there was the clean, sharp call of fresh blood; a tang in the air that made my skin tingle and my senses sharpen and the rest of the world winnow away into nothingness.

Ezra's eyes cut back to the water bottle.

He's trembling with need.

"Or maybe I'm wrong. Maybe vampires *don't* exist." I stand up, hooking my backpack over my shoulder, and reach for the bottle. Ezra's breath catches as I carelessly screw the lid back on, turning to leave. "Sorry to bother you. I'll take this and go."

I'm halfway to the door before I hear the rasp of Ezra's voice. "Wait."

Adrenaline pumps through my veins, my nervous system flooding with the stuff. It's painfully obvious that my human body is built for flight, not fight.

Ezra hesitates for a long moment. I can feel his eyes on me.

"It was a girl," he finally says. "The one who . . ." He trails off, reaching up to skim his fingers over his neck. He sucks in a breath, his dark brown eyes finding mine. "I was waiting for Max to give me a ride home. We started talking . . ." He pauses, his fingers still pressed against the bite marks in his throat. "I thought it was a dream."

My breath catches in my chest.

"A girl?" I turn back, taking a step toward Ezra. My hand tightens around the water bottle.

For a moment, the bloodied rooftop flashes through my mind, hazy and dreamlike around the edges.

I push the fragment away, focusing on Ezra.

"Was she alone?" I press, taking another step forward. "Or was someone with her?" I remember the feeling I had yesterday, hurrying through the parking lot after school. Like someone was watching me. Like I was *exposed.*

"I don't think so," Ezra says. "At least, not that I saw."

I can feel my palms flickering with nervous heat, the water bottle suddenly growing slick in my grasp. "But you're not sure?" I ask. "You need to be *sure.*"

Ezra's jaw muscle twitches in response.

"I'm sure," he says. "She was alone. It was just . . . *a girl.*"

*Just a girl,* I think.

*A random vampire, passing through.*

*It wasn't him.*

*It wasn't Cassius.*

A wave of relief washes through me, so strong it nearly knocks me to the ground. I step forward, setting the water bottle down on the tray next to Ezra.

"Drink this," I say. "Then check yourself out of the hospital. *Now.* Don't let the doctors stop you."

Ezra tears his eyes away from the bottle, looking up at me. "What am I supposed to tell them?"

I shrug.

"You're a vampire now, Ezra," I say, turning on my heel. "If I were you, I'd get used to lying."

And I stride out of the room, leaving Ezra alone with his thirst.

# CHAPTER Eight

I DON'T SLEEP THAT NIGHT, EITHER.

Instead, I sprawl on top of my fake sateen comforter, staring up at the brownish water spot above my bed.

I've scoured the local news sites down to the bone, but there's no sign of Ezra's vampire anywhere. No unusual disappearances. No dead bodies washing up with the tide. Not a single "blood-crazed killer stalks Florida town" headline to be found. You'd be amazed how easy it is to track a vampire if you know what to look for.

I'm guessing that whoever turned Ezra has either left town, or they're already dead.

Most likely it was a newborn vampire; someone desperate, someone still driven by their near-constant need for human blood. Someone who turned Ezra by accident and then suffered the consequences.

And if they *weren't* a newly turned vampire, well . . .

Older vampires may be able to control their *bloodlust*, but the rest of it? The eternity of darkness, the never-ending loneliness, the rage and the guilt and the horror . . .

Eventually, even the strongest vampire can snap.

And once they'd realized what they'd done?

Let's just say, "Ezra's maker fleeing Florida in a haze of blood-soaked shame" is probably the best-case scenario here.

To be honest, part of me can't help wanting to skip town, too.

To pack my bags, gas up my car, and *drive.* To disappear, like I've done a thousand times before. Like I did in Lauterbrunnen, and in London, and in Rome . . .

Only this time, I wouldn't be running from my past.

I'd be running from my shot at a *future.*

From the solid warmth of Max. From Sarita's gleeful laughter and increasingly unhinged wardrobe choices. And even from Ezra. From whatever I might owe him.

I can't run away this time.

I *refuse.*

So, instead, I lie on my bed, staring up at the water mark until the first rays of sunlight finally fight their way through the curtains.

My legs are clumsy as I force myself up, my body aching in protest.

Lifting my chin, I head for the shower.

At least today's spirit theme is Pajama Day, which means that for the first time all week, I'm actually comfortable. Of course, being comfortable also means that I'm about two seconds away from falling asleep at any given moment.

Despite my best efforts, I doze through most of science

class and only manage to stay awake during history by pinching myself under the desk.

*Hard.*

Luckily, most of my teachers seem willing to cut me some slack. It helps that I've spent the last two semesters carefully cultivating my reputation as a solid B student: I'm polite, but not a suck-up; friendly, but not outgoing; smart, but not a genius. And, sure, my homework might *sometimes* be covered in cheeseburger stains, but at least I turn it in on time.

Well, usually.

When I'm not half dead with exhaustion, that is.

By the time lunch rolls around, my legs are covered in tiny pinch marks, and I'm yawning so much I'm genuinely worried that my jawbone might crack in half.

I'd forgotten how *tiring* being tired can be.

"Look what I found," Max says, plunking an enormous iced coffee down on the table in front of me. "Extra-large vanilla cold brew with a *splash* of sweet cream."

Summoning a smile, I reach for the drink.

"Thank you," I say. "You're a prince among men."

Max grins, sliding onto the bench beside me. He's wearing a thin plaid robe over a T-shirt and pajama pants, looking like an advertisement for Christmas morning.

I take a long sip of coffee, trying not to wince at the taste.

I've never quite had the heart to tell Max that I prefer my coffee black.

Besides, I'm sure the vanilla will grow on me if I keep drinking it.

"Did you get my message about Ezra?" Max asks, helping himself to one of my pretzels. Despite yesterday's ordeal, he's bright-eyed and bushy-tailed, his hair perfectly tousled and his smile turned up to eleven. "He's home. I guess it was a viral thing after all!"

I choke slightly on my drink, pushing away the memory of the thick coppery blood pooling in Ezra's water bottle.

"That's great," I say. "I'm glad he's feeling . . . better."

Surreptitiously, I reach up and tug on the sleeve of my pajama shirt. I can feel the bandage beneath the thin fabric, right at the crook of my elbow.

"Right?" Max says, chewing away in blissful ignorance. "Speaking of which, would I be the worst if I asked you for another favor? I told Ezra's teachers I'd bring his homework over, but I have weight training after school. Would you mind dropping it off before you come over for dinner?"

Right.

Dinner.

With Max's mom.

*Tonight.*

Is it bad that I'd completely forgotten about it?

"Wait a second," Max says, eyeing me suspiciously. "You didn't forget about it, did you?"

"Of course not!" I say manically. "I was just thinking, are you sure Ezra's up for homework right now?" I ask, keeping my voice as light as I can. "After all, he's barely home from the hospital."

Also, more importantly, *he just found out he's a freaking vampire.*

I'm guessing *homework* isn't exactly Ezra's number one priority at the moment.

I reach for a pretzel and absently break it into smaller and smaller pieces.

Do I feel bad for Ezra? Sure. But what happened to him isn't my fault. I barely know the guy, and I've already given him a *pint of my blood.*

What more could he want from me?

Across the cafeteria, I can see Sarita talking to Astrid, her hands flailing wildly through the air as she illustrates whatever point she's trying to make. Sarita's cheeks are flushed beneath the hood of her zip-up shark onesie, her short black hair escaping from the sides.

Astrid, on the other hand, is dressed like Ebenezer Scrooge, with a long, striped old-timey nightshirt and pointy sleep cap perched on top of her curly hair. She nods along excitedly with Sarita, pausing to brace herself against Sarita's arm as she laughs.

"Maybe you're right," Max says, his forehead momentarily creasing in concern. "But colleges still look at your second-semester grades. We can't blow off the rest of the year."

Right.

Colleges.

Max seems to take it for granted that everyone he knows is going. That we all have our futures mapped out for us as far in advance as he does.

Personally, I'm less concerned about *planning* for the future and more hoping that I *have* one.

I glance down at the dark green T-shirt he's wearing beneath his robe, still creased from its package.

"Wait," I say. "Is that . . . a *Dartmouth* shirt? Did you hear something?"

Max looks down, plucking ruefully at the T-shirt. "My mom got it for me, back when I first applied," he says. "I didn't have any other clean shirts. Wait, why?" he asks, looking eagerly back up at me. "Have *you* heard anything?"

"Oh. Um, not yet," I hedge, thinking of the stack of unfinished applications still waiting for me on my laptop. Max *may* or may not be under the impression that I've already finished them. "But I think community colleges are on a different admissions schedule."

There's no need to worry Max about the details.

I'm sure I still have plenty of time to figure out where I'm going next fall!

I mean, it's only *May*.

Max opens his mouth as if he's about to say something, but before he can get anything out, I'm nearly tackled by an incoming shark.

"Guess who has a date for prom?!" Sarita shrieks way too loud for the middle of the cafeteria—especially with Astrid still standing a few feet away. She grips my arm as she bounces up and down in place. "Spoiler alert: It's *me*!"

"Well, well, well . . ." Max says, crossing his arms in satisfaction. "So, you finally womaned up, huh?"

"Um, more like I *sharked* up," Sarita says, her cheeks still flushed with happiness as she gestures toward her onesie. "Did you know sharks can only swim forward? It's actually very aspirational."

"That's amazing!" I say, giving Sarita a hug. "Wait! We have to go prom shopping!"

"Not a chance," Sarita says seriously. "I'm wearing these pajamas for the rest of my natural-born life. Deal with it."

"Personally, I think it's a *fin-tastic* idea," Max chimes in. "We should *all* wear shark costumes to prom."

I reach for my too-sweet coffee, watching as the two of them banter happily back and forth with each other. It feels as if they're bobbing along on the surface of the ocean, no idea of the *actual* sharks circling beneath their feet.

Out of nowhere, my heart surges with sudden, fierce love.

Max and Sarita have no idea how dangerous the real world can be.

And, if I have my way, they never will.

I'll do anything to protect the life I've made here. To protect Sarita and Max.

*Anything.*

And in that instant, I make a decision.

"Text me Ezra's address," I say. "I'll go after school."

# CHAPTER Nine

THREE HOURS LATER, I FINALLY PULL UP IN front of Ezra's house.

According to Max's directions, Ezra lives in the mobile home park on the west side of town, in a dark blue double-wide with a tiny deck jutting off from the front door.

Luckily for me, there aren't any cars in the driveway; Ezra's stepdad is a long-haul trucker, and from what I've gathered, he's almost never here. Ezra's mom isn't really in the picture anymore, but I know he used to stay with his grandmother a lot, and I think he has an aunt down in Orlando.

I'm a little sketchy on the details; Ezra doesn't really spend a lot of time talking about himself, and I never asked. Plus, his social media accounts are pretty bare bones.

Which is fine.

I have a very healthy respect for other people's privacy.

And my own.

I remember the first time Max tried to post a picture of us. He . . . did not make that mistake again.

Climbing onto the deck, I knock loudly on the white-painted screen door.

"Ezra?" I call. "It's me, Lily! Are you in there?"

There's no answer from the other side of the door. For a second, a small part of me can't help being relieved. Maybe I don't have to be involved, after all. Maybe I can leave! I could even be *early* to dinner!

But then I remember Max's hopeful expression in the cafeteria. Damn him and his Disney Prince face.

Pulling open the screen door, I prop it with my foot and knock again, harder this time. "Ezra? Open the door!"

Still no answer.

Not that I was really expecting one.

Glancing around, I spot a suspicious-looking ceramic frog perched on the corner of the deck. Since Ezra doesn't exactly strike me as a "decorative frog" person, I follow my hunch and pick it up.

As expected, it's hollow, with a single metal key hanging from a hook inside.

"Ezra? I'm coming in," I announce, a warning note in my voice. "Please be wearing pants!"

Fitting the key into the lock, I twist the handle and let myself inside.

The front room is dark, the curtains drawn tightly against the late-afternoon sun. A matching couch and armchair are arranged in front of the TV, and a bunch of potted plants line the shelf beneath the window.

It's nice.

Well, if you don't count Max's giant panda, which sits

creepily slumped in the chair, its plastic eyes staring blankly up at the ceiling.

The kitchen, off to my right, is meticulously clean, dishes stacked neatly in the drying rack, and a single place mat is centered on the end of the small kitchen table.

An actual place mat, covered in a bright, '70s-style floral pattern and laminated in plastic.

I can't remember the last time I saw one.

For some reason, the sight of it, sitting there alone, breaks my heart a little.

"Ezra?" I call again, moving cautiously down the hallway. "It's me, Lily. Are you in here?"

I gingerly push open the first door I come to, but the bedroom is empty; Ezra's stepdad's, I'm guessing, from the looks of it. It's untidier than the rest of the house, with clothes stacked carelessly on the floor and a pile of unopened mail overflowing on top of the dresser. A thick layer of dust covers everything, giving the room a musty, unused smell.

I quickly close the door, feeling like an intruder.

Which, technically, I am.

"Hello?" I continue, making my way farther down the hall. A portable air-conditioning unit whirs loudly in the window; it must be cranked to the max, because the air feels clammy and refrigerated.

I pause in front of the last room, tapping softly on the door before twisting the handle open. "Ezra?"

It's hard to see inside at first; a wrinkled comforter is draped across the window frame, blocking the late-afternoon sun completely.

Feeling around next to the door, I find the light switch and flick it on.

The narrow twin bed is empty, the sheets twisted and creased, as if Ezra was thrashing back and forth in them. The rest of the room is painfully neat: bookshelves, double-stacked with thick paperbacks; a beanbag chair in front of a laptop. Postcards are tacked to the wall above his bed, dozens of them, from all different countries: Spain, Ireland, Laos, Zambia . . .

To the right of the bed stands a narrow closet, its accordion door pulled almost shut, a half-filled hamper shoved to the side in front of it.

"Ezra?" I whisper.

Inside the closet, something rustles in response.

I steel myself for what I'm about to find.

Then, taking a deep breath, I yank the accordion door open.

Ezra is huddled on the floor of the closet, his knees pulled tight against his chest.

He looks up at me, blinking in the sudden light. He looks younger; a scared kid, hiding in his closet, hoping the monster outside the door will go away.

But it's too late.

The monster is already inside.

"Usually when people don't answer the door, there's a reason," Ezra mumbles, turning his head.

My irritation with Ezra melts away, replaced by a wave of sudden pity.

I sink to my knees, my movements slow and cautious. "I know. And I'm sorry," I say. "But it's going to be okay."

Ezra laughs, a harsh, humorless sound. "Yeah. I'm pretty

sure we have different definitions of the word 'okay.' " He runs his hand through his hair, pushing back his tangled brown curls. He's wearing jeans and an old white T-shirt, stretched a little at the neck. His feet are bare, and for a second, I wonder if he's cold.

But of course not; he doesn't feel the cold anymore.

"Fair enough." I set my backpack down, arranging myself more comfortably on the floor. "How long have you been sitting in here?"

"I don't know," Ezra says, leaning back against the wall. A couple of shirts, hanging from the rack overhead, brush against the top of his head. "What time is it?"

"A little past five," I say, double-checking my phone. I need to make this quick if I'm going to get to dinner on time. "Max sent me with your homework."

"Of course he did," Ezra says, a bitter edge to his voice. "Because Max has no idea how to *mind his own fucking business*."

Well.

Clearly I'm not the only one who finds Max to be a bit . . . much, sometimes.

"We need to talk," I say. "But first, I brought you this." I reach into my backpack and pull out another water bottle. I wonder if it would be tacky to ask for the first one back.

Ezra's breath quickens, his eyes flashing darkly at the sight of it.

"Take it away," he says through gritted teeth. "I don't want it."

"Yes, you do," I say matter-of-factly. "It's been almost twenty-four hours since you've eaten. You need to manage your hunger, especially in the beginning. Or else . . ."

Ezra swallows. "Or else what?"

"Or else . . . bad things will happen," I hedge. I set the bottle down in front of Ezra, unscrewing the lid. "You're hungry," I say. "Take it. It's fresh."

He draws a shuddering breath. "Where did you get it?"

I push up my sleeve, showing him the recently changed bandage wrapped around the crook of my arm. "B positive. My blood type *and* my life philosophy."

Ezra squeezes his eyes shut, turning away again. "You shouldn't have done that."

"It's not like I had a ton of options." I pull my sleeve back down, covering the bandage. "You can't exactly waltz into a blood bank and shop off the rack these days." To be honest, my arm is sorer than I'm letting on; beneath my bandage, an ugly bruise is already forming, and there's a dull ache when I move too quickly.

It's unsettling how *fragile* such a small wound can make me feel.

"What about animal blood?" Ezra asks. "Pigs? Or cows? A butcher's shop, or something?"

"It doesn't work like that," I say. "It's not like in the movies. You need human blood."

"I need *human* blood," he repeats dully. "Because I'm not *human* anymore, am I?"

I don't deny it. Instead, I push the bottle closer to him. "Drink it. You'll feel better."

A long moment passes.

When he speaks again, his voice is low. "I don't want you to watch. While I . . . I don't want you to see me . . . drinking it."

I nod. "Okay." Shuffling backward, I move away from the closet. I rest my head against the bed and wait.

Behind me, Ezra hesitates.

But a second later, I hear his breath quicken as he picks the water bottle up. He drinks slowly at first, then faster, tipping the container back and swallowing greedily.

When the empty bottle falls to the carpet with a soft thud, I turn around.

Ezra is on his feet. His cheeks are flushed, his pupils dilated, his chest heaving beneath his T-shirt. The scared teenage boy hiding in his closet has disappeared; *this* Ezra looks ready to scale a mountain peak, one-handed.

I can almost see the pounding in his veins, the power flooding through him. The feeling, for one moment, of being totally and utterly *alive.*

Ezra takes a half step forward, his lips slightly parted, his dark eyes suddenly hooded.

Well.

They don't call it "bloodlust" for nothing.

"Better?" I ask in a manically cheerful voice.

Ezra pauses mid-step, then shakes his head as if he's trying to clear it. "Um, yeah," he says, reaching up to grip the back of his neck. "I guess so."

Thick black lines peek out from beneath his shirtsleeve: the edge of a tattoo on the inside of his bicep that I've never noticed before. His arm is lightly corded with muscle; his thin white T-shirt clings to his flat stomach.

I look away, clearing my throat.

Ezra's heightened emotions are obviously affecting me, too.

He sits down on the edge of his bed, putting a little more distance between us. "So, how does it all work?" he asks. "Being a vampire?" He looks over his shoulder, at the comforter draped across his window. "I can, like . . . never go outside again?"

I sit down on the other end of the bed, careful not to let my body touch his.

"Direct sunlight is . . . not great," I admit. "Luckily, you live in a post–polyvinyl butyral kind of world."

Ezra looks at me blankly.

"A post *what* kind of world?"

"Polyvinyl butyral," I repeat. "Did you know that most windows today block, like, ninety-nine percent of UV rays?" I make a little jazz-hands motion, waving my fingers back and forth in front of me. "As long as the building you're in was constructed after the 1950s, you're pretty much good to go."

Ezra swallows. "And if they're not?" he asks. "I, what . . . burst into flames?"

"Well . . . yeah," I admit. "Pretty much. But there are plus sides to vampirism, too," I add quickly. "Strength. Speed. You heal fast. Like, *fast*. Almost instantly, most of the time. And there's the whole chance-for-immortality thing, obviously. That's a perk."

"Great," he says dully. "Maybe I'll finally be able to beat *Call of Duty*."

"You can travel," I say. "See the world." I look up, nodding at the postcards lining the wall above his bed.

"They're from my grandma," he says. "She used to fly a lot, for work. She took me to Paris when I was a kid. We went to

Disneyland. Like, the Europe one." He manages a weak smile. "It kind of sucked."

"First of all, you're wrong," I correct him. "Disneyland Paris is awesome. And, secondly, there's more to Paris than theme parks," I assure him. "The Catacombs, Musée d'Orsay, La Tour d'Argent . . . *Quand il est allumé la nuit, c'est incroyable.*"

Ezra blinks at me. "You speak French?"

Whoops.

"My point is," I say, "there's a whole wide world out there. You can go anywhere. Do anything. Be anyone."

"You *do* realize you sound like a motivational poster, right?" Ezra asks, his voice incredulous. "I can't even get over the fact that *vampires* are real. What's next? Witches? Zombies? Werewolves? Leprechauns?"

*"Leprechauns?"* I repeat.

"Well, how am I supposed to know?" he demands. "Yesterday, vampires didn't exist, either."

Fair point.

"No leprechauns," I say. "No zombies. No werewolves, as far as I know."

"And witches?"

An involuntary shiver runs through me.

Ezra doesn't need to know about witches.

Not yet.

"Witches are . . . complicated," I hedge. "For now, let's stick to the basics. Vampire 101—you ready?"

He nods, pushing back his hair. I catch another glimpse of the edge of his tattoo, peeking out from beneath his sleeve. "Hit me."

"Unfiltered daylight? Bad." I hold up a finger, ticking it off. "Fire? Also bad. Wooden stake through the heart?"

"Bad?" he guesses.

"Very bad," I agree. "See? You're a natural!"

"Yeah, I feel like that one was kind of obvious," Ezra says, a ghost of a smile crossing his expression.

"True," I allow. "Okay, so, daylight, fire, stakes; those are the big three. Garlic, holy water, and crosses, on the other hand?" I ask, rapidly ticking them off. "Complete crap."

It's possible that I'm rushing things, but the faster I can speed him through this process, the better it will be for everyone involved.

One way or another, Ezra needs to come to terms with his new life.

And, more importantly, *I* need to make it to dinner on time.

"What about the 'crossing the threshold' thing? Like, does somebody actually have to invite you into their house?" Ezra asks as I pull my phone out, surreptitiously checking the time. "Because I walked right in here last night. I didn't even *knock*."

"Yeah. That one's tricky." I gesture around his bedroom. "A mobile home like this? No problem. Make yourself comfortable. But if the house has a foundation, you're going to need an RSVP from someone who lives there."

"Seriously?" Ezra asks.

I nod.

"There's a Bible quote about it," I say, trying to remember the exact wording. "Something about being built on a rock, I think?"

He crosses his arms against his chest, considering my answer.

"Well, that sucks," he says after a second. "So, what, rich people are safe, but if you live in a trailer park, you're open season for vampires? That's some plutocracy bullshit."

"I'm not the one who made the rules," I remind him. "But, yes," I agree. "It's pretty much some plutocracy bullshit."

This time, Ezra's smile actually makes it to his lips.

"Okay, so that's basically it," I say, a little too brightly. "Congratulations. You've officially passed Intro to Vampirism."

Ezra looks at me, his smile slowly fading.

"I don't get it," he says. "Why are you helping me? Don't get me wrong, I'm grateful and everything. But I always kind of thought that you didn't . . . *like* me."

"*You're* the one who doesn't like me," I correct him. "Besides, maybe I have reasons of my own."

Reasons that have nothing to do with Max, or Sarita, or even Ezra.

*A dark-haired girl. A rooftop. Blood.*

Wrapping my arms around myself, I suppress a shiver.

What's past is past.

But maybe, with my help, Ezra will still have a future.

"You're Max's best friend," I remind him. "What am I supposed to tell him and Sarita if I let you get yourself killed? If I let you kill someone *else*?"

For once, Ezra has no reply. I watch him as this new reality dawns on him. The rearranging of his future happening in real time. He hugs his knees tightly, and I can't help but notice the soft curve of his eyelashes, trembling ever so slightly as he blinks back tears.

"Maybe I should leave," he finally says, swallowing hard. "I can't hurt anyone if I'm *gone*."

It's a more tempting offer than I'd like to admit.

"Running away won't solve your problems," I say, fully aware of the irony in that statement. "If anything, it would make them worse."

Ezra opens his mouth to protest, but I cut him off.

"You won't make it a day if you don't know how to feed. How to stay hidden. How to be a *vampire*." I pause, willing my next words to be true. "I can keep you safe, Ezra. I can keep *everyone* safe. Please . . . let me help you."

"But *how*?" Ezra presses. "No offense, but you're *human*. How can you possibly know so much about vampires?"

*I'd do anything to protect Max and Sarita*, I remind myself. *Anything.*

*Even if it means telling the truth.*

"Because," I say. "I used to be one."

# CHAPTER *Ten*

H'S DINER IS TUCKED AWAY ON A QUIET BACK street, only a few blocks from the rows of tourist traps lining the boardwalk. The cracked vinyl booths are patched with strips of duct tape, and the paper napkins are jammed so tightly into the metal holder that it's impossible to tear one free without ripping it to shreds.

Max took me here on one of our first dates, when I moved to Sunrise Harbor at the end of last summer; we drank shaved espresso milkshakes and shared a plate of French fries.

Max let me have the last one.

When he kissed me at the end of the night, I could taste the salt on his lips, and everything about him felt new.

*I* felt new.

It was . . . intoxicating.

"Anywhere you like," the waitress says as Ezra and I step through the door, not even bothering to glance in our direction.

I pull my phone out, checking to see if Max has replied to me yet.

Lily

Sorry, something came up. Rain check??

Tell your mom I'm sorry!

It's been over twenty minutes, but there's still no response.

Biting my lip, I turn my phone on silent and slip it into my pocket.

My confession sucked the air out of Ezra's house, his bedroom growing unbearably small in a matter of seconds.

I wanted to be around people.

Somewhere bright, and loud, and busy.

Somewhere Ezra and I could at least *pretend* to be normal.

Luckily, May is the start of the rainy season here in Florida; though the sun hasn't set yet, the sky overhead is thick with rolling gray clouds. The air feels even heavier than usual, my skin clammy with the weight of unshed rain.

Ezra, still looking slightly traumatized by his three-second trip through the parking lot, heads for the nearest booth, but I shake my head; it's the booth where Max and I sat, all those months ago. "Let's sit over here," I say, leading Ezra toward one of the tiny tables near the bathrooms. The diner is busy for a weeknight, the booths crammed with laughing preteen girls and a group of surly old men sitting at the counter, nursing coffees.

The waitress follows us, plunking two glasses of ice water down on the table. "I'll be back in a minute for your orders."

Despite everything, my stomach rumbles at the thought of food. I take a drink of water, then set it down, shivering a little in the air-conditioning.

Across the Formica table, Ezra gives me a flat look. Then, wordlessly, he shrugs out of his jean jacket and hands it to me.

"I'm fine," I try to insist, but the air-conditioning is cranked, and my arms are covered in goose bumps.

"Don't be a martyr," he says. "Put it on already."

I hesitate for a second, then nod, taking the jacket from him and slipping my arms inside. It's too big for me, and I have to roll the cuffs a couple of times to stop them from covering my hands. I can already feel my goose bumps starting to fade.

Ezra leans forward, crossing his arms on the table in front of him. Square edges of his ink peek out from below his T-shirt.

I take another drink of water, purposefully glancing away.

Across the table, Ezra hooks his chair closer.

"Okay," he says. "We're here. Now *talk*." His palms are flat against the table, his body barely held in check. "What do you mean, you *used* to be a vampire? Like . . . past tense? As in there's a cure? As in you can *fix me*?"

My plastic glass clicks softly as I set it down on the Formica. "Ezra," I say quietly. "Have you ever heard the expression 'the remedy is worse than the disease'?"

"Have you ever heard the expression '*I don't want to be a fucking vampire anymore*'?" he asks. "I don't care how bad the 'remedy' is."

The familiar images flash through my mind before I can block them. Ezra doesn't know what he's asking for.

I grip the edge of the table, meeting his glare.

"Do you want to know why the world isn't overrun with vampires?" I ask.

Ezra blinks.

"Umm," he says. "No?"

"It's because making another vampire, *turning* a human being . . ." I say, ignoring him. "It's almost impossible to do. Most times, it ends badly for everyone involved."

"How badly?" Ezra asks.

"*Slow, agonizing death* kind of badly," I say. "The majority of vampires never turn another human being because altering a life like that—it has consequences. Not every vampire can do it."

Cassius had been the exception, a vampire both old enough *and* strong enough to successfully turn another.

Even so, he'd been sick for weeks afterward.

"And if the process *does* work, which, again, is rare, the original vampire is left practically defenseless. It takes most vampires months to recover their strength afterward."

Ezra pushes his hands through his hair, tugging on the ends of his curls. Across the restaurant, a table full of junior high girls are darting looks in his direction, elbowing one another in the sides between hushed snorts of laughter. I resist the urge to roll my eyes.

"I don't get it," he says. "If making a new vampire is so dangerous, why did that girl risk turning me?"

I consider how to explain. "Vampires aren't exactly known for playing well with others," I begin. "Apex predators and all that. But *humans*? Well, they're another story. A cure for loneliness and a walking Happy Meal all rolled into one."

Ezra shudders. "Awesome," he says. "Thanks for the visual."

I go on, forcing myself to be brutally honest.

"The problem with humans is that we eventually die," I say. "Over and over again, every single time. Watching it happen for centuries on end can have a . . . suboptimal . . . effect on a vampire's mental health."

"Suboptimal effect?" he repeats.

"I'm guessing that whoever turned you may have been experiencing a . . . slight break from reality," I say. "Vampires don't go around turning random humans for no reason. Either she had no idea what she was doing, or . . ."

"*Or . . . ?*" Ezra prompts, his voice grim.

"Or she knew *exactly* what she was doing," I say quietly, giving him an apologetic look. "She knew that trying to turn someone would probably kill her. And she simply . . . *didn't care.*"

Ezra sits back, the muscles in his jaw working back and forth as he processes the information.

"Well," he says at last. "That's unbelievably horrible."

"It gets worse," I warn him, fiddling with the edge of my glass. My nails are short and bitten as I run my fingers around the plastic rim, the polish chipped away at the ends.

"I told you that making a vampire is hard," I go on. "But, as it turns out, *unmaking* a vampire is even harder."

Ezra stops clicking his jaw. Around us, the diner vibrates with energy, but it's as if the air particles at our table have completely stopped moving.

"I need to know," he says. "If there's even a chance that I can go back . . ."

"It won't make things easier," I whisper. "I promise, Ezra, knowing the truth will make everything *harder.*"

"It's my decision, Lily," he says. "You have to let me make it."

I close my eyes, knowing that he's won.

And then I begin.

There had always been rumors, of course.

Cassius and I had been hearing them for as long as we could remember, whispers of miracle cures and snake oil promises, each more ridiculous-sounding than the last.

But this particular rumor couldn't be ignored; a single word repeated over and over again in the darkness.

*Bloodstone.*

It was a promise or a threat, depending on who you talked to. A magical artifact so powerful it could strip a vampire of its very fangs. At a cost, of course.

We spent *decades* searching for it.

With every year, our hope slowly waned, the light at the end of the tunnel growing darker and darker. Maybe the rumors weren't true. Maybe there *wasn't* a cure. Maybe we'd been fooling ourselves all along . . .

By the time I found it, I'd already given up.

The shard of bloodstone was tucked away on one of the bookshelves, hidden just behind an untouched first edition copy of *The Count of Monte Cristo.*

(Cassius was a collector, not a reader.)

How long had the stone been sitting there?

How long had Cassius been *lying* to me?

A week? A month? A year?

*More?*

My hands shook with anger as I reached for the bloodstone.

For something so light, it felt heavy in my hand. As if it carried the weight of Cassius's betrayal.

I didn't even stop to think. I rushed to the roof.

One floor below me, in the penthouse suite of our luxury apartment, Cassius was asleep. Our bed was piled high with crisp Egyptian cotton sheets, a foil-wrapped chocolate waiting expectantly on my pillow.

And I stood on top of the building, watching as the sky faded into the gray predawn light.

The fire door was propped open behind me, ready for me to dart inside at the first painful hint of actual daylight: IN CASE OF EMERGENCY, USE STAIRCASE.

I made sure to lock the door to the stairwell. I didn't want Cassius—or anyone else—to follow me. The rumored consequences of using the bloodstone were as numerous as where to find the stone itself. Whatever was about to take place, well, I didn't want anyone else to see it.

It was starting to drizzle.

Spring came unwillingly to London, most years. Fall wasn't much better, and the winters were straight-up miserable. Still, despite the weather, I kept coming back. Like a moth, drawn to the flame of my previous life, my wings fluttering uselessly against the glass.

I bent my head low against the passing rain, impervious to the cold.

The ritual had seemed so easy at first.

So *simple.*

With one quick motion, I pulled the edge of the bloodstone against my palm. Blood dripped to the floor of the rooftop garden. I watched it stain the petals of the lavender blooms below. I clenched my fist around the gem, feeling it crumble beneath my fingers as I whispered the incantation aloud.

And then, all at once, my mind went . . . blurry.

I remember slamming to the ground, the rough cement pulling at the knees of my trousers and scraping painfully against my palms. The world swirled sickeningly past, spinning me around and around in dizzying circles.

Every limb felt like it was on fire.

My skin was too tight, my throat too raw with sudden, overwhelming thirst. My veins ached and my body burned, crying out with desperate *need.*

At first, I didn't even notice the girl hurrying toward me, her eyes wide with concern.

"Are you okay?" she asked, crouching next to me. "Do you need me to call someone?"

No, no one else was supposed to be here. I tried to make sense of her blurry features, tried to place her unfamiliar voice. But then the wind shifted, blowing her scent in my direction.

Suddenly, my focus was razor-sharp.

And, like a razor, it *cut.*

I remember lunging.

I remember my teeth, ripping into her throat.

The light, dimming in her eyes.

Her long brown hair fanned against the concrete as she slumped to the ground, unmoving. I remember:

*A dark-haired girl.*

*A rooftop.*

*Blood.*

It was over in seconds.

I scrambled backward in horror, frantically wiping at the smear of warm blood on my chin. As if that would somehow wipe away the evidence of what I'd done. As if it would make her *alive* again.

I could already feel her blood curdling in my stomach.

Pain ripped through me, my body convulsing in agony. My hands scrabbled against the concrete as I leaned forward, trying uselessly to brace myself.

The thick black bile that spewed from my mouth was like nothing I'd ever known before.

I could taste the *wrongness* of it as I choked and gasped and clawed against the never-ending onslaught.

By the time it was over, there was nothing left of me.

I lay there on that rooftop waiting to die—*wanting* to die. But instead, I felt the raindrops hit my face.

It was morning.

And, for the first time in over a century and a half, I was cold.

No.

I wasn't cold; I was *freezing.*

Shivering uncontrollably, I wrapped my arms around myself, tears dripping through the blood still smeared across my cheeks.

Next to me, the girl stared unseeingly up at the sky.

The dawn was unfolding in waves of shimmering red and gold.

The sliver of sunlight peeking over the London skyline was the most beautiful thing I'd ever seen. And I had just done the most terrible thing imaginable.

I looked down at my still-bleeding hands uncomprehendingly.

With every breath, I could feel a dull stab of pain.

With every *breath.*

My hands trembling, I reached up, pressing my palm flat to my chest.

Beneath my fingers, my heart was racing, my lungs rising and falling in a rhythm I'd almost forgotten.

I was alive.

And the girl next to me would never be again.

I take a deep, shuddering breath, looking at Ezra from across the table.

"And after all of that, I walked away," I say. "I knew the bloodstone was dangerous, and I took it, anyway. I don't even know her *name*, Ezra. All I know is that she's *dead.* Because of me. Because of what *I* did."

*A life for a life*, I think dully.

Ezra reaches across the table, but I pull away, flinching at the thought of his touch.

"Lily," he says. "It's not your fault. You couldn't have known."

"Maybe not," I say, blinking back tears. "But you *can.* And I'm telling you, the bloodstone isn't a cure. It's a *curse.*"

# CHAPTER Eleven

I WAIT FOR EZRA'S EYES TO FILL WITH JUDGMENT. With disgust. With *loathing.*

After all, I just confessed to killing *an innocent girl.*

Ezra should hate me as much as I hate myself.

He should realize that he can't even stand to *look* at me.

But for some reason, his gaze doesn't even falter.

"It doesn't matter, anyway," I say, glancing away in confusion. "Even if you *were* willing to kill an innocent person, you'd still need to find another piece of bloodstone."

"So what?" Ezra asks. "It's a rock. Rocks are *everywhere.*"

"Not like this one," I say. "It's a shard of the original stone placed above the burial site of the ancient Irish chieftain Abhartach. Ask anyone today, and they'll say Abhartach was a myth, but I think you've figured out by now, some legends are real."

Across the table, Ezra swallows. "He was a vampire?"

"Abhartach was the *original* vampire," I answer. "According to the stories, he wouldn't stop coming back from the dead and demanding 'blood tributes' from his people. It ended up being . . . a whole thing."

In the end, they stabbed the guy through the heart with a sword made of yew wood, buried him upside down, covered him in thorns, and placed the bloodstone boulder over his grave.

"*That's* the rock you're looking for," I say. "A piece of Abhartach's original headstone."

"Okay, so we go to Ireland and bring a chisel," Ezra says.

"The gravestone disappeared sometime around the seventh century," I say. "It took over a hundred years for me to find a single shard. I don't even know if another one *exists*."

We both straighten as the waitress stalks back over to our table, pad in hand. "What can I get you?"

I summon my smile like armor, beaming up at her as if I don't have a care in the world. "I'll have the pecan waffles with a side of bacon, please. And a hot chocolate, extra whipped cream."

She nods, not even bothering to look up. "For you, hon?"

"Coffee," Ezra says. "Black."

"And a large side of French fries," I add. "Please."

"I'm not hungry," Ezra starts to say, but I wave him off, waiting until the waitress walks away.

"You're at a restaurant," I remind him. "Try to *blend*."

Ezra sits back in his chair, picking at a loose edge of the tabletop.

For a moment, there's silence, punctuated only by the giggles of the junior high schoolers at the next table over.

In my back pocket, I can feel my phone buzzing.

I don't reach for it.

"The girl on the rooftop," Ezra says at last. "She was the first person you . . ."

"Killed?" I finish, the word tasting like bile in my throat. "Yes. She was . . ." I pause, swallowing hard. "She was the only one."

Ezra leans forward, his eyes searching.

"How long?" he asks. "How long did you make it before . . ."

I take a deep breath, letting it go with a *whoosh.* "I was turned in 1867."

The waitress walks past, dropping a pitcher of syrup off at the edge of our table without stopping.

"1867," Ezra repeats. "Are you serious?"

"As a heart attack," I say. "Which, for the record, you don't have to worry about anymore. Vampire perk."

He ignores my joke.

"That's . . ." I wait while he counts the decades off in his head. "You've been alive for over a hundred and fifty years?"

"Technically, I was dead for most of them," I say, swinging for the fences.

Ezra doesn't smile.

"Tough crowd," I mutter aloud.

"That's impossible," Ezra says bluntly. "You look . . . you're *my* age."

"And I've been your age for a very, very long time," I agree.

Ezra sits back in his chair, still looking at me like I'm one of P. T. Barnum's sideshow attractions. Or whatever the equivalent of that is, nowadays. I want to say . . . reality dating shows?

Shifting uncomfortably in my chair, I pull Ezra's jacket more closely around me.

"So, how did it happen?" he asks abruptly. "This Cassius guy, the one who found the cure. Was he the one who turned you?"

I try not to flinch at Cassius's name.

"He saved me," I say automatically, repeating the words that I've told myself so often. "If it hadn't been for him, I would have died."

"Of what?" Ezra asks.

I trail my finger through the water left behind by my glass, tracing the outline of a rectangle on the table in front of me. The same shape as the small window above my hospital bed, so grimy with soot and dirt that only the faintest rays of light seemed to penetrate.

The room was dank and airless, the stench of unwashed bodies and unemptied chamber pots mingling with darker scents: bandages crusted with dried blood, maggots crawling beneath them, and the sharp, putrid stink of gangrene.

My hair was heavier then, sweaty and lank, past my shoulders, my entire body screaming with pain.

"It was a fire," I explain. "In the factory where I worked, cutting matches. In a good week, I could make eight shillings. In a bad week, well . . ."

I blink hard, trying not to remember the heat and the noise and the stench of the factory floor. The way my wrists ached, and my fingers trembled with exhaustion, and just the sight of the lecherous foreman could make my stomach clench with nerves.

"They were mostly bad weeks," I say, trying and failing to force a smile.

"Noted," Ezra says, his voice careful.

"Back in the day, matches were dipped in phosphorus," I go

on, taking a deep breath. "There must have been a spark or a mistake or . . . I don't even know. Whatever it was, I'm told the entire place went up like a tinderbox. I have no idea how I made it outside. That's where Cassius found me . . . there on the pavement. I was . . . I was still *burning*."

I can only remember flashes of it: the horrible, strangely colored phosphorus flames, wreathing my entire body. A half-choked scream of terror escaping from my lips. A tall, shadowy figure, appearing out of nowhere, wrapping me in sudden darkness.

"Cassius managed to smother the worst of the flames with his cloak, but by the time he got me to the hospital, it was already too late."

I remember a cool hand, pressing against my forehead. Gentle fingers smoothing back my hair. A soft prick on my neck, and a voice, whispering in my ear that everything would be all right.

Cassius's voice. His tall, inky silhouette wavering in the fluttering gaslight.

*A dream*, I thought.

My own guardian angel, come to save me.

"He didn't have to save me. He didn't even *know* me. But he did. And when I woke up the next morning, I was healed. It was a miracle," I say. "Believe me, not a lot of people walked out of the hospital back then. But a few days later . . ."

"You started puking blood," Ezra finishes for me.

The waitress, who's suddenly appeared at our table again, doesn't even blink. Ezra mumbles a thank-you as she sets two mugs down on the table, but she's already halfway across the diner, writing up another ticket.

I'm telling you, if waitresses ruled the world, there'd be a lot less bullshit.

"So, then what?" Ezra asks, his coffee cup untouched in front of him.

I wrap both hands around my own mug, letting the warmth spread through my body. There's a huge dollop of whipped cream on top, from a can, obviously, but still sprinkled with cocoa powder. I take a sip, savoring the taste.

Hot chocolate: human perk.

"You have a whipped cream mustache," Ezra informs me.

"*You* have a whipped cream mustache," I reply nonsensically. I go to swipe my sleeve across my mouth, then remember that I'm wearing Ezra's jacket. Guiltily, I reach for a napkin instead. It gets stuck in the container, of course, the paper shredding in my hand. I wad it up, gingerly sponging my upper lip as Ezra watches. "Better?"

"Better," he agrees.

"So, yeah," I say, setting the mug down on the table but keeping my hands wrapped around it for warmth. It feels . . . *strange* . . . to be talking to Ezra about my past. I've never told anyone my story before. I've never *wanted* to.

It's odd; sometimes, when I'm with Max, I can almost pretend my past never happened.

"Cassius found me that night," I go on. "He explained what happened. What he'd . . . done."

Like Ezra, I hadn't believed it at first. I'd thought Cassius was a madman.

And then the blood began to call to me . . .

"Cassius took care of me," I say. "And I took care of him."

"What about your family?" Ezra asks quietly. "Your friends? Did you ever see them again? After you . . . turned?" His voice is even, but his hands have gone unnaturally still on the table as he waits for my answer.

I pause, biting my lip, debating what to say. But anything other than the truth is less than he deserves. "No. But it was a different time," I add quickly. "I didn't have any siblings, and I was a working-class girl in Victorian England. I couldn't *disappear* and then come back with some fancy gentleman at my side. Not without a lot of very hard-to-answer questions. And even if I'd wanted to, I wouldn't have been able to visit my parents; they died from pneumonia soon after."

*And heartache*, I think to myself, though I'd never say it aloud.

I remember my mother, the unruly waves of her hair and her surprisingly deep laugh. The way she liked to sing as we walked together when I was young. The way my father smelled like pipe smoke and couldn't stand the taste of butter. The soft crinkle as he spread his newspaper across the dining room table after dinner.

The memories are faded; blurred with time.

I don't even have a picture of them.

"So," I say, clearing my throat. "That's pretty much it. Cassius taught me how to feed without hurting anyone. How to stay hidden from the world. How to protect myself. It was . . . good. For a while, at least."

Until it wasn't.

I pause, taking another slurp of hot chocolate. The powder

is already congealing in thick clumps, the taste cloyingly sweet on my tongue.

I set the cup down, pushing it away.

Ezra sits back in his chair, looking at me. "So, how did you end up in Sunrise Harbor? You could have gone literally anywhere in the *world*, and you ended up in Florida. The armpit of the East Coast."

Florida.

The Sunshine State.

After a lifetime spent in darkness, I'd liked the ring of it. Florida was warm. It had beaches. Fresh-squeezed orange juice by the gallon. Hell, Florida had fucking *Disney World*.

It was perfect.

I shrug in Ezra's direction. "Maybe I like it here."

"There are literally three Applebee's in this town," Ezra says, holding up his fingers to demonstrate. "That's how much people here love Applebee's. So much that we need *three* of them."

I toss a sugar packet at his head.

He catches it easily, his hand actually blurring a little in the air. As I watch, he rips it open and dumps it into his coffee. He only takes one sip before pushing it to the side, grimacing.

"Is it me, or does everything except blood taste like dirt now?"

"It gets easier," I say. "After a while, you don't even notice the taste."

Ezra looks skeptical.

Probably rightfully so.

He slides the cup farther away. "So, you've really been alive for a hundred and fifty years, huh?"

"It depends on your definition of 'alive,' I guess."

"The stock market crash of 1929." He holds up his hand again, ticking his fingers off one by one. "The moon landing. The sinking of the *Titanic.* JFK's assassination. World War I. World War *II.* The fall of the Berlin Wall. You were there for all of them."

I roll my eyes.

"I'm not Forrest Gump," I say. "It's not like I was standing on the deck of the *Titanic* as it sank. I've never even been to Berlin. And I spent the entirety of World War I in Spanish Morocco."

He looks a little crestfallen.

"I saw *Star Wars* on opening night: 1977. Mann's Chinese Theater," I offer, not wanting to disappoint him completely.

I can still feel the floor, sticky beneath my feet, the whispers of the crowd fading away as the music began. The way my stomach swooped with excitement as the opening words crawled across the screen.

*A long time ago in a galaxy far, far away . . .*

It was only fifty years ago, but it feels like light-years.

Ha ha.

Do you see what I did there?

"So that's what you did with your immortality, huh?" Ezra asks. "Watched movies?"

I shrug. "Sorry if my afterlife wasn't up to your standards."

Across the restaurant, the clump of junior high girls are finally leaving, clustered together so tightly they resemble an octopus. They collapse into a fresh wave of giggles as they pass by our table, the most daring one risking a glance in Ezra's direction.

He doesn't even notice her.

"All I'm saying is would a little culture have killed you?" he asks me. "Maybe a quick whirl through a museum or two? Stopping by the symphony now and again? No offense; watching *Star Wars* is great and everything. But it feels like in a hundred and fifty years, maybe you should have *lived* a little more."

I toy with the handle of my mug, remembering the pillow of snow beneath my head as I gazed up at the northern lights in Iceland, watching the ethereal colors dance above me. The eerie blue glow of the phosphorescent grotto in Malta as the water lapped quietly beneath our boat. Hearing Sweet Emma Barrett play the piano for the first time, the music vibrating all around me and the air thick with cigarette smoke and possibility.

And then I think of Sarita, making me laugh so hard that I snort iced coffee through my nose. I think of Max, spinning me around in the air until I'm dizzy. Of Ezra, rescuing me at Mia's party with the single most ridiculous excuse in human history.

They're small moments.

Insignificant, even.

But somehow, it feels like they matter more.

"I'll take it under advisement," I say as the waitress arrives with the plates of food. I smile, thanking her, then reach for a piece of bacon, closing my eyes in ecstasy as I chew.

"Do you need a minute alone with that?" Ezra asks.

"Sorry," I say, cramming one of his French fries in my mouth, too. "I'm starving."

For a second, I can't help picturing my empty seat at Max's dining room table. I wonder how long they waited before eating without me.

I hope the pot roast wasn't stone-cold.

Guiltily, I reach for the pitcher of maple syrup. I pour it liberally over my waffles, making sure to fill every indentation. The devil is in the details when it comes to waffles. "Speaking of which . . ." I say, setting down the syrup and reaching for my fork.

"Speaking of what?" he asks. "Waffles?"

Stabbing a huge bite, I cram it in my mouth.

"Speaking of *you*," I say around my mouthful of delicious, delicious waffles. "I'm not a one-woman bloodmobile, Ezra. It's time for you to graduate to Vampire 102."

Ezra eyes me warily across the table. "Vampire 102?"

I grin, forking up another bite. "Intro to Feeding."

# CHAPTER *Twelve*

DESPITE THE FACT THAT THE SUN SET OVER AN hour ago, the restaurant parking lot still reminds me of a sauna. The second we step outside, I can feel my jeans sticking to my legs, a trickle of perspiration already making its way down my back.

I'd forgotten how much humans *sweat.*

Though I'm pleased to report that deodorant technology has come a *long* way in the past century and a half.

Peeling off Ezra's jacket, I hold it out for him. But Ezra's eyes are fastened on something behind me, scanning the parking lot with a strange, sudden intensity.

Despite the heat, a prickle of cold fear runs down my back.

"What?" I ask, turning to peer into the darkness. "What is it?"

Across the parking lot, a car door slams. I tense, my keys cutting into the palm of my hand.

A second later, a middle-aged couple in matching Panthers jerseys cuts in front of us, making their way into the diner.

Sheepishly, Ezra and I turn to look at each other.

"Sorry," I say, shaking my head back and forth to clear it. "I'm a little . . . paranoid these days."

"Tell me about it," Ezra says. Taking the jacket from me, he slides into the car.

I do the same, flinching at the temperature inside. If the parking lot feels like a sauna, the inside of my Ford Fiesta feels like *the surface of the sun*.

"One sec," I say, fumbling to turn the key in the ignition. For some reason, I feel even clumsier than usual. "Let me turn on the air."

"It's fine," he says. "I'm not hot. Or cold. Or . . . *anything*." He looks down at his arms, turning them back and forth. "I could be standing in a snowstorm right now, and I wouldn't even feel it. Is that normal?"

"Vampire perk," I say, finally getting the engine to turn over. Hot, humid air begins to flow through the vents, somehow making the interior of the car even more sweltering than before. "You are now officially impervious to weather."

Reaching behind me, I awkwardly wiggle my phone out of my back pocket.

Ezra looks down at the jean jacket in his hands. "Well. I guess I can get rid of this."

Wistfully, I think of my silver beaded flapper dress, a hint of smoke still clinging to the fabric after all these years.

The ridiculous hat I wore to view Queen Victoria's funeral procession, almost two feet wide and heaped with snowy-white silk flowers. She'd banned black at her funeral and was buried in her wedding veil.

I always had a soft spot for her and Prince Albert.

"Keep it," I say, finally managing to free my phone. "Trust me; good denim never goes out of style."

My heart sinks as I realize that Max still hasn't replied.

I thumb quickly through the rest of my messages, most of them from Sarita—she must have decided against the shark onesie, after all, because she's sent a billion pictures of herself modeling possible prom outfits at one of the local vintage stores. I scroll through them as quickly as I can, nixing the obvious noes (head-to-toe leopard print, a Dick Tracy–style zoot suit, a literal *wedding dress*) and giving a thumbs-up to a simple red slip dress, the best option by far.

Then, clearing my throat, I drop my phone into the cupholder.

"Don't forget your seat belt," I say.

The fabric-covered bucket seats of my car are so small that his fingers almost brush against mine as we reach for our buckles.

"Sorry about the mess," I babble, my voice slightly too loud. How can sitting next to Ezra in a car feel more intimate than *feeding him my blood*?

Grabbing the (mostly) empty Burger Queen bags at his feet, I toss them onto the floor behind me.

"Don't worry about it," Ezra says. "A messy car isn't exactly high on my list of problems right now." Reaching out, he taps the bobblehead that sits on the dash, watching as it wobbles back and forth.

"Princess Leia," he comments.

"I told you," I say, throwing the car in gear. "*Star Wars* forever."

The vents are still blowing hot air, circulating the scent of leftover hamburgers through the car.

For a moment, I allow myself to think about my 1957 Maserati 300S, with its buttery-soft leather seats and its cherry-red exterior. Cassius surprised me with it for my birthday one year; another of his typical over-the-top gifts.

God, I loved that car.

They only made twenty-six of them, ever. It went from zero to sixty in less than five seconds, and I swear, the first time I drove it, I felt like I was flying.

I wrapped it around a tree not too many years later; in the end, all that was left was the steering wheel.

Well, and me, I suppose.

"So, where are we going, anyway?" Ezra asks, still watching the bobblehead with a slightly mesmerized expression. "Some sort of . . . blood bank, or something?"

"It's nine p.m. on a Wednesday," I say, flooring it out of the parking lot. Ezra grabs the edge of his seat as I careen around the corner, pushing my Ford Fiesta to its limits. "Do you really think *blood banks* are open right now?"

"Er . . ." Ezra says. "I don't know. Maybe?"

"The answer is no," I say. "They're not. Also, blood banks have cameras. They have security systems. They have *validated parking*. Breaking into one is, like . . . a last resort kind of thing."

"Got it," Ezra says. My Princess Leia bobblehead wobbles drunkenly on the dash as I speed toward the beach with reckless enthusiasm. A row of overpriced tourist bars lines the street; they may have different names, but they're all the same, with dimly lit corners, watered-down mixed drinks, and shitty dance music pounding through a PA system at top volume.

Ezra gives me a look as we pull up in front of the largest one.

"Club Wett?" he reads aloud, his voice thick with disbelief. "Are you serious?"

"Um, excuse me," I say, cutting the engine. "Do I look like the kind of person who would joke about a place called *Club Wett*?"

Ezra looks physically pained. "Please tell me we're not actually going in there," he says.

I nod toward the folding sign propped outside the door. The words **18+ NIGHT!** are emblazoned across it in neon pink letters.

"Yeah," I tell Ezra. "Unless you have a fake ID that can get you in somewhere else, this is our only option."

Ezra leans back against the headrest, closing his eyes. "Awesome."

"I know it's embarrassing, but this location is ideal," I say. "It's dark, it's loud, it's depressingly crowded . . . It's the perfect place to learn to feed. And you *do* need to learn how to feed, Ezra," I add, my voice softening. His white T-shirt is practically glowing in the neon light from the overhead sign, his curly hair flopping messily over his forehead. "Preferably *before* I develop anemia."

Ezra opens his eyes, turning to look at me. His hands are clenched on his seat again, his fingers biting into the cheap fabric cover.

"I know," he says, his voice serious. "You're right. I'm . . . nervous."

The interior of the car is hot and still, the thumping bass music from the club reverberating softly through the floor.

The space between us seems to have shrunk into nothing.

I can't help thinking of the first time I ever saw Ezra, sliding into the seat next to mine during study hall on the first day of school. It wasn't even lunchtime yet, but my cheeks already ached from smiling at everyone I met, and the sound of my own name had already lost all meaning.

As Ezra turned in my direction, I automatically summoned another smile, waiting for him to introduce himself.

But instead, he just . . . looked at me.

It sounds ridiculous, but for the first time all day, it felt like someone was actually *seeing* me.

No.

That's not true.

For the first time in a *century*, it felt like someone was actually seeing me.

It felt . . . nice.

No, better than nice.

It felt *right*.

But before I could say anything, Ezra turned away.

A second later, a blond-haired boy sat down in front of me, his grin so bright that it felt as if I was staring directly into the sun.

By the end of the week, Max and I were dating.

And the next time Ezra looked at me, it was like he didn't see me at all.

"I don't want to hurt anyone, Lily," Ezra whispers now,

his soft voice bringing me back to the present. "I don't want to hurt *you*."

My breath hitches in the silence.

"Ezra . . ." I say. "I—"

My phone buzzes again, rattling insistently against the plastic cupholder.

For a long moment, neither of us move. And then Ezra pulls back as I reach for my phone.

Max has finally texted me back:

Max

For the record, the pot roast was delicious.

As I shove my phone into my pocket, Ezra pushes his hand through his hair, looking away.

Whatever moment we might have had, it's already passed.

"Promise you won't let me go off the rails?" Ezra asks, his hand already on the door handle.

I nod, my fingers clumsy as I reach for my seat belt clasp.

"Trust me," I say aloud. "It's going to be fine."

# CHAPTER Thirteen

A BALDING BOUNCER SITS ON A STOOL NEXT to the door of Club Wett, his scalp lit up blue and green by the neon lights above.

Ezra pulls his driver's license out of his wallet, handing it over to the bouncer as I scrabble for my own *slightly* less legal one.

It's shockingly easy to buy a fake ID these days; all you need is fifty bucks, a post office box, and a certain . . . moral flexibility.

The bouncer grunts, marking our hands with a bright **UNDER 21** stamp before waving us through.

The inside of the club feels like a seizure waiting to happen.

The dance floor is lit by choppy, multicolored strobe lights and crowded with young people, a tangle of sunburnt skin and sweaty armpits and *way* too much body spray. This early in the night, it's mostly high school kids, with a few obnoxiously drunk frat guys mixed in just for fun.

"Okay," I say aloud, raising my voice to be heard above the music. "Good. This is good!"

"I think you and I might have different definitions of the word 'good,' " Ezra calls back.

Rolling my eyes, I pull him toward the under-twenty-one bar. "Two waters?" I ask the nearest waitress. "Bottled, please."

She doesn't even break stride as she reaches below the bar and shoves two lukewarm waters vaguely in our direction.

"Eighteen bucks."

Gritting my teeth, I drop a twenty on the bar, then lead Ezra toward the quietest corner I can find. Gingerly, I settle down on a cracked plastic barstool, making sure no part of my bare skin actually touches anything.

"Okay," I say, sliding one of the water bottles toward Ezra. "Look around. What do you see?"

Ezra obediently glances around the club. "I don't know," he says. "Terrible music taste? Rampant venereal disease? *Way* too many male tank tops?"

"People," I correct him, cracking open my water. "You see *people.* Also known as 'dinner.' "

Ezra leans forward, burying his head in his hands.

"Could you make it sound any creepier?"

"I hate to break it to you, Ezra, but you're the walking undead," I say bluntly. "It doesn't get much creepier than you. Think about it; you're a violation of the natural order. Your very existence is *obscene.*"

Ezra blinks, pushing his hair back. "Wow," he says. "Has anyone ever told you that you're *terrible* at pep talks?"

*"But,"* I add, ignoring him, "none of that is your fault. You didn't ask to be a vampire. And underneath it all, you're still *you*. So, you have a choice." I hold up one hand, weighing the first option. "Choice number one: You can be a martyr. Choose not to drink blood. Slowly and painfully waste away into dust."

"Please tell me the second option is better than the first," Ezra says.

"Choice number two," I say, holding up my other hand. "You go on a murderous blood-filled rampage, leaving a trail of half-drained corpses in your wake."

"So that's a no on the 'better option' thing, huh?" Ezra asks.

"There's always the *third* choice," I say, dropping my hands to the table, then immediately regretting it. I pull away quickly, wiping my palms on my jean shorts. "You learn how to feed. The *correct* way. Without hurting anyone. Without anyone even realizing what you've done."

Ezra nods in relief. "Yes. I'll take door number three, please, Vanna."

"Wrong game show. But I like your instincts. So," I say, gesturing toward the dance floor. "Who here looks good enough to eat?"

Ezra looks pained. "Is there any possible way to answer that without sounding like a massive perv?"

I grin. "Nope."

"Great," he says. Sitting up a little straighter on his stool, he scans the club, his eyes roaming helplessly over the crowd of teenagers. "I don't know," he says. "No one?"

I give him a look.

"Fine," he says. "*Everyone.* Are you happy?" He drops his head to the table, his shoulders slumping. "I hate this."

"It gets easier," I say. "Don't look at their faces. Concentrate on their heartbeats. If you concentrate, you can hear the blood pumping in their veins."

His head still flat on the table, Ezra gives me an incredulous look. "Are you serious?" he asks. "Have you heard the music in here? It's like the Thunderdome. But *louder.* How am I supposed to hear someone's *blood pumping in their veins*?"

"You're a vampire now," I point out. "The laws of science don't apply to you anymore. So, *try.*"

Ezra sits up, peering dubiously around the club again. After a moment, I see his eyes slowly widen, his gaze darken with hunger.

My own pulse quickens in response.

"Okay," Ezra breathes, holding himself very still.

"You hear them, don't you?" I ask.

He pauses, nodding, slowly licking his lips. "What do I do now?"

For some reason, I'm having a hard time concentrating.

"Now, you, um . . . learn to glamour someone," I say, pushing a lock of loose hair behind my ear. Then, thinking better of it, I quickly pull it forward again, hiding the bare curve of my neck.

Better safe than sorry.

"What?" Ezra tears his eyes away from the crowd to look at

me. “You mean, like . . . hypnotize them? Because I hate to break it to you, but I’m not a fucking *magician*.”

“First of all, magicians are awesome,” I say. “And secondly, glamouring someone is easy. You just have to lean into your natural charm.”

Ezra gives me a flat look. “Yes,” he says. “Because I’m known for my natural charm.”

“Your *supernatural* charm,” I correct myself. “Think of it this way: There’s a reason everyone thinks vampires are sexy, right?”

“Wait. You think I’m sexy?” Ezra asks.

Beneath the strobing lights, I can feel my cheeks flushing.

“I’m talking about vampires in *general*,” I say. “Not *you* specifically.”

“Sure,” Ezra says, obviously enjoying himself. “Whatever you need to tell yourself.”

“The secret to glamouring someone is eye contact,” I explain, grinding my teeth. “All you have to do is get the other person to relax. Your vampire senses will take care of the rest.”

“What do you mean, ‘relax’?” Ezra asks, his voice dubious. “Like . . . offer them a neck massage?”

I roll my eyes.

“*Flirt*, Ezra,” I say. “You’re supposed to *flirt*.”

“Right,” Ezra says, lowering his voice in an attempt to sound smooth. Self-consciously, he tosses his head to the side, flicking back the curls that have spilled over his forehead. “I, um, I knew that.”

As I watch, he flicks his head again with forced swagger, nearly falling off the stool this time.

It's like watching a train wreck happen in slow motion.

Only worse.

"Okay, this is officially tragic." I stand up, gesturing toward Ezra. "Practice on me."

"Oh, thank God," Ezra says in his normal voice. He pushes himself off his stool to face me. "Yeah. I can do that."

Awkwardly, he adjusts the collar of his T-shirt.

"So, uh . . . how do I start?" he asks.

"Are you asking me how to flirt?"

Ezra gives me a look. Stepping forward, he closes the distance between us.

"Hey," he says, sticking out his hand. "I'm Ezra."

"Lily," I say, taking his hand.

Despite the heat of the club, Ezra's fingers are cool against mine. I suppress a shiver as his thumb accidentally brushes my wrist, my nerve endings jumping suddenly to life.

*Get a grip, Lily.*

"Lily," Ezra repeats, his fingers still tangled with mine. "Like the flower."

My heartbeat slows. I can feel the music reverberating through the floor, the beat pulsing relentlessly in my veins.

*Ezra*, I remind myself hazily. *It's EZRA.*

"I've always liked lilies." His words flow around me like water. "They seem . . . *sharp*."

I tilt my head in confusion.

"They're *spikier* than other flowers," Ezra explains quickly, stepping closer. "But that's what makes them beautiful."

My cheeks heat. Even when his fangs emerge, slipping over

his bottom lip, I can't look away. Ezra's eyes are pools of liquid darkness.

I can feel his other hand slipping around my waist, his grip the only thing keeping me upright. The only thing keeping me from floating away.

In the strobing darkness of the club, Ezra's fangs are almost glowing.

All the breath leaves my body as I imagine tilting my head to the side. I can feel his fangs scraping softly against my bare neck. Can feel them *plunging* into—

"Er, Lily?" Ezra asks in concern. "Are you okay?"

I come back to the present abruptly, blinking up at Ezra in confusion. Somehow, the club seems even louder than before, the strobe lights spinning garishly around and around the dance floor.

"I'm great," I say, smiling brightly. "That was really, uh . . . great." I give him an awkward punch on the arm. "Really good first try." I step backward, slipping from Ezra's grip.

Ezra shoves his hands in his pockets, looking relieved.

"Are you sure?" he asks. "It wasn't too much? The whole *flower* thing? Because I kind of . . . took a swing."

"I'm sure," I say. "In fact, I think you're ready for the big leagues."

Ezra blinks. "What?" he asks. "Right now?"

"No time like the present!" I turn away from him, scanning the dance floor. It's even more packed than before, a sea of glow-in-the-dark necklaces and backward baseball caps and . . . *Oh. My. God.*

Smack in the middle of the dance floor, a familiar face turns in our direction.

"Is that . . . *Noah Coates*?" Ezra asks in a slightly strangled voice.

Unlike Ezra, Noah *clearly* owns a fake ID; I can practically smell the Captain Morgan fumes from here.

As Ezra and I watch in silent fascination, Noah throws his head back, letting out a loud *"Whooo!"* He whips his shirt off, waving it back and forth around his head like the world's most ineffective lasso.

"Wow," I say. "Being the head of the prom committee must be more stressful than I thought."

"You have to admit," Ezra says, "if nothing else, he's *going* for it."

As Noah gives another loud "Whoo!" I grab Ezra's arm, yanking him away from the dance floor before Noah can see us. The last thing we need right now is to be recognized by someone from school.

Especially someone who owns his own *megaphone.*

"What are you doing?" Ezra asks as I pull him toward the rear exit of the club. "Shouldn't we get out of here?"

"Not yet," I say determinedly.

We fall in step behind a college kid in a backward Gators cap. As he pushes open the heavy metal door into the parking lot, he's already pulling drunkenly on his vape.

"Really?" Ezra asks, wrinkling his nose in distaste. *"Him?"*

"Please don't be all weird about glamouring a guy," I say.

"Because I hate to break it to you, but they're, like, fifty percent of your food base."

Ezra shoots me a look of annoyance. "It's not that," he says. "He looks kind of . . . douchey."

"Of course he does," I say, pausing with my hand on the door. "But he also looks like *dinner*."

# CHAPTER Fourteen

CHECKING TO MAKE SURE THAT NOAH IS STILL occupied on the dance floor, I push open the door, leading Ezra into the dimly lit back parking lot. Despite being so close to the beach, I can't smell the ocean; instead, the humid night air reeks of asphalt and cool mint vapes, with the lingering tang of fresh vomit.

College Guy is leaning against the back of his truck, a thin cloud of haze surrounding him as he scrolls through his phone.

"Remember, it's all about the eye contact," I say softly. "Ask him for a light or something."

Ezra gives me a look. "Seriously?" he asks. "You're a hundred-and-fifty-year-old teenager, and you don't know how *vapes* work?"

"The longer you drink from someone, the harder it is to stop," I say, hardening my voice. "Count to thirty in your head, okay? *Thirty seconds.* You don't want to accidentally drain him."

Ezra jogs in place for a minute, slapping his hands against his thighs. "Okay," he says aloud, obviously trying to convince himself. "Okay, yeah. I can do this. But wait," he adds, turning to look at me. "What if he's expecting it?"

"What if he's expecting a *vampire attack*?" I repeat. "You do know that, like, ninety-nine point nine percent of the population doesn't even *believe* in vampires, right? Plus, look at him," I say encouragingly, gesturing toward the stranger. "He's, like, six two. He's not going to be expecting anyone to mess with him."

Lucky him.

I remember when I wasn't afraid of the dark.

I remember when I *was* the dark.

Ezra closes his eyes. "For the record, this is a terrible idea, and I'm definitely about to get beaten up."

I think of Ezra's magnetic pull in the club. The heady swirl of his eyes fastened on mine, and the liquid blackness that I wanted to disappear into.

"Trust me," I say, swallowing hard. "All you have to do is get him to look at you. The rest will take care of itself."

Ezra takes a deep breath, visibly bracing himself.

"Fine," he says. "But . . . don't watch, okay?"

"I've seen worse," I say, shrugging. Ezra looks down, shuffling his feet. "I won't look," I add. "Promise."

He jumps up and down a few more times, then turns to make his move.

*"Thirty seconds,"* I hiss after him as he sets determinedly across the parking lot. "I'm *serious*, Ezra!"

I can just barely see him nod in the distance.

Without vampire hearing, I'm too far away to know what Ezra says as he approaches, but out of the corner of my eye, I see College Guy's shoulders relaxing.

Ezra takes a step closer, a tall, slim figure in the moonlight, his white T-shirt flashing beneath his jacket.

As promised, I turn away, taking the opportunity to scan the parking lot for any visible cameras. Somehow, despite the lack of security, I still can't shake the feeling that someone is watching us.

I hear a muffled cry of surprise and begin to count.

One . . .

Two . . .

Three . . .

Four . . .

Somewhere behind me, Ezra's entire life is changing.

After this, he'll never be the same person again.

He'll never be a *person* again, full stop.

Ten seconds.

Twenty.

The breeze off the ocean has picked up, the stale, garbage-perfumed air blowing loose strands of hair around my face.

I feel sick to my stomach.

I shouldn't have made Ezra do this yet. Not here. Not like *this.*

Clenching my hands at my sides, I force myself to keep counting.

Thirty seconds.

Thirty-five.

*Forty.*

Ezra should already be making his way back to me. But when I turn to look, I spot him lunging forward again, sinking his fangs more deeply into College Guy's neck. Even in the dim glow of the barely lit parking lot, I can see the blood pouring down his neck, spilling greedily from the wound Ezra has torn open in his hunger.

"Ezra!" My lungs seize. I break into a run, my sneakers slapping against the pavement. "Stop!"

College Guy is losing too much blood, too quickly. I watch as he slumps, unmoving, against the side of the truck, his head lolling to one side. *No, no, no.* The scene is all too familiar.

"Ezra!" I yell, skidding to a stop behind him. *"Ezra!"*

Up close, the college kid looks even worse; his skin is pale and clammy, his eyes flickering weakly up and down. I reach for Ezra's arm with both hands, trying to pull him away.

"Ezra! You need to stop! *Now!*"

He growls low in his throat, shaking off my grip.

Gritting my teeth, I grab his arm again, yanking backward with every ounce of strength I have left. He doesn't even notice.

*"Ezra!"* I cry desperately. "You're going to kill him!" I think of the packed crowd inside the nightclub; of the dozens of people who could walk outside at any moment. My stomach lurches as I imagine the look on Noah Coates's face as he watches Ezra sink his teeth into someone else's throat.

We need to move.

*Now.*

I give another useless tug on Ezra's arm, my senses flooding with frustration and fear. He growls again, louder this time, turning to glare at me. His dark brown eyes are blank with hunger, the irises tinged with red. Blood smears his mouth, dripping down his chin.

"Ezra—" I try not to let my terror show on my face. *"Please,* you have to stop," I beg.

Wrenching free from my grip, he whirls toward the truck. I lose my balance, stumbling backward. My palms scrape painfully against the pavement as I catch myself, but I scramble to my feet again, determinedly ignoring the ache.

This isn't happening.

I'm not *letting* it happen.

I promised Ezra that everything would be okay.

For *once* in my life, I'm going to keep my promises.

Racing forward, I hook my elbows over the back of College Guy's truck, boosting myself up to scan the open cargo bed.

There's not much: a few lengths of twine, an abandoned dog dish, and a tarp . . . neatly folded and weighted down with a brick.

Bingo.

Grabbing the brick, I drop from the truck and brace my back foot against the curb.

Holding tight, I take aim.

Then, with everything I have, I swing the brick through the air, smashing it against the side of Ezra's head.

He crumples to the ground, momentarily incapacitated.

Darting forward, I step over his body, barely managing to catch College Guy before he hits the asphalt, too. He sags forward, his knees buckling beneath him.

As I stagger under his weight, he makes a sort of low, groaning noise.

Panic splices through me, threatening to cut me in half.

Forcing myself to stop shaking, I manage to open the door of the truck with one hand and shove the kid inside, pushing his legs in after him. He slumps to the side, falling across the bench seat. My fingers slip through the warm, wet blood that covers his neck, searching desperately for a pulse.

He's pale but still breathing.

For *now*, anyway.

He needs help.

Fast.

I scan the ground for his phone, then hold it up to his face to unlock it. Dialing 911, I drop the phone on the seat next to him, leaving the line open.

At my feet, Ezra is stirring, one hand pressed tentatively to the side of his head. "What happened?" he asks, looking up at me. "Was that a *brick*?"

I grab Ezra's hand, helping him pull himself upright.

I take a last look at the unconscious college kid, swallowing down a sickly wave of nausea. No matter what happens to him, I already know that I'll see his face in my dreams for the rest of my life.

"Come on," I say, looping Ezra's arm around my shoulder. "We're leaving. *Now.*"

# CHAPTER *Fifteen*

WE RIDE HOME IN SILENCE.

For the first time that I can remember, my hands aren't steady on the wheel. The tepid air that floats through the vents does nothing for my nausea and even less for the film of sickly sweat that now drenches every inch of my body.

If *I'm* this shaken, I can't even imagine how Ezra is feeling.

As I pull up in front of his house and kill the engine, I'm expecting him to bolt from the car the second it stops.

But to my surprise, he doesn't even reach for the door handle.

The stillness stretches between us, each second ticking by with excruciating slowness. Finally, I can't stand it anymore.

"Ezra, look," I say. "I know that was . . . bad, okay? But it's not your fault. It was *mine*."

I take a shallow breath, pushing away the image of the college kid's half-drained body, draped unmoving across the seat. Ezra and I could already hear the sirens as we pulled away from the club; for all of our sakes, I pray they got there in time.

The front of Ezra's white T-shirt is dark with dried blood.

It's probably stained for good.

"How is it not my fault?" he asks woodenly. "I'm the one covered in blood. I'm the one who *attacked* someone."

"It was *my* fault," I repeat, my voice firm. "Okay? *Mine.* I should have been watching you. I should have remembered how hard it is to . . . *stop* . . . in the beginning." The guilt presses down on me, flattening my voice and robbing the air from my chest. "The first time is the hardest, Ezra," I whisper. "I promise, it'll get easier."

Ezra stares at the dashboard.

"That guy is going to be fine," I say. "Honestly." I force a smile, trying to get Ezra to look at me. "All he needs is a little . . . blood transfusion."

Ezra finally turns, his expression flat.

Now that I think about it, he might have a point about my pep talks.

"I could have killed him," Ezra says. "I *would* have killed him, if it wasn't for you. I wanted to."

"But you *didn't,*" I remind him. "And that's what matters."

"Because you *smashed me in the head with a brick,*" Ezra says.

I look down, fiddling with the edge of my seat belt.

The movement catches Ezra's eye; to my surprise, he reaches out, gently turning my hand over.

My palm is scraped from the pavement where I fell, a long scratch running the length of my hand.

Wordlessly, he traces his thumb across the scrape.

Despite the heat of the car, I shiver.

"I hurt you," Ezra says softly.

"It's only a scratch," I whisper back, not quite trusting my voice. "I'm fine."

He drops my hand, turning away. "No thanks to me," he mutters, his voice thick with self-loathing.

"Ezra," I say. "Wait."

But he's already reaching for the door handle. "I'm sorry," he says, not looking at me. "It'll never happen again. I swear."

I open my mouth to reply, but he's already halfway out the door. As I watch, he disappears inside, the screen door falling shut behind him with a hollow clang.

I look down at my hand.

Despite the coolness of Ezra's fingers, my skin feels warm where he touched me. I tell myself to stop being ridiculous.

Shaking my hand out, I reach for the keys.

There's nothing more I can do for Ezra tonight.

I've already done enough.

The Comfortable Choice Motor Lodge, situated across from the strip mall on the edge of town, is neither comfortable nor a choice; it *is*, however, the only place I can afford on my part-time Burger Queen salary and alarmingly empty bank account.

My room is at the far side of the parking lot, near the ice machine. It's small, dark, and smells vaguely like cat pee, even though pets technically aren't allowed.

I rent by the month from a charming older gentleman named

Rick, who has no qualms about a seventeen-year-old girl paying for a motel room with cash, openly watches porn behind the desk, and takes every possible opportunity to try to look down my shirt.

Yeah.

Rick's a classy guy.

Cutting the engine, I pull my phone from my pocket. Max's text is still open on the screen, and, for a moment, I consider calling him.

But it's too late for that.

Instead, with still-trembling fingers, I search for any updates on the boy we left bleeding to death in an empty parking lot. There's nothing so far, officially or otherwise.

Still trying to convince myself that no news is good news, I lock the doors to my car and stride toward my room, glancing automatically over my shoulder. It's almost midnight, but the night air is thick with salt and humidity.

Despite the darkness, I can't help feeling exposed.

I quicken my steps, avoiding the cigarette butts that litter the ground in front of the motel. Did I mention Rick also smokes?

Yep.

He's delightful.

It's a relief when I push open the door to room 7 and step inside, dropping my keys on the dresser. I'm already reaching for the light switch when it hits me: the familiar scent of cedar and cloves, clinging to the air.

Spice & Wood aftershave, an ounce of which costs more than my monthly rent.

Slowly, I force myself to turn around, already knowing what I'll find.

Cassius Raith is sprawled on the edge of the bed, his long legs crossed lazily at the ankle in front of him.

Vampire.

Sire.

*Ex-boyfriend.*

"Is it my imagination," Cassius asks, starting in the middle of the conversation, like no time has passed at all, "or does this place smell like cat pee?"

I wonder how much it cost to bribe Rick for a key to my room.

Twenty bucks?

*Ten?*

I let the motel door fall shut behind me, leaning against the cheap metal frame for support. "What are you doing here, Cassius?" To my surprise, my voice is almost steady.

An amused look crosses his handsome face.

His hair is slightly longer than the last time I saw him, falling almost to his chin in thick black waves. His blue eyes are mocking and bright against his pale face, his loud floral-patterned shirt unbuttoned practically to his waist.

On anyone else, it would look ridiculous.

On Cassius, it looks . . . beside the point.

"What am *I* doing here?" he asks. He sits up straighter, spreading his hands wide, and gestures around the dingy motel room with long, elegant fingers. A musician's hands in another life. Or several other lives, actually. "The question is, what are *you* doing here, Lilliana? I've been here for twenty minutes, and I can already feel the will to live leaching out of me. I mean, my god, *Florida*?" he asks. "Were you *really* so desperate to get away from me?"

The thin silver bracelets around his wrist jangle as he flops dramatically back on the bed, stretching his arms out. His shirt rides up at the bottom, revealing an expanse of smooth, flat stomach.

I take a deep breath, trying not to vomit. "Cassius, I—"

"Oh, relax," he says, cutting me off. "I'm kidding." Looking down at the bedspread beneath him, he wrinkles his nose. "Do I want to know the last time this comforter was washed?" he asks. "No, wait, don't tell me. Let's keep the mystery alive."

"If I'd known I was expecting company, I wouldn't have given the maid the day off," I say, keeping my voice purposefully light.

Cassius hoists himself up on his elbows. He tilts his head to the side, his eyes running slowly up and down my frame. "You look good, Lilliana," he says. "You look . . . the *same*."

"It's Lily now," I say, folding my arms across my chest. "Just Lily."

He pulls himself up from the bed, straightening so quickly I don't even have time to blink before he's standing in front of me, his face inches from mine.

"*Lily*," he says experimentally, drawing a few extra syllables out of the name. His breath is soft on my neck; his body, in front of me, radiates coolness. "I like it. It suits you." Reaching up, he gently tucks a loose strand of my hair behind my ear.

I go absolutely still as he runs his fingers carelessly down my neck.

"You're so warm now," he says. His thumb strokes across my

skin, pausing at the hollow of my throat. "So . . . fragile." His head dips forward, his lips grazing my neck. "So *human*."

For a second, time seems to stop.

Prickling heat floods through me, making my palms burn and my fingers twitch. Ignoring the warmth pooling in my hands, I reach up, pushing him away from me.

Cassius steps back, laughingly raising his hands.

"You're right," he says. "I wouldn't want to step on anyone else's toes. Tell me, *Lily*, are the rumors true? Are you really dating the *quarterback*?"

Heat licks through my veins again, lapping at my palms. I can feel the warmth pulsing in my fingertips, my skin tingling in response.

Max.

Cassius knows about Max.

Of course he does.

Cassius knows *everything*.

"Max doesn't play football," I say, my voice as level as I can manage. "He's captain of the swim team."

"Of course he is," Cassius says, suppressing another smile. "My mistake."

The familiar scent of his cologne is making my head ache. I almost find myself wishing for the Axe body spray that Rick slathers on by the gallon instead.

"How did you find me, Cassius?" I ask. "I'm *human*. The sire bond is broken. My blood doesn't call to you any—"

But even as I say the words aloud, I can see the puzzle pieces falling into place:

*Me, snarling down at Max, my pencil poised menacingly above his chest.*

*Me, gazing into the camera of a phone, blinking in horrified realization.*

*Me, scrambling to my feet, my cheeks flushed the same virulent shade of pink as my costume.*

*Me, me, me.*

*Over and over and over again.*

*All over the internet, for anyone to see.*

"You'd be amazed how easy it is to find someone these days," Cassius says, sidestepping the question. "Well, given enough time and money, that is." He tilts his head to the side, giving another shrug. "Luckily for me, I have endless amounts of both."

Swallowing my rising nausea, I straighten my shoulders. "If you're waiting for an apology, you're out of luck," I say. "*You're* the one who betrayed *me*, remember?"

His head snaps up, his carefully cultivated facade cracking before my eyes.

"Is that what you think?" he asks. "I would *never* have betrayed you, Lilliana. *Ever.*"

His earnestness takes me by surprise.

"You *hid the cure* from me," I say, trying to regain my footing. "You knew how much it meant to me, Cassius. How long I'd been looking for it!"

"I wasn't *hiding* anything," Cassius says impatiently. "I was waiting until I had enough of the cure for *both* of us!" He shoves his hand into his pocket and then thrusts something in my direction.

I look down at the sliver of jagged rock, the red-flecked stone shockingly dark against his pale skin.

*Bloodstone.*

It's another piece of *bloodstone.*

"I . . . I don't understand," I falter. "How did you . . . *Where* did you . . ."

"It doesn't matter," Cassius says, sliding the bloodstone back into his pocket. "You could have waited for me, Lilliana," he says, his voice rough around the edges. "You could have *trusted* me."

I blink hard, driving away sudden tears.

All this time, I've assumed Cassius betrayed me.

But what if *I* was the one who betrayed *him*?

"I-I'm sorry, Cassius," I say at last. "But maybe it's better you weren't there. The cure . . . Something went wrong with it. There was a girl . . ."

For a moment, the familiar memory threatens to overwhelm me.

"She wasn't supposed to be there," I say, struggling to get the words out. "*Nobody* was supposed to be there. I don't know what happened, but I couldn't help it. I couldn't *stop.* I . . . I . . ."

Cassius is already stepping forward, folding me into his strong, cold embrace.

"Hey," he says softly, against the top of my head. "It's okay, Lilliana. It's all okay."

Despite everything, I can feel myself sagging into his familiar touch.

"It's not okay," I insist. "I *killed* her, Cassius. She's dead because of me."

He pulls back, looking down at me with searching blue eyes. "It's okay, Lilliana," he says again, smoothing my hair away from my face with gentle fingers. "I *know.*"

I look up at him in confusion, trying to make sense of his words. "What do you mean, you *know*?"

"I found the girl," Cassius says. "On the rooftop, after you disappeared. I . . . took care of it."

*"Her,"* I say raggedly, after a pause. "You mean you took care of *her*."

Cassius nods. "I'd do anything for you, Lilliana. *Anything*."

"But why?" I whisper. "I stole the bloodstone from you, Cassius. I stole your only chance to be *human*."

He shrugs, giving me a rueful look.

"You were the one who wanted to be human," he says. "All I ever wanted was to stay with you."

The words knock the wind out of me, leaving my chest tight and aching.

"I'm sorry," I repeat, each word scraping painfully against my throat. "I'm so sorry. I shouldn't have left. No matter what happened."

"It was . . . less than ideal," Cassius admits. He forces his lips upward, the smile not quite reaching his eyes. "No goodbye, no explanation . . . not even a forwarding address?" He looks around the room. "Although, given your choice of accommodations, I can't say I blame you for that last part."

For the first time, I see the grungy motel room through his eyes. "It's not the Ritz," I concede.

"If you needed money, I could have given it to you," Cassius says. Inside his pockets, his hands are balled into fists, straining at the expensive material. "I would have given you anything, Lilliana. I would have given you *everything*, if you'd let me."

"I know," I say, swallowing hard.

After a long moment, he nods.

"It's fine," he says. "Water under the bridge and all that."

"Cassius . . ."

"*Lily* . . ." he mimics, a ghost of his old smile crossing his handsome face. "Really. All I've ever wanted is for you to be happy. And for some reason, *this*"—he pauses, sweeping his elegant hands around the dingy motel room—"seems to make you happy."

He takes a step forward, letting his smile drop, along with his hands.

"It does, doesn't it?" he asks, the mockery wiped clean from his voice.

After a long minute, I nod.

"Yeah," I say softly. "It does."

"Then all is forgiven," he says. "Well, on one condition, that is."

This is the Cassius I recognize; he always did come with strings attached.

"What condition?" I ask cautiously.

He lifts his eyebrows, wagging them roguishly in my direction. "Come out with me, tomorrow night," he says. "We can paint the town red, one last time. Besides," he adds. "You still owe me a goodbye."

"I'm not sure if that's such a great idea," I say carefully. "I'm not a vampire anymore, remember? And, besides, I have work."

Cassius snorts so loudly that I worry it'll wake the other guests. I watch as he zeroes in on the khaki shirt neatly folded over the side of my desk chair. "I'm sure the . . . *Burger Queen* . . . can make it one night without you," he says. "Or, if you need me to, I could always speak to your boss." His forehead wrinkles in mock concern. "Do you report directly to the queen herself, or should I work my way up the royal chain?"

I hesitate.

For so long, I thought Cassius had wronged me. That *he* was the villain. But I'm the one who ran. I'm the one who *killed*. And he's the one who fixed it. He saved me . . . again.

I flinch as a flicker of hurt crosses his handsome face.

"Well," he says. "If the pleasure of my company isn't enough, I suppose I can always throw in some bribery."

Reaching into his pocket, he pulls the shard of bloodstone free.

"Come out with me tomorrow night," he says. "And the bloodstone is yours. I'm sure your new . . . friend . . . would appreciate the gift. Ezra, is it?"

I stare down at the dark, red-flecked jewel.

For a moment, I'm back on the rooftop, feeling the pain, and the fear, and the *hunger* slamming into me all over again. I almost choke on the memory of the girl's warm blood pouring down my throat.

I can't let Ezra know what that feels like.

I *refuse* to.

"I already told you," I whisper. "The stone is *cursed*."

Cassius smiles.

Slipping the bloodstone back into his pocket, he steps forward and drops a soft kiss on my cheek. "Haven't you heard,

Lilliana?" he whispers softly into my ear. "Curses are meant to be broken."

And, before I can open my mouth to respond, he's gone, leaving only the faint scent of cedar behind.

"It's Lily now," I whisper aloud to the empty room. "*Just* Lily."

# CHAPTER Sixteen

I LIE AWAKE FOR MOST OF THE NIGHT, TURNING Cassius's words over and over again in my head.

*Haven't you heard, Lilliana? Curses are meant to be broken.*

If Cassius is right, it means Ezra could be cured. That he could get his life back without *taking* someone else's.

But what if he's wrong?

Nothing ever comes for free.

A report of tonight's "incident" has finally made it onto the local news sites. College Guy has a real name: James Whitney. I read through the article multiple times, greedily devouring words like "stable condition" and "full recovery" before sending it to Ezra.

He doesn't respond.

I must eventually fall asleep because I wake in a startled panic to the sound of my alarm. I rush through my shower as quickly as possible, cursing the motel's shitty water pressure as I awkwardly swivel my head back and forth, trying to rinse the last of the shampoo from my hair.

The scent of Cassius's aftershave still lingers faintly in the room; for once, it's a relief to step outside into the sweltering heat of the humid morning air.

Even though I'm feeling slightly nauseated from lack of sleep, I swing through Dunkin' on my way to school and order an extra-large black coffee over ice. At the last minute, I throw in a donut for Max, as well.

Luckily for me, ambushing him with baked goods works *slightly* better than ambushing him with a pencil.

Having inhaled the entire donut in seemingly one bite, he kisses me briefly before pulling me into a tight hug.

"Sorry about my text last night," he says against the top of my head. "It was kind of an asshole move."

I close my eyes, letting the familiar scent of chlorine and Max's fabric softener wash over me.

*Of course* he's *the one apologizing.*

"*I'm* the asshole," I say firmly. "I'm sorry, Max. I . . . I got caught up in something, and I lost track of time. Does your mom totally hate me now?"

"Of course not," Max says. He pulls back, grinning down at me. "At most, she hates you, like . . . eighty-five percent."

I pretend to smile back before I kiss him again, hard enough to make us both forget about last night.

Hours later, when we decorate for prom, I can still taste the sickly sweet sugar on my lips.

I look down at my phone again, checking to see if Ezra has returned any of my messages.

But of course not; I'm still on read, exactly like the last twenty times I checked.

On the other side of the gym, Noah Coates lies across the bottom row of bleachers, nursing a large Gatorade and looking decidedly worse for the wear.

Even if he *had* seen Ezra and me at the club last night, I'm guessing he wouldn't remember us.

Still, I keep my distance, just in case.

Looking back down at my phone, I tap out yet *another* message for Ezra.

Lily

EZRA. I KNOW YOU'RE SEEING THESE. ANSWER YOUR PHONE ALREADY.

On the floor across from me, Sarita leans forward, shamelessly trying to catch a glimpse of my screen. "Who are you texting so much?" she demands, her brush hovering over the **LOVE AMONG THE STARS** banner that we're working on. "And why do you look so *grumpy* about it?"

"It's nothing," I say shortly, sliding my phone back into my pocket. "I'm checking on Ezra."

"In all caps?" Sarita asks. Unlike me, who gave up on my rhinestone-bedazzled cowboy hat somewhere around fourth period, she's still wearing her miniature top hat from today's Wacky Hat Day, perched rakishly at the crown of her head.

Unsurprisingly, it looks amazing on her.

"He isn't answering," I say, dipping my own brush into the bucket of paint with slightly more force than necessary. "What if he, um . . . got sick again? Or what if he slipped and fell in the shower?" I ask, gaining steam. "He could be unconscious on the bathroom floor *right now*."

Sarita pulls out her own phone, typing one-handed as she holds her dripping paintbrush over the bucket.

A second later, it buzzes in response.

The phone, that is, not the paintbrush.

"Oh, look," she says, showing me the screen. "Ezra's fine."

I think of the last time I saw Ezra, his shirt splattered with someone else's blood. Of the look on his face as he traced the scrape on my palm. Of how he disappeared into the darkness without a second glance.

Ezra may be a lot of things right now, but I'm guessing "fine" is not one of them.

"Well . . . good," I say, outlining the first *S* in **LOVE AMONG THE STARS**. Even to my own ears, my voice sounds unconvincing. "At least he's responding to *one* of us."

Across the gym, I can see Max on top of an alarmingly rickety-looking ladder, stringing glittery cardboard stars with the confidence that can only come from years of perching on the edge of a high dive.

Catching sight of me, he offers a tentative grin.

I smile brightly back at him, pretending as hard as I can that everything is fine.

"Something weird is going on between you two," Sarita says. Narrowing her gaze in my direction, she idly fiddles with her necklace. "Don't bother trying to deny it; I can *feel* it in my bones."

"Deny *what*?" I ask. "Max and I are fine."

"I was talking about you and *Ezra*," Sarita says.

"That's ridiculous," I say. Ducking my head, I concentrate on tracing the outline of the *T*.

Despite scrubbing it earlier, there's still a faint smudge of ink on the back of my hand.

"Nothing is going on between Ezra and me," I say firmly. "We don't even *like* each other."

She gives a little snort, dipping her brush in the bucket again. "Sure," she says. "Keep telling yourself that."

I sit back on my heels, accidentally dripping paint on the edge of the banner.

"What is *that* supposed to mean?" I ask.

Sarita stops working as well, tipping her head to one side. Her miniature top hat bobs jauntily in response. "Has Max ever talked about his last girlfriend?"

I glance toward the ladder, watching as Max reaches up to hang another glittery star.

It's odd; I've spent so long hiding from my past that it never even occurred to me to ask about his.

Or, maybe, if I'm being honest with myself, I didn't *want* to know.

"No," I admit. "He hasn't."

"Yeah," Sarita says dryly. "That's because there *isn't* one."

I jerk my head back toward her so quickly that I almost give myself whiplash. "What do you mean, there *isn't* one?" I repeat. "How is that possible? *Look* at him," I say, gesturing toward the ladder. Max's back muscles flex beneath his T-shirt as he reaches up again, his blond hair glinting in the gym lights. "He's *Max Hutchinson.*"

Sarita glances toward the ladder, biting her lip.

"You know that Max's dad died a few years ago, right?"

"Yeah," I say, nodding. "Of course."

I may not be the best girlfriend in the entire world, but I'm not a *total* asshole; I've seen the pictures of his dad lining the walls of their house. In every single one of them, he's beaming into the camera, looking tanned and happy and healthy. The original Max 1.0.

"It was a heart attack, right?" I ask Sarita. "Nobody even knew he was sick."

Maybe it's a good thing that Max can still remember his dad the way that he looks in the photos.

Or maybe Max would have given anything for a few more memories, no matter how painful they were.

Sarita nods. "Apparently, a lot of kids kind of . . . shut down when something like that happens. But Max did the opposite." She swirls her paintbrush idly through the bucket of paint, sending a slow ripple outward. "He was always a joiner, but he started throwing himself into activities. Swimming. School. Volunteering. *Everything.* All of the adults were like, 'Look how well he's doing! Kids are so *resilient*!' "

Sarita glances in Max's direction. "No one but Ezra and I seemed to realize he was *miserable.* That he was only going through the motions. For *years.* Until you arrived."

I remember a blond-haired boy sitting down in front of me, his smile so bright that it felt like I was staring into the sun.

"I had no idea," I say, guilt creeping up the back of my throat. "Max never said anything."

*And I never asked.*

Oh, God.

Maybe I *am* a total asshole.

"He doesn't really like to talk about it," Sarita says with a shrug. "I'm only letting you know because Ezra is Max's best friend. And he saw how . . . hollow . . . Max was, before you got here." She picks up her paintbrush again, giving me a speculative look.

"What are you saying?" I tighten my grip on my paintbrush, trying to ignore the heat building in my palms.

Sarita gives another shrug.

"All I'm saying is what do you think is more likely?" she asks. "That Ezra doesn't like you? Or that he would give up *anything* to help Max?"

Two hours later, I climb awkwardly out of my battered Ford Fiesta, handing the keys to a waiting valet. Standing beneath the soaring marble facade of Cassius's luxury hotel, it's hard not to feel underdressed in my black tank dress and sneakers.

Then again, I'd probably feel underdressed in a ball gown.

Not that I own a ball gown anymore.

Well, unless you count my cheap *poofy* prom dress.

Which I don't.

Straightening my shoulders, I make my way up the hotel's wide, palatial stone steps, concentrating very hard on not tripping over my own feet. It's been a while since I've been somewhere so . . . *fancy.*

I'm guessing a single night's stay in one of the hotel's suites costs more than a month at my motel.

Knowing Cassius, he's probably rented out an entire floor.

Nodding toward the uniformed doorman, I pull my cardigan on, bracing myself for the familiar blast of air-conditioning.

The hotel has obviously gone with the "more is more" philosophy of interior design; everywhere I look, there are glittering crystal chandeliers and carved marble fountains, tufted velvet settees and enormous gilt-edged mirrors.

No wonder Cassius chose this place; it's loud and extravagant and the *tiniest* bit gaudy.

Exactly like him.

The hostess leads me past the polished oak bar toward a private banquet room at the back. I wonder if Cassius even bothered glamouring her or if his platinum-edged credit card was enough to dazzle her on its own.

I step through the door to find that Cassius is already waiting for me, sprawled comfortably in one of the plush booths ringing the edge of the banquet room. One long arm is stretched across the top, his fingers tracing lazy circles in the velvet.

Even from a distance, I can feel the magnetic pull of his smile.

As I near the booth, Cassius stands up, stretching like a panther. He's wearing dark pants and a loud, bird-print silk shirt, unbuttoned halfway to the waist.

"At last!" he says, beaming. "The party can begin!"

My eyes drop to the ice-cream cake resting incongruously in the middle of the table. It's been sitting for too long, the ice cream puddling over the edges of the cheap cardboard tray. I can make out the words **HAPPY RETIREMENT, WALTER!** piped on in bright green icing across the top.

"For me?" I ask dryly. "You shouldn't have."

"It came with the room," Cassius admits. "But don't worry. I'm sure Walter wouldn't have wanted it to go to waste."

I give him a look, but he only grins.

The hostess has disappeared, leaving us alone in the massive banquet room.

Drink in hand, Cassius saunters forward, pressing a cool kiss on my cheek. "You look lovely, Lilliana," he says. "Thank you for coming."

"I don't really remember having a choice in the matter," I say wryly.

"Don't be silly," Cassius says, raising his glass. "There's *always* a choice."

He takes a long sip of his drink, thick red liquid sloshing against the rim.

"Seriously?" I ask. "*Blood?* With all these people around?"

Cassius's lips quirk upward at the corners. "I hate to break it to you," he says innocently. "But some of us are *still* vampires."

I narrow my eyes, glaring at him.

"Oh, don't be cross, Lilliana. This is supposed to be a celebration, remember? In fact . . ." Cassius sets his glass down on the table. Giving me a rakish look, he sweeps into a low bow, offering me his hand. "May I have the honor of this dance, Miss Morris?"

"No way," I say, my voice firm. "You know I don't dance, Cassius. And besides," I add, gesturing around the empty room, "there isn't even any music."

Cassius steps forward, slipping his hand around my waist. "There's always music," he says. "You just have to *listen*."

His feet sure enough for us both, Cassius launches us into the opening steps of a familiar old-fashioned dance.

"God, I miss *waltzing*," he says, turning me expertly around and around in a rhythm only he can hear. "Nobody *waltzes* anymore, have you noticed?"

I cling tighter to his shoulders as we whirl past one of the booths, narrowly avoiding the edge of the table.

"What was the name of that village we stayed at, in Switzerland?" Cassius asks, not missing a beat. "The one with the dance hall."

"Lauterbrunnen," I say, the name springing automatically to my lips. Cassius has always been terrible at names; it's a source of pride for him, the fact that he can't be bothered to learn them.

Cassius twirls me again, sidestepping another table. "Remember the absinthe?" he asks. "The Swiss were wild for it, back then. We drank it like it was water."

Despite myself, I can't help a smile from tugging at the corner of my lips. My feet are barely touching the ground, my heart racing in my chest. I'd forgotten how *free* Cassius could make me feel sometimes.

"I remember," I say aloud. "You jumped off the Staubbach Falls because you were convinced you could fly."

Cassius laughs, *really* laughs; a loud, boyish sound that echoes eerily through the empty room.

"I maintain that I'm right," Cassius says, whirling me away again. "All those tales about vampires turning into bats can't be complete myth."

I remember Cassius wading into the icy water at the top of

the falls. His hat was long gone, black hair flying everywhere, his overcoat catching in the wind. His cheeks were flushed with drink and blood, his expression already triumphant as he cupped his hands to his mouth, shouting to be heard over the roar of the falls beneath him.

"Watch me fly, Lilliana!" he'd yelled, right before he jumped, fearless, over the edge.

"You sank like a stone," I say. "If I recall correctly, you broke most of the bones in your body on the rocks below."

With a flourish, Cassius dips me backward, momentarily stilling his manic waltzing. "If I recall correctly, you were an excellent nurse," he says, a smile still playing on his lips as he remembers. "You had the innkeeper make me barley soup. It was disgusting. But I liked it there. Why did we ever leave?"

I pull myself upright, the half smile fading from my lips. "The innkeeper's wife."

*Alda*, I suddenly remember. That was her name. She smiled constantly, her cheeks so big and red they were like apples.

Until she stopped smiling forever.

Pulling Cassius's hands from my waist, I step backward, out of his reach. I can feel anger radiating through my fingers.

For a moment, we eye each other across our makeshift dance floor, the silence growing louder and louder between us.

"It was an *accident*, Lilliana," Cassius says at last. "A terrible accident that happened more than a *century* ago." He cocks his head to the side, his black hair gleaming. "Do you want me to apologize again? Because I will. Tell me what you want me to say, and I'll say it."

All of the giddiness leaves my body in a single *whoosh*.

"Nothing," I say tiredly. "I don't want you to say anything."

In the booth behind us, the remains of the cake are a ruined mess, the melted ice cream dripping slowly onto the floor.

"This was a mistake," I say. Raising one hand, I gesture toward the lavish room. "This isn't my world anymore, Cassius. I don't *belong* here."

"But what if you could?" he asks, taking a step forward. "*Belong?* What if you were a vampire again?"

I know it's physically impossible, but I swear, for a moment, my heart stops.

"What?" I whisper.

"Be honest, Lilliana," he says, taking another step. "Is being *human* really all it's cracked up to be?" He attempts a lopsided grin. "Working for minimum wage? Living in some seedy motel room? Watching your pathetically short life slip through your fingers, day after day?"

"Cassius, I—"

"What if I turned you again?" he asks, interrupting me. His hands are jammed in his pockets, his words falling from his mouth one after the other, almost too quickly to understand. "It would be like before. Everything could go back to the way it was. You and me against the world. *Forever.*"

Deep in my chest, I can feel my heart beginning to beat again. I focus on the reassuring rhythm, letting it ground me.

"You can't . . . We don't even know if that would work," I say, struggling to explain. To find the right words, the ones he'll finally understand. "Even if it *could*, I wouldn't want it to."

"Of course you would," Cassius says dismissively. He surges forward again, his fists straining against his pockets. "You haven't thought this through, Lilliana. What happens if you get hurt? If you get *sick*?"

"I'm only seventeen years old, Cassius," I say, trying to smile. "I'm not going to get sick."

"You don't know that," he retorts, his voice sharp. "Humans get sick, Lily. Humans *die*."

"Everyone dies eventually," I say with a shrug. "Even you, Cassius."

Cassius closes the distance between us, his eyes darkening dangerously. The scent that surrounds him is achingly familiar: cedar and cloves and the sharp, ever-present tang of blood.

"I'm sorry, Lilliana," he says. "But I refuse to accept that."

And before I can even register what's happening, he strikes.

# CHAPTER Seventeen

CASSIUS'S GRIP IS LIKE AN IRON VISE AROUND my wrists.

"This isn't how I wanted it to happen, Lilliana," he whispers, his breath cool against the side of my neck. "But you'll thank me later. I *know* you will."

There's a manic light shining in his eyes, an unnatural calm to his voice that makes me shudder.

"Cassius," I say, my throat dry with fear. "What are you doing?"

Desperately, I try to look away from his mesmerizing gaze, from the swirling ebb and flow of his icy blue eyes.

I can't.

He reaches up, yanking my head painfully to the side. "You're a *vampire*, Lilliana," he growls. "And I'll prove it to you."

"Cassius, *stop*." I can feel the panic clawing at my throat, can feel myself falling deeper and deeper into his thrall. "Please. You need to *stop*."

“Don’t worry,” Cassius whispers, the edges of his fangs already curving over his bottom lip. “This will only hurt for a moment.”

I gasp as his fangs sink into my neck, slicing through my skin, cutting deep. The pain is sharp and sudden, and I recoil at the shock of it, the *brutalness.*

For a moment, everything is suspended.

I feel like I’m underwater. The world has slipped away; the throbbing in my hands is gone. There’s only the thrum of my heartbeat and the sound of my blood pulsing in my ears.

I want to fight the current swirling around me, but it’s easier to let go.

To let myself float away.

Maybe Cassius is right.

Maybe I—

“Lily!”

Ezra’s voice appears out of nowhere, dragging me back to the surface.

Over Cassius’s shoulder, I see a blur of sudden movement. I have enough time to shout “Ezra, no!” before he tackles Cassius away from me, both of them crashing to the marble floor below.

For a brief moment, they roll back and forth, tousling for control. Ezra somehow ends up on top, his long, lean arms shaking with the effort of pinning Cassius to the ground.

Cassius looks up at Ezra in complete unconcern.

“The famous Ezra, I presume?”

“Presume *this,* asshole,” Ezra snarls.

And, drawing his fist back, he brings it crashing down on Cassius's face. There's a thick *crunch*ing sound as Cassius's nose breaks.

Cassius laughs, spitting blood onto the floor.

He's obviously toying with Ezra.

And even worse, he's *enjoying* it.

"Is that all you've got?" Cassius asks. "How . . . disappointing."

A low growl escapes from Ezra's throat.

"Ezra, stop it!" I yell, knowing the words are useless even as they leave my mouth. "He has the cure! He can *save* you!"

Ezra's head snaps toward mine in surprise, a bead of sweat dripping down his forehead.

"The *cure*?" he asks. "You mean . . ."

*"Bloodstone?"* Cassius interrupts, wrenching one arm free from Ezra's grasp. He reaches into his pocket and grabs the shard, then waves it tauntingly in front of Ezra's face, the sharp edges glittering in the chandelier light.

As I watch in horror, he tightens his grip, his long, elegant fingers closing inexorably around the stone.

*"No!"* I cry, but it's already too late.

Cassius laughs again. He opens his empty hand, showing it to Ezra and me like a magician showing off a new trick.

Fine, crushed powder rains softly to the carpet.

"Oh, dear," he says. "How clumsy of me."

No.

No, no, no, no, *no*.

"Cassius," I whisper. "What have you *done*?"

"What have *I* done?" he repeats. "*You're* the one who did

this, Lilliana. You're the one who ruined *everything*." He wipes his hand clean on his expensive silk shirt, his eyes glittering with fury.

"You took the bloodstone from me," Cassius says. "And now I'll take it from you." Letting his hand fall to the floor, he looks me straight in the eye. "I swear on my grave, Lilliana. I'll grind every last piece of bloodstone to dust before I let you have it."

Ezra grabs Cassius's arm, pinning him to the ground again.

"Max and Sarita are on their way!" he calls. "Don't wait for me! Just *run*!"

A fresh stab of fear lances into me.

No.

Max and Sarita can't be on their way.

They can't be anywhere *near* this place.

Cassius laughs again, a low, musical sound that echoes tauntingly through the enormous room.

"Don't go now, Lilliana!" he calls. "The party's just starting!"

Ezra's entire body is taut with rage as he draws his fist back and slams it into Cassius's face again and again and again. *"Leave. Her. Alone,"* he spits, punctuating each word with another punch.

He pauses, his breath heaving in his chest. His knuckles are raw, his face flecked with Cassius's blood.

Cassius smirks up at him, his nose cracking as it resets itself from Ezra's onslaught.

"Finished?" he asks.

Before Ezra has a chance to answer, Cassius reaches up,

pushing Ezra off him with a casual *flick.* My hands flood with heat as Ezra flies through the air and crashes heavily into a nearby booth.

Cassius is already on his feet, scooping Ezra up with one hand. *"That,"* he says, tossing Ezra through the air like a rag doll, "was a mistake."

Ezra bounces off the wall before hitting the ground again, the back of his head smacking loudly against the marble floor. A groan of pain escapes his lips, but Cassius is already on him, lifting him high into the air.

My neck is throbbing with pain, blood dripping between my fingers.

Blood.

I'm so sick of *blood.*

I'm so sick of *all* of this.

When Ezra hits the floor this time, he doesn't make a sound; his head is bent at a strange angle, his body slumped motionless next to an overturned chair.

I pull my hand away from my neck, wavering a little as I try to find my balance. How much blood have I lost? How deep did Cassius go?

*Not deep enough to kill me.*

I stumble blearily toward Cassius.

He hauls Ezra to his feet again, Ezra's head lolling drunkenly to one side.

Cassius isn't going to stop.

Not unless I *make* him.

The heat in my palms has turned to fire now. I can feel it biting at my fingertips, straining eagerly through my veins.

Cassius spares me a look over Ezra's shoulder, his eyes glittering triumphantly.

"Say goodbye, Lilliana."

Instinctually, I raise my palms in front of me.

"Goodbye," I whisper.

And then I let go.

# CHAPTER Eighteen

IT'S NOT PRETTY.

Fire sears through the room in front of me, a messy wave of purple-tinged flames that spills from my palms, scorching everything in sight.

Cassius is blown off his feet, the blast knocking Ezra in the opposite direction.

I can smell something burning; it takes a long minute to realize that it's Cassius.

He shrieks, batting uselessly at his ridiculous bird-print shirt. The air around him crackles with heat, consuming everything in its path.

I can feel the back draft, the pulsing heat that reminds me of standing too close to a fire.

Only I *am* the fire.

It's like nothing I've ever felt before, like nothing I even knew I *could* feel before.

It's terrifying, and surreal, and . . . *powerful.*

I flex my hands experimentally, another tumultuous burst of strangely colored flames pouring from my palms in response. The air ripples around me, waves of heat pushing outward from my body.

On the floor in front of me, Cassius howls like a wounded animal.

He's in agony, his skin blistering beneath his shirt into angry, bubbling welts. Strips of silk tear away as he claws at the buttons, ripping the cloth frantically from his chest. Beneath his snarl of pain and anger, I can see fear lurking below.

*"Lilliana!"*

My stomach twists with sudden, sickening guilt.

The fire spilling from my palms gives a final wild surge, then sputters uncontrollably to a stop.

I fall forward, catching myself against the floor with one hand.

All at once, the chill of the air-conditioning rushes back in, making me gasp with shock.

Beneath the remnants of a broken table, Ezra groans, trying to lift his head.

Cassius is already climbing to his feet, his ruined shirt still smoldering against his skin. I don't even have time to flinch before he's on top of me, jerking me to my feet. His arms snake around my body, trapping me in an iron grip once more.

"Lily, Lily, Lily," he says. His voice is light, a tinge of exasperation skimming the surface. I can hear the anger bubbling beneath every syllable. "What *are* we going to do with you?" His face is smeared with blood, but his expression is calm, his cool blue eyes assessing.

I push against him, fighting his grip, trying desperately to raise my hands in front of me once more.

Cassius's lips curve upward into a smile.

"One day," he says, "we'll laugh about this."

Behind him, I catch a glimpse of movement; Ezra's fingers twitching ever so slightly. The feeling must be returning as his spine knits back together.

Any second now, and he'll be on his feet, going after Cassius again. But Cassius is done playing with him.

This time, he'll kill Ezra without a second thought.

He'll kill Max.

He'll kill Sarita.

He'll kill anyone and everyone to get what he wants.

And what he wants is *me.*

I clench my fingers into useless fists, feeling the slow tears beginning to trickle down my cheeks.

The past six months come rushing over me: the taste of French fries and Max's salt-tinged kisses. Sarita's ridiculous cowboy boots, glittering in the streetlight above us. Ezra's cool fingers, tracing the length of my palm.

What made me think that I deserved any of it?

I was telling Cassius the truth before.

I don't belong in his world, but I don't belong in this human one, either.

And I never will.

"Promise you won't hurt anyone else," I say, blinking my tears away. "Promise me that if I go with you, you'll *stop.*"

Triumph gleams in Cassius's eyes, cold and victorious. "I'm

not the only one who's *hurt* people, Lilliana. But a promise is a promise," he adds, his grip tightening. "And, unlike you, I actually *keep* mine."

I close my eyes, bracing myself for the icy plunge of Cassius's fangs.

But instead, there's only the crackle of flames.

"Lily!" calls a familiar voice. "Get back!"

I open my eyes, flinching away from the sudden heat.

Cassius hisses, snarling in pain.

Sarita stands in the entrance of the banquet room, one hand clutched tightly around her necklace. The other is raised in front of her, a narrow beam of white-hot fire spilling tightly from her palm.

She looks like an avenging angel in cut-off shorts, her ridiculous fucking top hat still perched jauntily on top of her head.

"Get back," she orders me again, her face blank with concentration.

Energy pulses around Sarita, the air in front of her shimmering with heat. Cassius scrambles away from the deadly flames, tripping in his haste.

From *Sarita's* deadly flames.

But that would mean she's a . . .

*"Witch,"* Cassius spits. "I'll tear you limb from limb."

If Sarita is here, Max can't be far behind.

"Sarita, listen to me!" I cry frantically. "You need to *run*!"

Ignoring me, she takes a step forward, the band of pale fire barely missing Cassius's feet. "Try it," she says to the vampire. "I'm *begging* you."

She's breathing heavily, but her shoulders are straight, her eyes clear. Her other hand is still tightly clutched around her necklace, her knuckles white with effort.

"You have no idea who you're playing with," Cassius hisses. "Lily and I are *off-limits* to your kind."

"I don't know what you're talking about," Sarita says. "But the rest of my coven are already on their way. If I were you, I'd leave *now.* While you still have a *chance.*"

For a moment, Cassius hesitates. But as she takes another step forward, his bravado flickers.

He staggers to his feet, clumsy for once in his life.

"This isn't over, Lily," Cassius says. "I *promise.*"

And before I can blink, he's gone.

# CHAPTER Nineteen

SARITA DROPS HER HANDS, LOOKING SUDDENLY unsteady on her feet. As she takes a hesitant step forward, I can see her eyes widening at the sight of my neck. "Oh my God. You're *bleeding.*"

"It's fine," I say automatically, pressing my hand to my neck. "I'm fine." My fingers come away coated with sticky blood.

*Well,* I think unsteadily, *I guess Cassius was right about painting the town red.*

"What about Max?" I ask. "Is he okay?"

"He's parking the car," Sarita says, hurrying forward. "And you're *not* fine." Pulling what looks like a used Kleenex from her pocket, she begins to dab ineffectually at my throat. "That was a *vampire*, Lily. You got bit by a freaking *vampire.*"

I'm still staring at her, blood trickling down the length of my arm.

"You're a witch," I say.

Sarita's forehead crinkles in surprise.

"Um . . . yeah?" she says. "I'm nowhere near as powerful as *you*, but . . ."

"Here, I've got it." I take over pressing the soaked tissue against my neck while my exhausted brain tries in vain to keep up with her. "Wait, what do you mean?" I ask.

Sarita sits back on her heels, gazing at me incredulously. "You *do* know that you're a witch, right? You *have* to know. *Right?*"

A witch.

Sarita is a *witch*.

She thinks *I'm* a . . .

"No," I say. "That's not . . . I can't be . . ." I swallow hard, bloodied hands dropping to my sides. "I *can't* be a witch."

"Um, yeah, you can?" Sarita says. "In case you didn't notice, we both used witch fire. Emphasis on the *witch*?"

I look down at my hands, remembering the heat that poured through them, the wild purplish flames that spilled everywhere. They'd been different from Sarita's. Wilder, more *chaotic*; an uncontrollable blaze so hot it could keep a *vampire* at bay.

*Witch fire.*

But that would mean . . .

A weak groan echoes through the banquet room, cutting my thoughts short. Sarita gasps as Ezra begins to stir, shoving aside the pieces of debris half covering his body.

"Oh my God," she says, her hands flying to her mouth in horror. "*Ezra!* What happened to you?!"

Ezra gives another groan, pulling himself up into a sitting position. "Cassius," he says woozily. "*Cassius* happened to—"

He stops midsentence at the sight of my throat, his eyes pinpointing with sudden need.

Unsteadily, I raise one hand to my bloody neck. "Ezra?"

He looks away, but not before I see his fangs sliding sleekly over his bottom lip.

"No," Sarita says. She stumbles backward, away from both of us. "No, no, no, no, *no*."

Ezra holds his body unnaturally still, struggling to regain control. Steeling herself, Sarita raises her palm. I can already feel the heat building in the air around us.

"Sarita, wait," I say, scrambling forward. "Don't! It's *Ezra*!"

Sarita turns to peer at me in disbelief.

"Not anymore," she says. "Ezra is gone, Lily. This . . . *thing* . . . is wearing his face."

Regaining control, Ezra turns to look at us. The ugly bruise on his cheek is already fading, dried blood flaking from the cut on his forehead.

He watches Sarita's raised palm uncertainly, his eyes cutting to mine in confusion.

"Lily?" he asks. "What's happening?"

"That isn't Ezra," Sarita says, chanting the words aloud to herself like a mantra. "Ezra is *gone*."

Wincing, I stand up, stepping slowly in front of her. "Sarita, listen to me. You don't have to do this, okay?"

Sarita's hand is shaking. "You think I *want* to?" she asks me. "We can't save him, Lily. There's nothing left to *save*."

I take another cautious step forward, putting myself between her and Ezra. "I don't know what you've been told, but it's *wrong*,"

I say. "Ezra is still *Ezra*. I can explain everything, if you give me a chance."

Sarita hesitates, her expression torn.

"How?" she finally asks, still not lowering her hands. "How can you be *sure*?"

I steel myself for everything to change.

"Because," I say simply, "I used to be a vampire, too."

Sarita's eyes widen in shock.

For a long moment, everything hangs in the balance.

And then a familiar voice echoes through the room.

"Um . . . guys?"

Max stands in the doorway of the banquet room, looking around in utter bewilderment.

"What the fuck is going on?"

Unsurprisingly, Sarita's house is warded to the hilt.

The three of us stand awkwardly on the stoop behind her, carefully not looking at one another as Sarita closes her eyes, concentrating on the wards.

I prop myself up against the railing, my body aching with exhaustion. The wound at my neck has settled into a dull throb, the edge of my dress crusted with dried blood.

Taking a shallow breath, Max looks purposefully away. Beneath his tan, his skin is pale and clammy-looking.

Ironically, Max is . . . not great with the sight of blood.

"Were we planning on going inside at some point?" Ezra asks

Sarita. "No pressure, but there's a good chance Lily is about to *bleed out*?"

Max clenches his eyes shut, taking another determined breath.

"I'm fine," I say tiredly. "It stopped bleeding a while ago."

I think.

Sarita turns icily to Ezra. "I'm sorry, do you *want* to die a horrible, painful death?"

"Er . . . no?" Ezra says hopefully.

"Then you're going to have to wait, aren't you?" Sarita says.

Closing her eyes again, she turns resolutely away. I can hear her muttering something under her breath.

It doesn't sound like part of a spell.

Unless spells have a *lot* more cursing than I thought.

Finally, Sarita gives a sharp nod. "There," she says. "Done." Pushing open the door, she steps inside.

"Sorry," Max says, tossing an apologetic glance in my direction. His eyes turn vaguely glassy at the sight of my blood-encrusted neck. "I need water or something."

He hurries through the door, practically running down the hallway toward the kitchen. But when Ezra goes to follow him, something happens; as he reaches the doorframe, he hits a barrier, his body abruptly slamming up against nothing.

Sarita backs away from him warily, nearly tripping over the pair of Doc Martens she's left lying in the middle of the hallway.

"What the hell?" Ezra says, testing the invisible boundary with his hand.

"Invite him in, Sarita," I say. "I already told you, he's not going to hurt anyone."

"Are you sure we can't call my mom?" she asks, biting her lip. "She's the head of our coven. She can help us."

"Even if it means helping a vampire?" I ask.

Sarita hesitates.

"Shit," she says. "Do you know what she's going to do when she finds out I've let a *vampire* in the house?" There's a slightly hysterical edge to her voice that I've never heard before. "She's going to *disown* me. Like, I'll literally be an orphan. I'll be Oliver Twist, wandering around with a little bowl, asking people for porridge. *Porridge.*"

"It's actually gruel," Ezra says. "In the book, anyway." Sarita and I both look at him. "What?" he asks, shrugging. "AP Lit."

I lift my eyebrows, signaling him to read the room.

Ezra stuffs his hands into his back pockets. "Right," he says. "Sorry."

Sarita swallows. "You get one chance," she says. "*One.* But if you so much as *look* at me wrong, I'll stab you with a table leg. Understood?"

Ezra nods. "Understood."

"Okay," Sarita says. She takes a deep breath. "Then . . . come in. I guess."

Ezra visibly braces himself, then steps through the door.

Sarita lets out her breath with a loud *whoosh.* "This is . . . too weird," she says, turning on her heel. "I'm going to check on Max."

I step inside, carefully shutting the front door behind me.

The click of the lock is surprisingly loud, and I can feel a strange *prickle* run through me as the wards slam back into place.

I'm abruptly aware of how close Ezra is standing to me. The hallway is narrow, the tasteful gray walls lined with pictures of Sarita and her mom: the two of them smiling at the Grand Canyon, smiling in front of a lighthouse, smiling at Graceland . . .

They look like a regular, happy family. Nothing about the photos scream "supernatural vampire killers." Which, I guess, is the point.

The thought of *Sarita* being a witch is surreal enough.

But what if she's right about me?

What if *I'm* a witch, too?

The thought is too ridiculous to even contemplate. I've spent my entire life *running* from witches. I can't *be* one.

It's not possible.

"Hey," Ezra says, stepping forward. "Are you sure you're okay?"

My hand goes automatically to my neck. "I'm fine," I say. "It looks worse than it is."

Probably.

Ezra takes another step forward, coolness radiating outward from his skin. "I didn't mean your neck," he says. "Although it looks . . ." He trails off as his eyes drop to my collarbone.

I hold very still as Ezra regains his composure. After a long moment, he nods.

"Bad," he says, dragging his eyes away from my throat. "It looks *bad*. But I was talking about you. That was . . . pretty messed up back there."

"Pretty messed up" feels like the understatement of the decade.

"I'm fine," I lie. "Really. It's a flesh wound."

"If you say so. But we should get it cleaned up." Slipping past me, he heads for the guest bathroom.

"There's got to be some stuff in here," he says, opening the side cupboard and beginning to rummage through the contents. "Like . . . medical shit? Sarita's mom is a doctor, right?"

"She's a podiatrist," I say, staring at my reflection in the mirror above the sink. And a *witch*, apparently. "She has foot stuff."

I look terrible. My neck is worse than I thought: two deep puncture marks, drawing their way upward into open gashes. Even by vampire standards, it's an ugly wound.

Cassius wanted to do more than turn me.

He wanted to *hurt* me.

I sink down on the edge of the bathtub, feeling suddenly shaky.

Ezra has moved on to the cupboard under the sink, muttering to himself as he ransacks the drawers for supplies. "Success," he says, a first aid kit clutched in his hands.

His look of triumph fades at the sight of my face. "Lily?" he asks quickly, kneeling next to me. "What is it? You're not going to faint, are you?"

"I'm fine," I say, grasping the edge of the tub with my hands. "It's . . . deeper than I thought."

Ezra's expression tightens. With precise, controlled movements, he opens the first aid kit, sorting through the contents. "You should have told me you were meeting Cassius," he says, ripping open an alcohol wipe with more force than is strictly necessary. "I wouldn't have let you go alone."

"Nobody *lets* me do anything," I say sharply. "Okay? It wasn't your decision to make."

I should have left when I realized something was wrong.

That *Cassius* was wrong.

I've always known he was capable of hurting people.

I just never imagined he was capable of hurting me.

Ezra unfolds the alcohol wipe with agitated fingers, accidentally tearing the thin material in half. Reaching out, I still his fingers with my own.

"Did I ever tell you about the time I saw Charles Dickens?" I ask.

Ezra blinks at me. "Charles Dickens?"

"The author?" I say. "*Oliver Twist*? Small, gruel-eating orphan? The one we were talking about before?" Letting go of his hand, I cup mine in front of me like I'm holding an invisible bowl. "Please, sir, I want some more?" I quote in an exaggerated British accent.

The side of Ezra's mouth tilts upward. "Please tell me that's not your real accent."

"It was 1869," I say, sidestepping the question. "His farewell tour. Dickens was dying, but he didn't know it yet."

He looked terrible, I remember; only fifty-seven, but his body already gaunt, his face drawn with exhaustion. It wasn't long after that that the seizures began; in a few months, he was dead.

"So, what was he like?" Ezra asks, clearly humoring me.

"I don't really remember," I admit. "It was pretty soon after I turned; I spent the entire talk staring at the neck of the woman in front of me."

"Yeah," he says wryly. "I know the feeling." With calmer hands, he takes another alcohol wipe and tears it open. "This might sting a little bit."

"You don't have to do this," I say. "There's a mirror right there. I can do it myself."

"Call me old-fashioned," Ezra says, gently swabbing my neck with the alcohol wipe. "But I've always believed you *shouldn't* leave a girl alone to cope with her gaping neck wound." He momentarily stills. "Actually, that joke doesn't really work now that I'm a vampire, does it?" he asks, beginning to dab again.

I bite my lip as the alcohol hits my skin, trying not to flinch at the sting.

"On the plus side, you've got time to workshop it now," I say.

"Well, that's true," he says seriously, reaching for a bandage. "I'm young and handsome forever, right?"

"Like James Dean," I say as he smooths the bandage carefully over my neck. "Only . . . not dead. Or, at least, not *totally* dead," I amend.

He smooths the bandage one last time, his fingers chill against my skin, then sits back on his heels, surveying his work. "I think that should do it," he says. "It doesn't look like it's bleeding anymore, at least." He eyes the stained neckline of my dress. "You might want to borrow some clothes from Sarita, though."

"Glass houses," I point out, gesturing toward his T-shirt. For the second night in a row, it's covered in dark splotches of blood; a Jackson Pollock painting come to life.

Ezra looks down, plucking at the material. "Please say I don't need an invitation to get inside a laundromat."

I laugh, even though the joke isn't funny.

Deep down, I know we're both pretending.

We're pretending that everything is normal.

That nothing has changed.

That we're still *friends.*

But it's a lie.

Ezra and I *aren't* friends.

We never were.

"Lily . . ." Ezra says.

He's inches away from me. If I wanted to, I could lean forward. I could close those inches between us. I could—

"Lily?" Max's voice sounds from the living room, making us both start. "Are you, um . . . okay in there?"

Ezra and I both bolt to our feet, nearly knocking into each other as we do.

"I'm fine!" I call back to Max, my voice sounding strange even to my own ears. "Be there in one sec!"

Ezra and I hover awkwardly in front of the open door, both of us trying to motion the other through first. Finally, my cheeks reddening, I duck my head and hurry into the hallway.

Sarita and Max are already in the living room, Sarita sprawled in a leather armchair while Max perches uncomfortably on the edge of the enormous sectional sofa.

As I step into the room, Max bounces to his feet, looking flustered.

Yesterday, he'd already have been hurrying forward to wrap his arms comfortingly around me. But today, he shoves his hands in his pockets, eying me warily from across the room.

"Are you sure you're okay?" he asks, grimacing slightly as he nods toward my neck.

"Oh," I say, reaching up to finger my freshly bandaged wound. "Um, yeah, I'm good."

It's literally impossible for this conversation to be any more excruciating.

I sit down on the other end of the sofa, leaving as much room between us as possible. After a second, he sits down again on the other side.

Ezra settles for the doorframe, leaning against it with one shoulder.

No one says anything.

The clock on Sarita's mantel ticks loudly in the silence, counting off the seconds with irritating slowness.

"So," Max finally says. "On a scale of one to ten, how pissed should I be that you guys have been lying to me?"

Sarita bites her lip. She's finally removed her ridiculous top hat, though I can still see the indent from the headband in her hair.

"To be fair, I did *tell* you I was a witch," she informs Max. "It's not my fault that you didn't believe me."

"We were in second grade," Max says. "And it was Halloween!"

"It still counts," Sarita mutters, fiddling with the chain of her necklace.

My eyes drop to the familiar crystal pendant, sudden realization dawning in my chest.

"Oh my God," I say, closing my eyes. "I can't believe I didn't see it before."

I think of the heavy silver rings on Sarita's fingers, glinting in the streetlight outside Mia's house. The necklace she never takes off. The scent of her homemade perfume, drifting across the living room even now.

"Lavender and angelica root for protection," I say dully. "Quartz to focus your power. And silver for . . . what?"

Sarita peers down at her rings.

"They don't actually do anything," she admits, wiggling her fingers. "But I like the look of them."

"You knew something weird was going on between Ezra and me," I say, thinking back to earlier, in the gym. "Those were your exact words. 'Something weird.' "

Good lord.

Was that only *this afternoon*?

"I wasn't sure what it was, exactly," Sarita says. "I could sense something *wrong*. And then tonight, when I tried to scry deeper . . ." She pauses, twisting one of her rings around her finger. "I could see you at the hotel. I knew you were in trouble, so I called Ezra to find out if he knew anything. But I swear, if I'd known how serious it was, I never would have brought Max."

"Awesome," Max says, folding his muscular arms against his chest. "This is all really great for my self-esteem, guys."

He turns to look at me.

"Last night, when you blew off dinner," he says. "*This* is what you got 'caught up' in? *Vampire* shit?"

I nod miserably.

"I was, um . . . I was teaching Ezra how to feed."

Max's jaw twitches.

"You mean he drank your—"

"No!" Ezra cuts in, shaking his head. "We went to a club, down by the shore. There was this guy, in the parking lot." He pauses, squeezing his eyes shut, like it pains him to remember. "He . . . *I* . . . I couldn't stop drinking from him. I almost killed him."

"But you *didn't*," I say firmly. "He's in stable condition, remember? He's going to be *fine*."

Max's jaw twitches again.

"Let me get this straight," he says. "After months of us dating, my mom *finally* invited you over for dinner. But instead of coming, you decided to go to some shitty nightclub. With my *best friend*. Where, apparently, the two of you almost *killed* some guy."

"I already told you, he's in *stable condition*," I snap. "And you're missing the point. I was trying to keep you *safe*, Max."

*"By lying to me?"* he asks incredulously.

Ezra rocks guiltily back and forth on the soles of his sneakers.

"If it helps, this is all new to me, too. I had no idea that witches existed, either," he says. "All Lily told me was that they were 'complicated.' "

"Complicated?" Sarita asks, looking insulted. "There's nothing *complicated* about it. We're good. Vampires are bad. End of story."

"*End* of story?" Max repeats. "I don't know how the story *starts*!"

I look down at my hands. Despite the quick rinse I gave them in Sarita's sink, they're still stained with blood.

Metaphorically speaking, it's not a great sign.

"Sarita's right," I say, still looking at my hands. "Witches aren't complicated. Witches are very, *very* simple. They're powerful. They're well-organized. And they're put on this earth to do one thing."

"What one thing?" Ezra asks, glancing between me and Sarita. "Witches are put on this earth to do *what one thing*?"

I look up at Sarita.

She looks down at her cut-offs again, suddenly very interested in the loose strings hanging from her thigh. "Oh, you know," she says, her voice casual. "Hunt vampires?"

# CHAPTER *Twenty*

"IN THEORY, ANYWAY," SARITA GOES ON, THE words tumbling out more quickly. "I'm only seventeen. I'm not even a full-fledged coven member yet."

I pause, flipping quickly through my jumbled memories. "So, back at the hotel, when you told Cassius your coven was already on its way, you were . . ."

"Lying my ass off," Sarita confirms. She tilts her head, giving me a curious look. "Speaking of which, what was Cassius talking about back there? When he said you were both 'off-limits'?"

I shake my head, trying to clear it. "I have no idea," I admit. "But I'm guessing that 'Cassius' and 'rational thinking' parted ways a while ago."

"Hold up," Ezra says, turning toward Sarita. "If you're not even a member of this coven thingy, why did you try to kill me?"

"Oh, I don't know," she replies, her voice thick with sarcasm. *"Because you're a vampire?!"*

"*I* was a vampire," I point out. "For over a century and a half. Does that mean you're going to try to kill me, too?"

On the other side of the couch, Max is staring at me like he's never seen me before.

It . . . does not feel great.

"Of course not," Sarita shoots back. "I . . . I don't understand. How could you possibly have been a vampire? You're a *witch*."

"I don't get it," Ezra says. "Why is *one* impossible thing more impossible than the *other* impossible thing?"

"*All* of these are impossible things," Max says. "Why am I the only one who sees that?"

"It's impossible because witches are one with nature," Sarita explains, her voice taking on the same slightly superior tone that people use when they're talking about Peloton. "Our powers come from the earth itself, and we can only use them if we maintain the natural balance. Vampires, on the other hand, couldn't care less about balance. They take what they want, when they want, with *no* regard for consequences," Sarita finishes dramatically. "Basically, they're a scourge on the natural world, and their very existence threatens us all."

"Great," Max says, burying his head in his hands. "My friends are all completely unhinged."

"Seriously?" I ask Sarita.

"What?" she says, crossing her arms defensively in front of her chest. "Witches are natural and vampires are unnatural. I'm sorry, but it's the truth!"

"So, witches *use* magic," I say. "And vampires *are* magic. You don't happen to see a conflict of interest there?"

Sarita narrows her eyes in my direction.

"Whatever," she says. "That still doesn't explain how you *used* to be a vampire. Vampires can't turn back," she adds firmly. "It's not *possible.*"

"For the last time," Max practically shouts. "*None* of this is possible!"

I swallow hard, my fingers curling in on themselves as I try to prepare myself.

This is it.

As soon as they learn the truth, Max and Sarita will never look at me the same way again.

I'll be lucky if they'll even look at me *at all.*

Across the living room, Ezra's dark eyes lock with mine. Subtly, he gives an encouraging nod.

I take a deep breath, steeling my nerves.

"Actually," I say. "It is."

My story comes quicker this time, the hazy memories taking shape without me clawing at them. The exasperation slowly fades from Max's face, his expression turning grim as I fill him and Sarita in on the details of my life.

And death.

And life again.

"I always knew that Cassius could be possessive," I finish, my hands clenched tightly on either side of me. "But I never imagined he could do something like this. Attacking me, trying to *turn* me. It's . . ."

"Incredibly fucked up?" Sarita says, nodding wisely. I can see Max mulling my story over and over in his head, still trying to convince himself it's not true.

I remember doing the same thing, all those years ago.

"Yeah," I agree, forcing myself to concentrate on the present. " 'Incredibly fucked up' pretty much covers it."

"Are you sure Cassius doesn't have any bloodstone left?" Sarita asks hopefully. "Maybe he didn't destroy it *all.* Maybe there's still a piece big enough to—"

"I'm sure," Ezra interrupts, his voice flat. "The asshole ground it to powder right in front of my eyes. It's gone."

"Oh." Sarita sits back, slumping dispiritedly against the chair.

I grit my teeth, the sound of Cassius's mocking laughter still ringing in my ears. Was this his plan all along? To crush my spirit, along with the bloodstone? To make me beg for Ezra's life before he took *mine*?

"Uh . . . Lily?" Max says, leaning away from me.

I look down; my fingers are digging into the sofa cushions next to me, the smell of burnt acrylic already filling the air.

It takes me a second to realize the couch is smoking.

"Shit," I say, quickly pulling my hands away. "Sorry." *Stop it,* I think, clenching my fingers into fists. *Stop it, stop it, stop it.*

"Holy shit!" Sarita says. "My mom is going to *kill* me."

Max stares down at the ruined fabric, his eyes wide.

I clench my fists tighter, the heat pulsing in my palms again.

"Hey, hey, hey," Ezra says, stepping forward in concern. "It's okay! Try some deep breaths. In for three, out for five." He demonstrates, moving his hands along with the rise and fall of his chest. "See? It's easy."

"Please," I snap. "You don't even *need* to breathe."

Still, I try to do what he says, forcing myself to drag in a breath and blow it out, counting in my head. *One. Two. Three. Four.*

By the time I reach five, the warmth in my hands has begun to fade, leaving my palms stinging and red.

A small tendril of smoke curls its way toward the ceiling, fading slowly away into nothing.

For a moment, no one says anything.

And then Max pushes himself up from the couch, already reaching for his keys.

"Welp," he says. "That's it. I'm calling it a night."

I wince, tucking my hands beneath my legs. "Max," I plead. "Wait."

"For *what*?" he asks, his hands wheeling wildly through the air. "For you to set the armchairs on fire? For Sarita to claim that *mermaids* are real? For Ezra to *rip my fucking throat out*?"

His words fly through the air like shrapnel, hitting everyone in their path.

Max takes a deep breath, looking away. "I'm sorry," he says, his voice quiet. "But clearly, none of this has anything to do with me. So, I'm *leaving*."

"What about Cassius?" Ezra asks, pushing himself away from the wall. "He's still out there! Destroying whatever bloodstone is left won't be enough for him. Sooner or later, he'll come for Lily!"

"And what then?" Max asks, exploding. "According to you, he's a *centuries-old vampire*. And I'm a *high school senior*! What am I supposed to do, challenge him to a fucking forensics debate?"

Forget the shrapnel.

It feels like a *bomb* exploded in Sarita's living room.

"Fuck you, Hutchinson," Ezra says shakily. "You're acting like an asshole."

Max laughs. "*I'm* acting like an asshole? Do you even hear yourself? In case you don't remember, I'm the one who took you to the hospital when you got sick. I skipped school for you. I fucking *sat by your bedside* like some . . . like some old-timey Victorian *ghost*."

There's a pause.

"Wait," Sarita says. "Do you mean a *nanny*?"

But Max is already plunging ahead, the floodgates finally open. "For the record, I *still* can't get the bloodstains out of my Jeep. And this is how you thank me? By lying to me? By avoiding me? By running around with my girlfriend behind my back?"

I feel myself flush.

Technically speaking, Ezra and I haven't done anything wrong.

But none of us are interested in technicalities right now.

"Lily was *helping* me," Ezra says. "I know it's hard to believe, but not everything is about you, Max."

"Okay," Sarita says, standing up. She glances anxiously between Max and Ezra. "Let's all . . . calm down. Does anyone want some tea?"

"What's that supposed to mean?" Max demands, ignoring Sarita's offer.

Ezra pushes his hands through his hair, his shoulders taut with frustration. "It means not all of us have perfect little lives, okay?"

"Fuck you," Max says, his voice shaking a little. "My life isn't perfect."

"Oh, yeah?" Ezra says. "*Join the club.* In case you haven't noticed, Max, I don't live in a fucking McMansion. My mom's not around to tuck me into bed with a glass of warm milk. And the reason I don't give a shit about my GPA is because I *can't pay for college.*" Ezra glares at Max, his eyes dark with anger. "Did you know your Jeep is worth more than my house? *Literally.* I looked it up one time."

"My mom has chamomile tea," Sarita says, wringing her hands uselessly in front of her. "It's *very* calming."

"Funny, you weren't complaining about my Jeep when I was picking you up for school *every single day for the last three years,*" Max says, although some of the bravado has gone out of his voice. "You didn't seem to have a problem with it then."

"It's not about the damn Jeep!" Ezra roars, his voice so loud that even I can't help flinching.

Ezra takes a long breath, noticeably calming himself.

"You're my best friend, Max," he says. "But my life can't *revolve* around yours." He runs his hand through his hair again, glancing in my direction. "Not anymore, at least."

I swallow hard, my palms flooding with sudden heat.

Max stands still, taking in Ezra's words.

In all the years they've been friends, I wonder how many times Ezra has stood up for himself before.

"Max," I say. "*Please.* Cassius wants to hurt me. And he knows the best way to do that is by hurting the people I love."

"So, what?" he asks. "We're supposed to hide in Sarita's house? Forever?"

"Not *forever,*" Sarita protests. "Cassius already told you he was going to destroy the rest of the bloodstone. If we can figure out where he's going, we can . . ."

She trails off, waving her hand vaguely through the air.

"Do *what*?" Max demands again. "Stop the evil vampire? Save our friend? Magically *fix* everything?"

"Er . . ." Sarita says. "Yes?"

Max tips his head back, letting out a frustrated groan. "This isn't one of your ridiculous movies, Sarita. It's *real life*. You can't keep me here."

Ezra steps in front of the living room door.

"Actually," he says. "We can."

To my horror, Max steps forward as well, shoving Ezra square in the chest.

Ezra doesn't even blink.

"Get out of my way, Cruz," Max says, his knuckles white around his keys. "I already told you, I'm *leaving*."

"No," Ezra says patiently. "You're *not*."

The two of them stand head-to-head, eyeing each other angrily. Ezra may be taller, but Max's shoulders are wider, his arms muscled from a hundred early-morning practice sessions with a personal trainer, a thousand extra laps in the pool. In any fair fight, Max could probably wipe the floor with Ezra and not even break a sweat.

But this isn't a fair fight.

When it comes to vampires, it never is.

"Please stay, Max," I say softly. "*Please*. If anything happened to you, I'd never forgive myself."

For a long moment, Max hesitates.

At last, he gives a reluctant nod.

"Fine," he says shortly. "On one condition."

Relief floods through me. "Anything," I say.

Max finally turns, looking directly at me. "When this is over, you never speak to me again."

The lump in my throat is nearly unbearable now.

"I'll do you one better," I manage to say. "As soon as I know you're all safe, I'll leave Sunrise Harbor for good."

# CHAPTER Twenty-One

"WAKE UP!" SOMEONE SAYS, SHOVING ROUGHLY at my shoulder. "Wake up, wake up, wake up!"

Blearily, I bolt upright, the bandage on my neck tugging in protest.

"Sarita?" I ask, blinking warily around the guest room. "What is it? Is everything okay?"

"Everything's fine," Sarita says, yanking the duvet cover back with a practiced flick of her wrist. "Well, not really," she adds. "Everything kind of sucks. But I made breakfast!" Grabbing my hand, she pulls me out of bed with enough enthusiasm to practically dislocate my arm. "Come eat it before it gets cold."

Groggily, I follow Sarita into the kitchen, smoothing my hair down as best I can. Like every other room in Sarita's house, it's decorated in tasteful shades of gray and white, with an enormous Sub-Zero refrigerator and a kitchen island big enough to have its own address.

Judging by the state of the countertops, Sarita has been up for a while.

Yawning loudly, I slide onto one of the leather barstools. "Where are Ezra and Max?"

"Max is still sleeping," Sarita says, busying herself with something on top of the stove. "And Ezra's down in the boiler room."

I blink, trying to process Sarita's words. "Why is Ezra in the boiler room?"

"I'm not really sure," Sarita says. "He kept talking about something called polyvinyl butyral and asking what year our windows were installed. I think he's worried about . . ."

"Burning to a fiery crisp?" I finish, picking pieces of eggshell from the marble island and dropping them into a nearby scrap bowl.

*Tornadoes* do less damage than Sarita cooking.

"Exactly," she says, setting a plate down in front of me with a flourish. "Anyway, eat up!"

I look down at the loaded plate, poking cautiously at a piece of toast.

"Are these . . . fried eggs?"

"No," Sarita says smugly. "They're eggs caramelized in a Parmesan cream sauce and topped with fresh thyme."

"So, fried eggs," I translate.

"With toast," Sarita points out, taking the seat next to mine. "I used the good bread." Picking up her fork, she scoops up an enormous bite, balancing the eggs precariously on a piece of toast before stuffing it in her mouth.

"Thanks," I say, staring down at my plate. I can't remember the last time I ate; despite everything, I'm starving.

I fork a small mountain of eggs into my mouth, my eyes widening in shock.

"Good, right?" Sarita says smugly, taking another bite. "The secret is butter. Well, and cream. And cheese. I guess there are a lot of secrets."

I stop listening, concentrating on shoveling all of the food from my plate to my stomach in the least amount of time possible.

It doesn't take long.

Sarita watches as I scrape the side of my fork across my empty plate, trying to scoop up the last of the cheese. Wordlessly, she pushes her still half-full plate across the table toward me.

I take it gratefully.

"You know," she says. "If you leave Sunrise Harbor, I won't be able to make you breakfast anymore."

Suddenly, I'm not quite as hungry.

"You literally told me all of the ingredients," I point out, lowering my fork. "And besides, you always knew this was coming. Senior year is almost over. Things were bound to change, no matter what. You're moving to Rhode Island!"

"You're aware of the fact that Rhode Island isn't actually an *island*, right?" Sarita asks. "Well, most of it, anyway. And even if it *was*, they make these things called 'airplanes' now. You can visit me at RISD all the time! Astrid's already planning to."

"Astrid is going to school in *Boston*," I say. "She'll be an hour away, not halfway across the country."

"You could come, too!" Sarita says, her voice pitching upward with excitement. "Max is going to Dartmouth, right? You could find a school that's nearby! We could all still be together!"

I think of all the half-finished college applications cluttering my laptop. If I'm being honest with myself, maybe I never intended to finish them.

"Maybe," I say, forcing a smile. "But in the meantime, you saw what Cassius was capable of last night. As long as I'm here, in Sunrise Harbor, none of you are safe."

She tips her head to one side, subconsciously reaching for her necklace. "We could always tell my mom what's happening," she says. "Cassius wouldn't stand a chance against her coven."

"Neither would Ezra," I point out again. "You know as well as I do that they'd kill first, ask questions second. They're *witches*."

"So am I," Sarita says quietly. "And so are you."

The eggs I've eaten are suddenly threatening to come back up.

This is ridiculous.

I can't even *hear* the word 'witch' without wanting to vomit.

How can it be possible that I *am* one?

I peer down at my hands, turning them back and forth in front of me. "If you say so," I mumble, dropping them to my lap.

"Oh, come on," Sarita says. "Don't say you still can't feel it. I could sense the power running through you the first day you walked into school. You're practically *radiating* it."

"Great," I say sarcastically. "I'm Chernobyl."

"Um, hello?" Sarita says. "*I'm* supposed to be the dramatic one, remember? Besides, you don't have anything to worry about. I saw you last night." She shakes her head ever so slightly, reaching up to play with her necklace. "I've never seen witch fire that strong before. Like . . . *ever*. Magic like that shouldn't have even been *possible* without a circle to help you focus. It's like you're a *super witch* or something."

I don't *want* to be a super witch.

I don't want to worry about vampires, and death, and *blood.*

I want to drink warm keg beer, and almost flunk history class, and wear ugly polyester pants to my shitty minimum wage job.

Is that too much to ask?

"I want to be . . . a girl," I say. "A normal *human* girl."

The words come out a little too forcefully. Like if I say them loud enough, they'll somehow be true.

"Witches are still human," Sarita says gently. "We've just got a few . . . upgrades."

Still feeling nauseated, I reach for one of the books lying in the middle of the island, surrounded by dirty dishes. The leather-bound spine crackles with age, the cover peeling up at the corners.

"What are these, your recipe books?" I ask, looking in vain for a title. The delicate pages are filled with old-fashioned cursive, the ink faded so badly that it's almost impossible to read.

"Coven ledgers," Sarita says. "I thought I might be able to find a way to track Cassius. Some sort of advanced scrying spell or something."

"And?" I ask, flipping the page.

Sarita shakes her head. "Nothing," she says. "But then I started thinking about what you said last night. About how witches *use* magic, but vampires *are* magic? I always thought that when a witch kills a vampire, the magic sort of . . . *dissipates.* But you were right; according to these ledgers, the magic goes to the witch." She pauses, looking vaguely ill. "I don't understand. The earth is supposed to *grant* us our magic. We're not supposed to *take* it."

There's a subdued tone to Sarita's voice that I've rarely heard before, her last words barely a whisper.

I run my finger across the page, tracing the cobweb-like script. I was always a terrible writer; I didn't have the patience that penmanship required. My letters were routinely blotched with drops of spilled ink, the edges of my fingers smudged black.

"Maybe there's a reason no one ever talks about it," I say. "Sometimes it's easier to ignore the truth. Even if it's staring right at you."

I can't help thinking of Ezra, his face inches from mine as he bandaged my wound last night.

About how easy it would have been to lean forward.

Resolutely, I push away the image, turning back to Sarita.

"Yeah," she says with a sigh. "I'm beginning to suspect there's a lot I haven't been told." She props her elbows on the counter. "Speaking of which, what was it *really* like?" she asks. "Being a vampire?"

I pause for a long minute, wondering how honest to be with Sarita. How honest to be with *myself.*

"It's hard to explain," I say. "When Cassius first turned me, I felt . . . powerful . . . for the first time in my life."

If I close my eyes, I can still feel the heavy weight of my petticoats tripping me at every step. I can remember the way the tops of my buttoned boots chafed at my legs and my high lace collar scratched against my throat. For years, I walked around in a literal cage; the fine boning of my corset crushing my ribs in a viselike grip. I didn't draw my first real breath until after I had died.

Being a vampire offered me the first taste of freedom I'd ever felt; an escape from the endless expectations of polite society and stifling social mores.

Cassius made me laugh; not the polite, stifled laughter that I'd heard all my life, but the kind of deep, *real* laughter that shook my whole body and made me gasp for air I didn't need anymore. He taught me how to ride a horse, how to win a game of cards, how to hold my head high when I walked into a room.

They say money can't buy happiness, but they're wrong. In those early years, Cassius's money bought us freedom. It bought us *adventure.* Fast horses and, later, faster cars. Sumptuous apartments and endless wine.

"There was nowhere we couldn't go," I say. "Nothing we couldn't do. It was . . . *intoxicating.* And then . . ."

"Then?" Sarita prompts me.

I swallow hard, staring unseeingly down at the counter in front of me.

The leftover eggs are beginning to harden on the plate.

"And then it *wasn't,*" I say simply.

At first, Cassius didn't understand. He thought I was a problem to be solved, a riddle he needed to find the answer to.

As if a change of scenery or a shiny new car would make me forget the aching *hollowness* inside me.

"I wanted to be human," I say aloud. "And Cassius wanted to be with me. Maybe he thought that finding the cure would change everything. That it could somehow *fix us.*"

Cassius had been wrong.

"Deep down, I always knew there was something . . . broken . . . in him," I say. "I didn't realize how badly."

I remember the innkeeper's wife, in Lauterbrunnen, the one with the apple-red cheeks. I think of the moment her cheerful smile finally faded from her face.

How many others had there been?

How many people did Cassius *kill*?

"He's a monster," Sarita says matter-of-factly.

"Maybe," I say. "But that doesn't mean *all* vampires are monsters. Don't believe everything you read about them being a . . ." I pause, glancing down at the page in front of me. "Dark scourge of humanity?" I read aloud. "Seriously?"

Sarita reaches over, firmly closing the book.

"Yeah," a voice says over my shoulder. "Could we maybe save the 'dark scourge of humanity' stuff until *after* I've had coffee?"

I turn to see Max standing in the kitchen doorway, his dark blond hair still wet from his shower. He's wearing the same clothes as yesterday, his rumpled T-shirt turned inside out.

Even from here, I can see the dark circles beneath his eyes.

"Max." I stand up so quickly I nearly knock my chair over. "Hey. You're up. How did you, um . . . sleep?"

"Er, good," he says, not quite meeting my eyes. "I slept . . . good."

"Good," I repeat, my head bobbling up and down like the Princess Leia bobblehead in my car. "That's . . . good."

"Well," Sarita says, looking between us. "I'm glad *this* isn't awkward at all."

Max turns to the fridge and grabs a carton of orange juice. As Sarita and I watch, he screws open the top and gulps the juice down straight from the container.

Sarita gives him a look.

"You realize no one else is going to want to use that now, right?" she asks. "It's literally *covered* in your mouth germs."

Max lowers the juice, staring blankly down at the carton.

"Shit," he says. "Sorry."

Setting the juice carefully down on the counter, he begins paging through Sarita's ledger. "What's this?" he asks. "Like . . . witch stuff?"

Sarita and I exchange glances.

"Yeah," she says. "It's witch stuff."

"I still can't believe any of this is actually real," Max says, still flipping through the book. "Vampires. Witches." He pauses, squinting down at the spidery handwriting on the page in front of him. "Fucking mystical bloodstones. It's wild."

A strange jolt runs through me.

"Wait," I say. "They mention *bloodstone* in the ledger?"

Stepping forward, I grab the book unceremoniously from Max's hands. The handwriting on the page is cramped and faded, but still legible.

Oh my God.

*Oh my God.*

"Lily?" Sarita asks, her voice cautious.

I flip to the next page, almost tearing the delicate paper in my haste.

"Hey!" Sarita says. "Be careful with that! I'm not even supposed to be touching it!"

I keep reading, my heart beating faster and faster with each word.

"What is it?" Max asks, looking between the two of us. "What's going on?"

"I'm not sure," I admit. "But according to this book, witches have been squirreling away bloodstone for centuries."

Could Cassius have somehow found out?

Is *that* where he got the bloodstone?

"How do we know it's *the* bloodstone from Abhartach's tomb? It could be unrelated," Sarita points out. "Witches *love* to hoard gemstones. My mom owns, like, thirty-seven lunar crystals. She claims they're for the different phases of the moon, but the moon only has *eight* phases, so—"

"Sarita!" I say, interrupting her runaway train of thought. "*Think.* If the witches *had* been collecting bloodstone, where would they be keeping it?"

She blinks. "Um," she says. "I don't know. Lots of places?"

"Lots of places *where*?" I ask impatiently.

"Damascus? Beijing? Athens?" she guesses. "There are covensteads scattered all over the world. Especially in the older cities."

"What about St. Augustine?" Max asks. "It's the oldest continuously inhabited city in America."

We both look at him.

"Really?" he asks, reaching for the carton of orange juice again. "Am I the only one passing US history?"

"Max is right," Sarita says. "I've only been a few times, but there's definitely a covenstead in St. Augustine. My mom's actually there right now, for her circle's annual gathering thing. You know, the 'conference' I told you about?"

St. Augustine.

It's only about ninety miles away, straight up the coastline. If I'm driving, we can be there in less than an hour.

"Your mom's van has tinted windows, right?" I ask Sarita.

Her eyes narrow suspiciously.

"Yeah," she says. "Why?"

I snap the book closed in front of me. "Call your mom," I tell Max. "You're going to need another excuse."

He lowers the carton. "Uh . . . why?"

"School's canceled," I say. "We're going on a road trip."

# CHAPTER Twenty-Two

"SO," SARITA ASKS CHEERFULLY, "WHO'S READY for a *heist*?"

As Sarita tosses a duffel into the trunk, I open the driver's side door and slide in. "For the last time, this isn't a heist." I say as she climbs in next to me. "We don't even know if the bloodstone is *there*."

It's probably not.

It makes no sense; why would a bunch of witches be *hoarding the cure to vampirism*?

Then again, *The Love Boat* made no sense, either, and it ran for almost a decade.

"Not to be a damper," Max says, buckling his seat belt. "But what happens if we *do* find the bloodstone? I thought you said it was cursed. We're not going to let Ezra *murder* someone, right?"

Through mutual unspoken agreement, we've all decided to pretend that last night's fight never happened.

Unfortunately for all of us, Sarita is the only one who can actually *act*.

"I agree with Max," Ezra calls from the back. "Murder is an *unacceptable* side effect, people!" His voice is muffled by the blankets he's insisted on piling on top of himself, despite the fact that the tinted windows are perfectly safe.

Well, as long as no one accidentally cracks one open, that is.

"No one is murdering *anyone*," I say firmly, reaching up to adjust the rearview mirror. "Cassius said there was a way to break the curse. All we need to do is *find* it."

Sarita wrinkles her nose. "And if your vampire ex-boyfriend was lying?"

I gun the engine of the minivan.

It whimpers pathetically in response.

"Then we'll cross that bridge when we come to it," I say. "In the meantime, let's blow this Popsicle stand!"

Sarita's wrinkles deepen. "What does that even—*aagh*!"

I flatten the gas pedal, roaring out of Sarita's garage like a bat out of hell.

"Residential street!" Max screams from the back seat, dramatically throwing his hands in front of his face. *"Residential street!"*

I slam on the brakes at the end of the driveway, patiently checking both directions. "Would everyone relax?" I ask, turning onto the empty side street. "I've been driving for over a century, remember? Besides, I have excellent reflexes."

I swerve to avoid an oncoming squirrel, the front right tire scraping loudly against the curb.

"See?" I say, quickly straightening the wheel. "That squirrel is alive because of me. A lesser driver would have squashed him flat."

Sarita closes her eyes, her fingers tightening around the door handle. In the back, Max is double-checking his seat belt.

"For the record, I hate this!" Ezra calls.

"For the record, piles of blankets don't talk!" I call back, my foot reaching automatically for the clutch. Which, of course, doesn't exist because we're in a minivan.

Drivers have no sense of *adventure* these days.

As I pull onto the main street, Max turns to look over his shoulder, scanning the road behind us.

"I told you, the squirrel's fine," I say.

He shoots me a look in the rearview mirror. "I'm not looking for *squirrels*," he says. "I'm checking to see if we're being followed."

Oh, right.

Yeah, that makes more sense.

"Thanks to Sarita, Cassius thinks there's an entire *coven* after him," I remind Max. "There's no way he'd risk going after the bloodstone in broad daylight. He's *angry*, not suicidal."

Knowing Cassius, he's probably holed up in his luxury hotel room at this very moment, licking his wounds.

Or, more likely, someone else's.

"Don't worry," Sarita says, twisting to look back at Max. "Lily and I will keep you safe. *Witch fire*, baby," she adds, wiggling her fingers for emphasis. "Get it while it's hot!"

I grip the steering wheel more tightly, trying not to remember the waves of undulating purple fire radiating outward from my body, or the acrid scent of Cassius's burning flesh.

I can feel my eye beginning to twitch; I'd do unspeakable things for a couple of aspirin right now.

"Maybe we should listen to some music or something," I say.

Sarita nods. "Good idea," she says. "I know the *perfect* heist soundtrack."

My eye gives another twitch.

"Again," I repeat. "Not a heist."

"Oh, really?" she asks smugly. "Then why are we wearing *heist* clothes?"

I spare a glance in her direction. For the first time, I notice that her shorts and T-shirt are both plain black. I look down at the leggings and tank top I've borrowed from her. Which, I'm now realizing, are also black.

My other eye twitches.

"If you want, I can go change into my school spirit outfit," Sarita says. "Although, fair warning, there are *definitely* pom-poms involved."

"Fine," I say with a sigh. "It's a heist."

She claps her hands in delight.

"Are we absolutely sure this is a good idea?" Max asks. "Because if we turn around right now, I can still make it in time for my calc test."

On the other side of the road, a cop car speeds past us, its red and blue lights flashing silently overhead. I tighten my grip on the steering wheel, trying to ignore my sense of impending doom.

"Don't be such a worrywart," Sarita says, reaching for her phone. "What could possibly go wrong?"

"Well," I say an hour later. "This can't possibly be right."

Leaning forward, I rest my hands on the steering wheel and

peer through the windshield. We're double-parked on a busy side street in downtown St. Augustine, the sidewalks already bustling with tourists despite the fact that it's barely even ten in the morning.

"The Witch's Cauldron," I say, reading the name hanging from the side of the storefront in purple loopy letters. A smaller handwritten sign in the window reads: *Crystals, candles, spell supplies, and more. Free tarot reading with $50 purchase!*

The store is nestled in the middle of one of the low stucco buildings that line the streets of the historic district, its pastel exteriors faded with age. There's a wine bar on one side, the back patio crowded with tables, and a used bookstore on the other.

"The Witch's Cauldron?" Max repeats. "Seriously?"

"What?" Sarita asks, looking innocently up from her phone, which she's been using to text Astrid nonstop for the entire ride. "Too much?"

"I don't understand," I say, shaking my head in confusion. "I mean, this is *St. Augustine*."

This city has been around since the *1500s*. It's been home to pirates, and smugglers, and the Underground Railroad. It's been invaded so many times that actual *historians* have probably lost count.

"We passed a literal *fortress*, like . . . five minutes ago," I go on. "Why would there be a covenstead *here*? It's basically a strip mall."

"Haven't you ever heard of hiding in plain sight?" Sarita asks. "Besides, witches have to make a living, too."

"What's going on?" Ezra calls from his (completely unnecessary) hiding spot beneath the blankets. "What are you talking about? Are we there yet? Should I come out?"

I squint at the front door, trying to make out the shop hours on the sign. "It looks pretty dark in there," I say. "I don't think they're open yet."

"Perfect," Sarita says. "Pull around through the alley." She leans forward, pointing toward the turn. "There's a parking garage in the back. I'm pretty sure it leads right to the basement."

I put the van into gear, maneuvering my way through the foot traffic. Thankfully, despite the bustle of sunburned tourists wandering overhead, the garage isn't quite full yet; I'm able to find a spot on the lower level, next to the elevators. *Technically* it's for compact cars only, but I truly believe that *any* car can be compact, if you want it badly enough.

"Okay," Sarita calls to Ezra as I turn off the ignition. "It's safe. You can come out now."

"Are you sure?" Ezra calls back.

"It's a *parking garage*," I say. "Trust me. This place hasn't seen natural light since 1972."

After a second, Ezra cautiously pokes his head out from the pile of blankets. He looks slightly worse for wear than I expected, his face drawn tight with stress. "Well," he says. "*That* ride sucked."

"Try being crammed into a steamer trunk for an entire transatlantic crossing," I say.

Ezra blinks. "I'll take your word for it."

Sarita unbuckles her seat belt. "Come on," she says. "We're wasting time."

"Remember," I remind Sarita. "You're opening the door for me, and that's *it*." Sarita begins to protest, but I steamroll ahead. "Ezra and Max, you wait here," I say. "We won't be long."

Ezra and Max glance at each other, the air between them simmering with unresolved tension.

I don't think they've said more than two words to each other all morning.

"Actually, I could use a cup of coffee," Max says, sliding open the door of the van. "Text me when you're done."

"Max, wait," I start to say, twisting around in my seat. But Sarita reaches for my arm, giving me a nudge.

"It's fine," she says. "Give him some time. Besides, it's broad daylight; he'll probably be safer out there, anyway."

I press my lips together, watching as Max strides toward the elevators, hitting the button just *slightly* too hard. When the doors open, he steps inside without a backward glance.

"Well, I'm not waiting here by myself," Ezra says. "This place is like murder central."

Cautiously, he opens the back of the van, one of the blankets looped over his head like an oversized kerchief. He peers around the parking garage suspiciously, jumping a little as tires squeal in the distance. A thin cloud of exhaust hangs low in the air around us, yellowish fluorescent lights buzzing above us. There's an uneven *drip drip drip* coming from somewhere overhead; probably the source of the musty smell in the air.

"Come on," Sarita says, nodding toward the row of doors lining the far wall of the garage. "And leave the blanket," she says. "You look like Mother Teresa."

Clearly affronted, Ezra drops the blanket and stows it in the back of the van.

"Are you sure we don't need, like . . . a key or something?" he asks, jogging to catch up with us. Thanks to the blanket, his hair has turned into a frizzy mass of curls. Self-consciously, he reaches up, trying to smooth it flat.

"I *am* the key," Sarita says. She stops in front of the right door, wiping her palms nervously against the sides of her shorts. "Here we go," she says. "Watch my back, okay?"

Ezra and I nod.

Sarita raises her hands, closing her eyes in concentration. As we glance nervously over our shoulders, Sarita begins to mumble under her breath. The moment stretches uncomfortably long, Ezra and I jumping with every slam of a car door. It's chilly in the lower level of the parking garage, the air clammy with trapped moisture.

The nervous energy that's kept me running through the morning is finally starting to fade, replaced by a dull, stomach-churning sense of dread.

This is a bad idea.

If we're caught, Ezra could be killed.

*All* of us could be killed.

And for what? The *possibility* of a cure?

I inhale slowly, ignoring the exhaust fumes as I try to calm myself down.

Ezra reaches out, brushing the back of his fingers ever so slightly against my hand. For such a light touch, it's surprisingly steadying.

"You okay?" he whispers, his voice soft in my ear.

I honestly don't know how to answer him.

"I . . ."

There's an audible *click* from the other side of the door.

Sarita opens her eyes. "Got it," she says in satisfaction. "Come on!"

"What?" I ask, jolting away from Ezra's touch. "No way! You guys are *staying here*, remember?"

Sarita looks at me.

"Lily," she says as if she's talking to a small child. "Be honest. Did you *really* think I was going to stay here?"

And, before I can even answer, she steps through the door.

Shit.

*Shit.*

My palms pricking with nervous heat, I hurry through the door after her.

And promptly run into her back.

"Sarita," I hiss. "I'm not messing around. Do you know how *dangerous* this could be?"

"Why do you think I'm not letting you do it alone?" Sarita asks, groping for the light switch. "Let me find the . . ."

Ezra reaches past her, flicking the switch on easily.

Vampire eyesight: definitely a perk.

"Oh, look," he says flatly as a single light bulb flickers to life overhead. "It's a broom closet."

To be fair, the room is *slightly* bigger than a closet.

It's full of dusty cardboard boxes and half-empty crates, Bubble Wrap spilling from their edges. A narrow stairwell leads into the shop itself, a pile of cleaning supplies heaped haphazardly on the landing.

Sarita grins and crosses the room. She runs her fingers along the wall before stopping at a seemingly random spot. Gently, she pushes on the plaster.

The entire wall swings open.

"Like I told you," she says, stepping forward, "witches are all about hiding in plain sight."

One after another, a series of overhead light panels *thrums* to life, casting the cavernous space into stark relief.

Holy shit.

It's absolutely *enormous.*

Sarita gives us a smug look, leading Ezra inside.

He whistles appreciatively, turning in a slow circle to look around. "Okay," he says. "Now *this* is some *National Treasure* shit."

I follow them into the room, staring in shock at the maze of display cases and row after row of gleaming, glass-topped cabinets. It's all stainless steel and spotless white floors, like a dental office on steroids.

Ezra peers curiously down at the nearest glass-topped display case.

"Um, guys?" he asks, his voice slightly higher than usual. "These wouldn't happen to be *human* teeth, would they?"

Sarita and I step forward. A strange wreath of hair, teeth, feathers, and bone rests beneath the display glass, fragile and yellowed with age.

"Ugh. It's a *ghirlanda,*" Sarita says, wrinkling her nose in disgust. "Sort of a DIY witch hex, from back in the day. Supposedly, if you put it in someone's bed, they'd die in their sleep."

Ezra looks up in horror. "Seriously?"

"Well, they didn't actually *work*," Sarita says. "It was the Middle Ages. People thought you could *sneeze out your soul*."

"If it doesn't work, why is it in the archives?" I ask.

Sarita shrugs. "I told you," she says. "Witches save *everything*."

"There's got to be some sort of system," I say, turning gladly away from the nightmarish human wreath. "A card catalog or something."

"A *card catalog*?" Ezra asks. "Seriously? *How* old are you again?"

"Give me a second," Sarita says. "Everything is digitized. There's got to be a computer somewhere." She heads purposefully across the room, winding her way through the maze of display cases. Ezra and I follow more slowly, peeking through the glass as we pass by. The room is clearly climate-controlled, the humidity filtered from the air, leaving it unnaturally dry.

The cases are crammed with artifacts. Most are mundane, like the rows of pressed herbs and carefully curated manuscripts, but I pass some pretty macabre collections, as well.

"This place gives me the creeps," Ezra says in a low voice, skirting wide around a display case full of desiccated ox hearts. "Like, come on, who needs *this many* ox hearts?"

I manage a half-hearted smile.

I know it sounds ridiculous, but I thought that being here might . . . trigger something in me, somehow. Like maybe, after all these years of not knowing I was a witch, being in a covenstead would feel like *coming home.*

But it doesn't.

It feels . . . *wrong.*

"You guys!" Sarita calls from the other side of the room. "Come look at this." She taps a laptop's screen triumphantly as we hurry toward her. "Cabinet H-37: Bloodstone."

I can feel my pulse quickening with excitement. "Which way do we go?" I ask, trying to keep my voice steady.

Sarita pulls up the coordinating filing system, squinting down at the screen. "Er . . . this way?" she says, sounding not altogether certain.

Still, we follow her, threading our way back through the cabinets again. "H-34, H-35, H-36 . . ." Sarita counts off, finally coming to a stop in front of one of the display cases. "H-37."

We all fall silent.

Beneath the glass, row after row of red-flecked bloodstones glow starkly against the background.

Oh my God.

There must be *dozens* of them.

Ezra leans closer, reading the top of the neatly printed label affixed to the front of the case. "Heliotrope. Sourced in Slaghtaverty, Ireland."

My breath catches in my chest.

I don't need a label to tell me that the shards of stone are real; I can feel it in my *bones.*

"What's in Slaghtaverty?" Sarita asks, sounding out each syllable as she reads.

"It's the burial site of Abhartach," I explain. "Also known as the original vampire." I feel sick, remembering the last time I held one.

*A dark-haired girl.*

*A rooftop.*

*Blood.*

"I don't understand," I whisper, dragging my eyes away from the case.

It makes no sense.

Why would Cassius have let me spend *decades* searching for a cure if he'd known where to find it all along?

Ezra is still bent over the case's label, his eyes darting quickly back and forth as he scans the block of text.

"What does 'transference' mean?" he asks. "It says the stones have been 'imbued for transference,' but it doesn't explain what 'transference' actually *is*."

We both turn to Sarita, who raises her shoulders defensively.

"Don't look at me," she says. "I already told you, I'm not a full-fledged member of the coven yet."

I eye the neat rows of stone, my forehead creasing as I try to think.

*Transference.*

*Transference.*

*Transfer—*

Overhead, a door falls shut with a muffled *thud*.

I freeze, my head snapping up in alarm.

A second later, a voice drifts down the stairwell. "See? I *told* you the ward had been triggered."

"I didn't say the ward *hadn't* been triggered," another voice snipes back. Is it my imagination or does it sound oddly familiar somehow? "You take these things so *personally*, Eloise."

*Witches?* Ezra mouths silently in our direction.

"Even worse," Sarita whispers back, the color draining from her face. "It's my *mom*."

# CHAPTER *Twenty-Three*

ADRENALINE COURSES THROUGH MY VEINS, MY fight-or-flight response kicking in instantly.

As per usual, I choose "flight."

*Hide,* I mouth, looking around frantically for a place big enough to conceal all of us. I can already feel the hysteria clawing at my throat.

*Why is everything in this place made of glass?*

It's too late, anyway; the unexpected visitors are already turning the corner of the stairwell. We freeze like proverbial deer in the headlights, staring wordlessly at the new arrivals.

"Sarita?" Maya stops dead as the rest of the coven files in behind her, staring at her daughter in shock. There are six of them total, by my panicked count.

Sarita lifts her hand, gamely waving. "Hey, Mom. What's up?"

Maya, still gazing at her daughter in disbelief, doesn't wave back. Despite the heat, she's dressed in a lightweight sweater set, complete with sensible flats and tasteful gold earrings. The women standing with her, on the other hand, are trying slightly *too* hard to look the part; there are lots of floaty black skirts and chunky amulets and long, swishy hair.

"Sarita," Maya says. "What are you *doing* here? And in the middle of a *school day*, I might add?"

"We were . . . We wanted to . . ." Sarita trails off, looking helplessly in my direction.

I swallow hard, feeling the bile burn against my throat.

Next to me, Ezra jams his hands into the pockets of his jeans, trying to look nonchalant.

"This is highly irregular, Maya," one of the swishy-haired witches murmurs. "She may be your daughter, but the rules still apply!"

"I am *well* aware of that, Agatha," Sarita's mom snaps. Her voice takes on a strange saccharine quality as she turns back to us, forcing a brittle smile onto her lips. "I know this all may seem slightly *odd* to you, but . . ."

Sarita mumbles something in a low voice, staring at her feet.

"What was that?" her mother asks sharply, the sickly sweet smile dropping from her face.

"I said, *they know we're witches*," Sarita says, her voice marginally louder.

"That's it," the woman named Agatha says. "I'm calling this in to the Council." Her long silvery hair is nearly to her waist, her arms weighted down with the same elaborately carved crystal bracelets that I recognize from the window display upstairs. She pulls a cell phone from the pocket of her skirt, her eyes narrowing purposefully.

"Put your phone away, Agatha," Sarita's mom snaps. "Or have you forgotten who's in charge of this coven?"

Despite the air-conditioning, a trickle of cold sweat slips down my back. Things are spiraling out of control; a snowball of fear and worry rolling faster and faster downhill, threatening to sweep us all away.

*Think, Lily. You need to THINK.*

But I can't.

No matter how hard I try, there's only static.

To my horror, a look of determination crosses Ezra's face.

*No. Not now.*

He wouldn't.

Would he?

With numb fingers, I reach for his hand, trying to stop him. But it's too late; Ezra is already stepping forward, my fingertips brushing nothing but air.

"Hey, Agatha," he says. He takes another step forward, toward the silver-haired witch. "That's, uh . . . That's a really pretty name."

Agatha glances up from her phone, unwittingly making eye contact with Ezra. I can practically see her pupils dilating in response.

"Thank you. I was named after my great-aunt," she says, licking her lips. "She raised miniature cocker spaniels."

"Wow," Ezra says. "She sounds really . . . cool."

Sarita looks between Ezra and Agatha in confusion.

"I'm sorry," she says. "But *what* exactly is happening here?"

*"Ezra,"* I hiss under my breath. "Get *back* here."

Ignoring me, Ezra takes yet another step toward the older witch. "Agatha," he says, his eyes still locked with hers. "You don't *really* need to call anyone, do you? This is all a big misunderstanding."

Agatha nods, lowering her cell phone obligingly.

"A misunderstanding," she repeats, a curious slackness to her voice.

Maya is staring at Ezra, her head tilted consideringly to the side. The bottom of her shiny dark bob grazes her shoulder.

My skin begins to prickle; I can feel every hair on my arms standing on end.

I must shift without realizing it, because Maya turns to look at me. Her gaze feels like a vacuum cleaner, sucking up every little crumb of information as it passes over me.

Her eyes land on the fresh bandage at my neck.

"You're hurt," she says. "What happened?"

"It's nothing," I say quickly, resisting the urge to cover the bandage with my hand. "A scratch."

I can feel my pulse quickening, my heart thumping erratically in my chest. The wound on my neck feels like a scarlet letter: *V* for Vampire Bite.

Ezra turns to look in my direction.

Too late, I realize he can sense my pulse speeding beneath my wrists, hear the sharp rush of my blood calling to him.

Shit.

When was the last time Ezra fed?

"Does anyone else feel that?" asks one of the long-haired women behind Maya, speaking for the first time.

The woman next to her gives a nod. "It's odd," she says, wrinkling her nose in agreement. "A sort of . . . *charge* in the air."

Maya is still looking at me, her expression unreadable. It feels as though she's looking *through* me.

My heart pounds, the blood careening through my veins like a river pouring through a canyon.

Ezra's eyes pinpoint with need.

No. No, no, no, no, *no.*

I turn toward him, willing him to stay calm.

To stay *hidden.*

But it's too late.

He's already slipped, his fangs curling sinuously over his bottom lip.

There's a moment of stunned silence.

And then all hell breaks loose.

# CHAPTER Twenty-Four

EZRA MIGHT AS WELL HAVE SHOUTED *VAMPIRE!* in a crowded theater.

It's complete chaos as the coven realizes what's happening, scrambling over one another in their haste to get away from us. At least two of the glass display cases are accidentally toppled over in the confusion, the sound of breaking glass nicely accompanying the high-pitched shrieks of alarm.

Agatha appears to be frozen in place, her phone still clutched in her hand. Sarita's mom flinches backward in shock, her polished exterior cracking for the first time.

"Vampire!" a redheaded woman cries, raising her hand to point in Ezra's direction. As if the *fangs* weren't enough to clarify which one of us she means. *"Vampire!"*

Ezra ducks his head, concentrating.

Within seconds, the fangs are gone. But the damage is already done.

As Maya raises her palms, I can already sense the heat beginning to gather.

"Ezra!" I cry, diving forward.

My head smacks painfully against the cement floor as we tumble to the ground, Ezra's taut body landing on top of mine.

A bolt of pale yellow flame flies through the air above us, singeing Ezra's shoulder.

For a moment, we lock eyes, something wordless passing between the two of us.

*"Mom!"* Sarita shrieks. "What are you *doing*?"

I rest my head against the floor, letting myself drift. Everything is going soft around the edges, and I'm suddenly tired.

I'm so tired.

Of *all* of this.

"He's a vampire, Sarita!" Maya shouts. "Get away from him!"

Ezra flinches as another wave of witch fire slams into him, knocking him a little to the side. The world swims overhead, Ezra's handsome face growing blurry above mine.

"Ezra," I try to say, but it doesn't sound right; it's a fun-house version of his name, thick and distorted and slow.

Inches from mine, Ezra's brown eyes darken in concern.

"Lily?" I hear a voice asking as the room tilts and whirls around me. *"Lily!"*

The floor is cold beneath my cheek, but my palms are hot with unspent energy. I can feel the witch fire already brewing inside me, the power sparking at my fingers whether I want it or not.

The warmth inside me is growing and growing and *growing*, every cell in my body begging for release.

*Ezra*, I think helplessly. *Run!*

Waves of uncontrollable fire roll outward from my aching

body, slamming into the nearby display cases and scorching the concrete floor black. Glass shatters in every direction, the sharp *crack*ing noise nearly drowned out by the dull roar of my flames.

I gasp, barely feeling the glass that rains down on us like water.

The world spins away again, plunging me into darkness.

I wake up with the worst headache of my life.

My stomach rolls with nausea, the veins behind my eyes throbbing with pain. My entire body feels wrung out, and the back of my head aches like I've been hit with a sledgehammer.

Or maybe a bottle of bottom-shelf tequila.

Groggily, I open my eyes.

"Lily?" Sarita swims into vision, hovering inches above me. "You're awake!"

The relief on her face is palpable.

And, quite frankly, a little alarming.

Was there a possibility I *wasn't* going to wake up?

"Try not to move too quickly," Sarita says, her voice anxious. "You hit your head pretty hard. I think you might have a concussion."

I squint blearily against the overhead light, trying to stop the world from spinning.

"I'm fine."

The words scrape painfully against my throat, my mouth

dry and sticky all at once. I take a deep breath, trying not to vomit.

Questions.

I need to ask *questions.*

Still dazed, I sit up a little straighter.

"What happened? Where are we? Are you okay?"

I blink back another wave of nausea. Am I asking the right questions? Are they in the right order? Is the order *important*?

"I'm fine," Sarita says quickly. "We're all fine. As fine as we can be, anyway, considering the situation."

"What situation?" I ask, reaching up to push my hair away from my face. Or, at least, that's the plan. Only, for some reason, *both* of my hands move, and I end up smacking myself on the nose.

I look down in confusion.

My hands are zip-tied in front of me with a thin strip of plastic, my wrists already chafing beneath the sharp edges.

"Yeah," Sarita says, showing me her own bound hands. "*That* situation."

It starts to come back to me . . . St. Augustine. The covenstead. The bloodstone. Sarita's mom . . .

Panic races through my veins, my stomach lurching wildly again.

Experimentally, I flex my hands, testing the boundaries of the zip tie. The plastic slices into the thin skin of my wrists, making me hiss with pain.

I force myself to stay calm.

"Where are we?" I ask Sarita, peering around the small, enclosed room, taking in the heavy desk, cushioned office chair, and rows of filing cabinets lining the opposite wall. "Is this some sort of . . . *office*?"

"Close," Sarita says, pointing toward the desk. "It's a microfiche room."

I blink, turning to look at the huge, old-fashioned newspaper reader sitting on top of the work surface. There's a thin layer of dust covering the top; it must have been a while since anyone's been in here.

"I think the coven might be panicking," Sarita goes on. "My mom hasn't even *checked* on us since she dumped us here."

*Us.*

My head snaps up in sudden realization. "Ezra," I say, my voice urgent. "What happened to *Ezra*?"

She gestures awkwardly toward the corner of the room.

I look over, panic flooding through me at the sight of Ezra's slumped body; his sneakers are barely visible beyond the edge of the desk.

"He's fine," Sarita says as I stumble to my feet, a wave of dizziness washing over me. "They didn't . . . My *mom* didn't . . . They didn't *hurt* him, or anything. At least, not yet."

She swallows hard, looking almost as nauseated as I feel; seeing this side of her mom must be hard.

Maya has never exactly given off the warm fuzzies, but she's always been nice enough to me, and it's obvious how much she loves her daughter.

When Sarita played a background villager in the school's

production of *Brigadoon* last fall, Sarita's mom came to see it six times.

*Six times.*

And Sarita didn't even have a speaking role!

I clutch the edge of the desk for support, the metal cold and slick beneath my palms. Ezra's head is bent at an unnatural angle against his chest, his face hidden by his mop of messy brown curls.

"Oh my God," I say. On unsteady legs, I lurch forward, falling to my knees in front of him. "Ezra? *Ezra?*" I push back his hair with slightly shaking fingers, ignoring the bite of plastic at my wrists. "Can you hear me?"

Ezra is completely unresponsive; his head lolls to the side at my touch.

The thick, acrid smell of smoke clings to his hair. Under his T-shirt, his shoulder is a mess of ugly-looking burns, his flesh raw red and blistered from the witch fire. I can still feel the heat radiating off him, bits of charred fabric sticking to his skin.

I bite my lip, my hands hovering uselessly above him.

"Diluted essence of rose hip," Sarita says quietly, coming to kneel next to me. "I'm not sure how much they shot him up with, but he hasn't moved since." She shudders at the memory. "You should have seen the syringe," she says. "It looked like some sort of horse tranquilizer."

The tension between my shoulder blades loosens slightly. Rose hip may be a powerful sedative, but the effect is only temporary.

Ezra will wake up.

Eventually.

"I don't understand," I say, forcibly pulling my hands away. "If the coven is so worried about Ezra being dangerous, why would they lock us in here with him?"

Sarita sits back on her heels, worrying at her bottom lip. "After what happened with Agatha, they're convinced we might be under his 'vampiric thrall,'" she says. "I tried to explain that Cassius is the one they should be worried about, but my mom wouldn't listen. It was awful, Lily," she adds in a small voice. "She couldn't even *look* at me."

"I'm sorry," I say, hating how useless the words sound even to my own ears.

We sit in silence for a moment, Sarita chewing harder on her lower lip.

"At least they didn't kill him," I offer at last. "There was an entire *room* full of witches. It would have been easy."

No vampire would stand a chance against an entire coven.

Especially not one as new as Ezra.

"Killing should never be easy," a voice says, crackling to life with a burst of static. "Even when it's a vampire."

I jump at the sound of the intercom, the motion making me even queasier.

Staggering to my feet, I turn to look at Sarita's mom. She's standing outside the microfiche room, peering tightly through the window in the door. As she catches sight of her daughter, her carefully controlled expression wobbles.

Two witches flank her on either side: Agatha, the one with the phone, and a blond woman I don't recognize. In her long floaty black skirt and dangling gold earrings, the blond looks like Stevie Nicks.

*Woo hoo*, I think. *Witchy woman.*

Sarita gives me a look; it takes a second for me to realize that I'm humming the tune aloud.

She may be right about the concussion.

"Maya," I say, forcing myself to concentrate. "Please, you're making a big mistake. If you let us out, we can explain everything."

I force my lips upward, trying to look friendly and approachable.

"What are you doing?" Sarita whispers.

"I'm *smiling*," I say under my breath, my jaw clenched tightly in a grin. "Because I'm *friendly* and *approachable.*"

"You look like a murderous clown," Sarita observes.

"It's *Dr. Peterson*," Maya says. "And I have no interest in your *explanations.*" Her voice is cold enough to freeze the entire Florida coastline. "You've put my daughter in mortal danger. And as far as I'm concerned, every single word coming out of your mouth is a lie."

I let the smile drop.

"For the last time, we're not *glamoured*," Sarita says, jerking her zip-tied hands in agitation. "I already told you, *Cassius* is the one you should be worrying about."

"My job is to worry about *you*, Sarita," Maya says. "End of story."

"Cassius knows about the bloodstone," I cut in. "He could be on his way here right now! Don't you understand? Everyone here is in *danger.*"

Behind Maya's shoulder, Agatha scoffs.

"I assure you," she says, "the covenstead is perfectly safe."

"Oh, really?" I ask. "Because I hate to break it to you, but we *walked right in.*"

"Mom, please," Sarita begs. "Cassius wants to destroy the cure. *All* of it!"

Agatha scoffs again, even louder this time.

"The bloodstone isn't a *cure*, you silly child. It's an *insurance policy.*"

I blink, trying to clear the spots at the edge of my vision.

Is it the concussion talking, or is Agatha making no sense?

"The High Priestess has already ordered the stockpile to be moved," Agatha continues self-righteously. "She's en route as we speak."

I can feel the blood draining from my face.

The High Priestess.

She'll kill Ezra before he can even blink. And then she'll turn on the rest of us, to be safe.

Agatha runs her beady eyes over me, looking hungry. "The High Priestess was very interested in *you*," she says. "Such power in a young, untrained witch. It's truly . . . *remarkable.*" She takes a half step forward, raising one hand in my direction. "I could *feel* the magic calling to me the moment I got close to you."

My heart lurches into my throat, the world swaying beneath my feet.

"Mom," Sarita says. "You *can't* turn Ezra over to the High Priestess. She'll *kill* him."

"For good reason," Maya snaps. "He's a *vampire*, Sarita. He deserves everything that's coming to him, and *more.*"

She stops, visibly centering herself.

"You don't need to worry, honey," she says. "The High Priestess will take care of everything."

I slam my hands against the window, my palms stinging as the doorframe rattles beneath them.

"Listen to me, Dr. Peterson. *Please.*" My voice sounds thinner than usual. Desperate, even to my own ears. "You need to let us out. *Now.* You may not believe that Cassius is a threat, but the High Priestess definitely *is.* When she arrives, she'll kill *all* of us. *Including* your daughter."

For a fraction of a second, Maya hesitates.

"Don't be ridiculous," Agatha snaps, next to her. "Your powers may be remarkable, but you obviously know *nothing* about our ways. The Council has very clear protocols when it comes to vampire containment. When the High Priestess arrives this evening, she'll . . ."

Agatha is still talking, but I've stopped listening.

I rest my forehead against the glass, letting the sound of her voice wash over me like white noise. My head is pounding with exhaustion, my temples throbbing against the window.

These silly, *silly* women, playing at being witches.

Every breath Agatha takes could be her last, and she's wasting it on sanctimonious *bullshit.*

"Mom," Sarita begs, interrupting Agatha's tirade. "Don't do this! Okay? *Please.*"

Maya raises one hand to her throat, shaking her head back and forth in distress.

"I'm sorry, Sarita," she says. "I really am. But you've left me no choice." She glances at Ezra, still blissfully unconscious in the corner. "Everything will be okay, honey," she says, looking away. "I *promise.*"

And before Sarita has a chance to answer, Maya turns, hurrying away in her sensible flats.

Agatha and the blond woman quickly follow, threading their way through the archives behind Sarita's mom. After a second, we hear the muffled thud of footsteps overhead, then the soft *clang* of the stairwell door closing shut.

The sound is ominously final.

Sarita sinks to the floor, looking utterly lost.

I force myself to push away from the window, my forehead leaving a greasy smudge against the glass. "Hey," I say, sitting down next to Sarita. Our hands are still zip-tied, but I nudge her knee reassuringly with mine, trying to smile. "You heard your mom. Everything is going to be fine. Okay?"

"But what about the High Priestess?" Sarita asks, her voice small. At the moment, she looks very, *very* far from fine. "You don't really think she'll *kill* us, do you?"

I close my eyes for a second, remembering Montreal . . .

Cassius and I had been living there for almost a year, making the city our own. We'd wander the neon sidewalks of the Plaza Saint-Hubert for hours, ducking into the tiny theaters that seemed to have popped up on every corner to watch French horror films. There were over a million people in the city at that point; it was an easy place to get lost and *stay* lost.

That evening, we'd stopped by Restaurant Bonaparte for a late-night dinner. Despite the hour, Cassius had ordered the ridiculous seven-course tasting menu; taking a bite here and there to keep up appearances.

I'd noticed the cool-eyed blond woman immediately, sipping martinis at the bar. She reminded me of Simone Signoret in *Diabolique*; I could smell her expensive perfume from across the room.

There was something about her that made me pause. Something . . . *predatory.*

It should have been obvious.

But it had been a long time since I'd felt like prey.

Cassius had noticed her, as well.

He'd been on edge all evening; darting glances in the woman's direction and swilling champagne like he was trying to drown himself. It was already late by the time they delivered our chocolate-drizzled mille-feuilles, the slices of pastry accompanied by tiny white cups of espresso.

I was reaching for the coffee when Cassius excused himself from the table.

*My apologies, Lilliana. I'll just be a moment.*

At first, I didn't think anything of it.

But a moment later, the woman followed him.

The sip of espresso I'd just taken tasted bitter on my tongue.

*Too bitter.*

The cup fell from my hand, the dregs seeping slowly through the crisp white linen tablecloth. I can still remember the way my stomach lurched as I stood up from our table. The way the floor swayed beneath me with every step, as if I were on the deck of a boat and not solid ground.

By the time I made it into the hallway, the drug had already taken hold.

I can only remember pieces of the rest: Cassius, his face

drawn, half collapsed against the floor. A white-coated waiter, slumped unmoving on the ground. The cool-eyed blond woman, striding toward me, the air around her already *crackling* with power.

The blast of witch fire threw me backward against the wall, the flames licking ravenously through the air.

The entire restaurant went up like a tinderbox.

I panicked.

It felt like I was back on that long-ago London street.

Like I was *dying* all over again.

To this day, I'm not sure how Cassius managed to get us out.

I have a vague recollection of tumbling down the steps of a dirty back stairwell, the doors spilling open into the frosty December air, the sky already lightening in the distance. The shock of plunging into the ice-covered Saint Lawrence River, the water so cold I could *almost* feel it.

Cassius, towing me beside him, his long arms cutting through the river with swift, sure strokes.

I read afterward that the fire was blamed on faulty wiring in the kitchen; I guess vampires weren't the only ones who had learned to cover their tracks by then.

Seventeen injured, and one dead: the poor white-coated waiter who'd happened to be in the wrong place at the wrong time.

The High Priestess hadn't bothered to save him. She'd *set an entire restaurant on fire*, just to take a shot at Cassius and me.

So, yeah.

I'm pretty sure the three of us are already dead.

I open my eyes.

"No," I lie to Sarita. "Definitely not. But to be on the safe side, we should figure out a way to get out of here."

"Maybe we can smash our way through the floor," Sarita offers. "Like they do in *The Raid*, when they're trying to escape that apartment building?"

"Maybe," I say, trying to sound encouraging. "Although we're already in the basement, so going *down* probably isn't our best option?"

"Oh," Sarita says, leaning her head against the wall. "Right. That makes sense."

We lapse into silence, peering dubiously around the room. Ezra is still slumped in the corner, completely unaware of our rapidly approaching deaths. Sarita was right; whatever dose they gave him, it's enough to drop a horse.

I need to think. I need to *concentrate.* I need to come up with some sort of plan. I need to *save* us.

But fear makes me slow.

My head is still pounding, thoughts swirling away before I can catch them. I feel like I'm suspended in water, treading desperately to stay afloat.

*Think,* Morris. *Think.*

There's got to be some way to get out of here. There's got to be *something* I can do.

Somewhere overhead, the basement door clangs again. A second later, the unmistakable sound of footsteps thud back down the stairs.

The High Priestess?

*Cassius?*

Panic claws at my throat, my breath coming in ragged gasps.

Sarita turns to me, her eyes wide with terror.

I can feel the guilt pushing down on me, a weight so heavy that it's as though I'm being crushed. My lungs contract, the air squeezing painfully out of my chest in a single, enormous *whoosh.*

"Sarita . . . I . . . I'm so sorry." The words come out in a short, painful gasp. "This is all my fault."

"Lily, stop. That's not true."

Sarita reaches for my hands, but I flinch away, squeezing my eyes shut. I can feel the tears coming now, hot and angry and completely, utterly *useless.*

"*No.* I lied to you," I choke out. "I lied to *all* of you. And now it's too late. I'm *too late.* She's already—"

I cut off with a gasp as a familiar blond head appears in the window, the person cupping their hands against the glass to peer inside.

At the sight of Sarita and me, Max's face clears.

"For the record," he says, his voice muffled through the glass, "you *suck* at heists."

# CHAPTER Twenty-Five

FOR A SECOND, I WONDER IF MY CONCUSSION is making me hallucinate.

"What are you guys even doing in here?" Max asks, using the intercom that Sarita pointed out to him. "Wait, is that a *microfiche* machine?"

I choke off a sob of relief as hysterical laughter whelms up inside me. Tears stream down my cheeks, mingling with snot on my upper lip.

Max's eyes widen in concern.

"Lily? What's wrong?" He does a double take at the thin strips of plastic binding our wrists in front of us. "Are you *prisoners*?"

Sarita finds her voice first.

"Max, what are *you* even doing here?"

"I saw your mom outside the witch store this morning," he says. "I was getting some coffee across the street, and she walked in with, like, a bunch of other women. I tried texting you guys, but you didn't answer."

I reach automatically for my phone, only to realize it isn't there.

"The coven confiscated them," Sarita explains, angrily pushing her short black hair behind her ear. "That narc Agatha is probably reading my texts as we speak."

"Well," Max says succinctly. "*That* sucks."

"Yeah," Sarita says, nodding in agreement. "It does. But go on," she says. "You saw my mom and the others go into the store."

"After a few minutes, a bunch of the women ran out again," Max goes on. "They were panicking so much, they didn't even close the front door behind them. So, I snuck inside the store and hid." He shrugs again, like *sneaking into a witch's covenstead* is no big deal. "Then, when your mom and the others finally left, I came looking for you guys. Speaking of which, where's Ezra?"

He pushes himself up on his toes to look through the window, peering around the microfiche room. As he catches sight of Ezra's sneakers, his face visibly pales. He looks suddenly younger, his face wiped clean with worry.

"He's fine," I say quickly. "But Max, you've got to get us out of here. Like, *now*."

Max nods. "Okay," he says. "Yeah."

I turn to look at Sarita, who eyes me back worriedly.

"I'm not sure how," she admits. "Even if I could get my hands free, there's some sort of warding on the room. Magic won't work in here."

I bite my lip, peering anxiously around the small space. The panic has returned, scratching at my throat like a cat, waiting to be let in. "What about the air vents?" I ask. "If we stack the chair on top of the desk, we might be able to—"

On the other side of the wall, Max pushes experimentally on the door handle.

It swings wide open at his touch.

Sarita and I gape at him.

"What?" he asks innocently. "You didn't try the door?"

Sarita recovers first. "Of course I tried the door!" she snaps. "It obviously locks from the outside!"

"Hey!" I yell, stamping my foot. "Focus up!"

"Right," Max says. "Sorry."

Following me toward the corner of the room, he crouches next to Ezra, his expression immediately sobering.

"Holy shit," he breathes, taking in Ezra's shredded T-shirt, the ugly burns marring his skin below. "Is he . . ." He pauses, swallowing hard. For a second, I think he might vomit. "He's okay, right?" Max asks, pulling himself together.

"He'll be fine," I say, willing the words to be true. "But we need to get him out of here. *Now.*"

Max nods. "Tell me what to do."

"Can you carry him?" I ask. "We need to get him back to the van."

He nods again, more confidently this time. "Yeah," he says. "One sec."

Bracing himself, he pulls Ezra's limp body into a sitting position. As Sarita and I hover in the doorway, Max scoops Ezra into his arms, grunting with the effort.

"Jesus," he mutters aloud, hefting Ezra's deadweight over

his shoulder into the fireman's carry. "It's like hauling a sack of rocks."

Staggering slightly, he heads in our direction, doing his best not to bang Ezra's head against the corner of the desk.

I mean, he *does* bang Ezra's head against the corner of the desk.

But he *tries* not to.

"This way," Sarita hisses, leading us back through the archival room toward the exit. We follow as quickly as we can, gingerly picking our way over the occasional pile of broken glass.

A familiar display case catches my eye; unbroken but empty.

I pause, all of my breath leaving my body in a sudden *whoosh.*

It looks as though Agatha has wasted no time in following the High Priestess's orders.

Every last shard of bloodstone is gone.

# CHAPTER *Twenty-Six*

"DO WE ACTUALLY HAVE A PLAN?" MAX ASKS, glancing in the rearview mirror. "Or should I keep driving around aimlessly?"

In the back seat of the van, I grit my teeth, pulling the sharp edge of a nail file across my upper forearm. "Hang on," I grunt as a line of blood wells beneath, a thin red scratch running parallel to my elbow. "I'm working on it."

In the mirror, Max's face pales.

He quickly looks away, concentrating on the road ahead of us.

I scramble over the armrest, positioning my elbow awkwardly above Ezra's mouth.

In the passenger seat, Sarita wrinkles her nose. "I thought feeding a vampire your blood was supposed to be *sexy*," she comments. "Like in the movies?"

I push my hair over my shoulder, accidentally smearing my ponytail with blood.

Sighing, I open Ezra's jaw.

"What?" I ask Sarita, jamming my arm into his mouth. "This isn't sexy?"

"Yeah," Max says. In the rearview mirror, he's turning slightly green. "I need some air. Does anyone else need some air?"

Without waiting for an answer, he rolls down the windows, letting the breeze whip through the van. On the highway, the air feels almost chilly, and our headlights shine bright ahead of us, keeping the darkness at bay.

We're all a little punch-drunk at the moment. According to the little red numbers on the dash, it's not even nine o'clock yet, but it feels as though a thousand years have passed since we woke up at Sarita's house this morning.

I flex my arm, speeding the trickle of blood flowing into Ezra's mouth.

Forget a horse; the coven must have given him enough rose hip to tranquilize an *elephant.*

Sarita twists farther around in her seat, giving me a worried look. "Are you sure he's going to be okay?" she asks. "He doesn't look so—*aagh!*"

She gives a little shriek as Ezra's eyes flick open, glowing eerily in the darkness.

"Jesus," Max says, the van swerving momentarily into the next lane. "Don't *do* that!"

Ezra reaches up, clamping his hands around my arm and pulling me close. He drinks hungrily, his body rigid with single-minded need.

I'm not going to lie; there may or may not be slurping sounds involved.

"Well," Sarita observes from the front seat. "*This* is officially disgusting."

I give Ezra another few seconds, letting my blood circulate through his sluggish system before pulling away.

To his credit, he only hesitates for a second before letting go; his memory of the parking lot is obviously still fresh in his mind.

As I sit back, drops of my blood stain the minivan's previously spotless upholstery; Ezra blinks, looking around in confusion. "What happened?" he asks, shaking his head back and forth to clear it. "How did we get in the van? Wait, how is it *night*?"

Max turns in his seat to look back at Ezra, the relief palpable in his expression. "Hey, man," he says. "It's good to have you back." The words are casual, but I can hear the undercurrent of emotion running through Max's voice. "You, uh . . . You scared me there for a minute."

Ezra slowly nods. "Sorry, man," he says. "I'll try not to do it again."

After a second, Max nods back, turning to face the road again.

"Anyway," Sarita says, completely oblivious to the touching moment Max and Ezra have just shared. "Long story short? My mom drugged you with powdered rose hip and then imprisoned us in a microfiche room."

Grabbing a wad of Kleenex from the center console, I press it against my arm, stanching the worst of the blood.

"Don't worry, I saved them," Max says, ducking away from Sarita's slap on the arm. "But now there's apparently some sort of 'High Priestess' chick after you? She sounds fucking terrifying."

Ezra blinks again.

"Wow," he says. "That's . . . a lot of information to take in."

He hesitates for a second, then forces himself to turn in my direction. "And the bloodstone?"

I shake my head, looking away.

Ezra, Sarita . . . even *Max*. They're all in danger now.

Because of *me*.

"It's my fault," I say. "All of this was all for *nothing*."

To my surprise, Sarita grins.

"Well," she says. "I wouldn't say *nothing*."

Plunging her hand down the front of her T-shirt, she pulls something free.

I stare uncomprehendingly at the shard of bloodstone clutched in her hand.

"Wait," Max says, the van momentarily swerving to one side again. "Have you been hiding that in your *bra* this whole time?"

"How . . . ?" I say. "How did you . . . ?"

Sarita clenches her hand triumphantly around the stone. "I *told* you it was a heist!" she says. "I lifted it while Ezra was trying to compel Agatha. *And* making a total ass of himself, by the way."

I still can't look away from the jewel in Sarita's hand.

In the soft light of the dash, it almost seems to glow.

"The sign thingy said the stone had been *imbued* with something, right?" Sarita says. "Maybe the stone itself isn't dangerous.

If I can figure out what the coven did to it, maybe I can undo it. I can *un-imbue* it!"

"Is that even possible?" Max asks dubiously. "Because I'm pretty sure 'un-imbue' isn't a word."

Sarita shrugs, handing the stone to Ezra. "There's only one way to find out."

Ezra freezes.

"Ezra?" I ask hesitantly. "Are you okay?"

"I thought maybe it would feel different," he says, not looking up from the bloodstone. "Special, somehow. But it's . . . a *rock*."

His hand tightens reflexively around the stone.

"Here," I say, reaching gently for the shard of bloodstone. "Why don't I . . . hold on to that?"

*Before you accidentally destroy it*, I add mentally.

Ezra nods, handing the stone to me.

I tuck it safely into my pocket, then grab another fistful of Kleenex, pressing them to my arm.

Ezra looks purposefully in the other direction.

"We need to find somewhere for Sarita to work," I say, thinking aloud. "Somewhere nobody will find us."

As terrifying as the High Priestess may be, the thought of Cassius tracking us down is even worse. *Especially* when he finds out his revenge has been snatched from his fingertips.

"Well, my house is out," Sarita says. "For obvious reasons."

"Hard same," Max agrees. "My mom is pissed enough at me right now."

"We need someplace no one knows about," I say. "Somewhere *safe*."

To my surprise, Ezra looks up. "I know the perfect place," he says. "Pull over. I'll drive."

Forty minutes and one stop at a convenience store later, the van is bumping down a glorified dirt path in the middle of nowhere, overgrown cypress branches scraping noisily against the roof of the van.

It's been almost ten minutes since we've seen another house; the swamp seems to press in on us from all sides, crowding the van into the center of the mud-rutted road. We left the ocean breeze behind long ago; the air here is muggy and still, heavy with moisture and smelling vaguely of rot.

"Is it me," Max asks as we bump our way over another huge rut in the road, "or is this place creepy as hell?"

"There's a definite V. C. Andrews vibe," Sarita agrees, slapping at an enormous mosquito that's made its way through her open window. "And not *Flowers in the Attic* V. C. Andrews, either. This is some old-school, *Pearl in the Mist* type of shit."

Max looks at her. "Literally none of that made sense to me."

Sarita swats at another mosquito. "That's because you're a philistine," she says. "V. C. Andrews is a national treasure."

"Where *are* we?" I ask, staring out the window in fascination. I've been in Florida for months, but I've never ventured farther than ten miles away from Sunrise Harbor. I'm used to fast-food restaurants and check-cashing storefronts, not cypress trees and swamps.

"My grandma used to own this place," Ezra says, his eyes trained on the road in front of him. Which, again, is a generous use of the word 'road.' "I spent summers here, when I was a kid."

"Oh, shit," Max says, turning to peer at Ezra in surprise. "This was your grandma's house? I remember you talking about it when we were little."

Ezra nods. "At some point, my mom sold it to some development group. As far as I know, they never did anything with it. It should be standing empty. Well, if it's still standing," he adds. "Like I said, I haven't been here for a while."

"Yeah," Sarita says as the van hits another massive pothole. "I'm guessing *no one* has been here for a while. For good reason. Do you even *know* how many snakes are out here?"

"Seven?" Max asks hopefully.

I'm still debating rolling my window up (snake bites: definitely *not* a human perk) when Ezra pulls off the road, bumping to an abrupt stop.

Through the bug-smeared windshield, I take in the small, derelict house in front of us. The stone bungalow is tiny and low to the ground, the walls made from crumbling river rocks and what now appear to be load-bearing wisteria vines. Waist-high weeds choke the yard, and the roof hangs heavy with rotting vegetation.

Ezra cuts the engine.

As if on cue, one of the shutters crashes to the ground.

"Well," I say aloud. "Welcome home."

# CHAPTER Twenty-Seven

FOR A LONG MOMENT, WE ALL TAKE IN THE ramshackle house in silence.

Aside from the frogs, that is.

Apparently, they won't shut up.

"Wow," Sarita ventures at last. "It looks really . . . cute?"

Ezra gives her a look.

"On the plus side, it's definitely empty," Max points out. He grabs two plastic shopping bags from the van, stuffed with convenience store snacks and a couple of cheap flashlights. "Come on, let's check out the inside."

To his credit, he wades bravely into the weeds, looking only mildly terrified at the possibility of what's lurking beneath.

Sarita pulls the last shopping bag from the back, then follows Max up the path, carefully picking her way over the uneven paving stones. I start after her, but I've only made it a few steps before I realize Ezra hasn't moved.

I turn to see him standing behind me, peering up at the

house, his hands shoved into the pockets of his jeans. Without the glow of the dashboard, it's hard to read his expression, but I'm guessing it falls somewhere between "brooding" and "also brooding."

"Are you okay?" I ask, slapping a mosquito away from my shoulder. "It must be weird, being back here."

*It must be weird being back here?*

*Wow.*

*Great job, Lily.*

*What an insightful comment!*

"Kind of," Ezra says, shoving his hands even deeper in his pockets. "I knew it was going to be in bad shape, but still. My grandma would lose it if she could see this place now."

I turn back, surveying the house. "It's not in *that* bad of shape," I lie. "It could use a little landscaping. And maybe a few coats of paint. And some structural work. Roofs are cheap these days, right?"

Ezra's lips curve reluctantly upward. "Again," he says. "*Staggeringly* bad at pep talks."

"First of all, I'm the LeBron James of pep talks," I say. "And secondly, you're smiling, right?"

Ezra's grin widens. "Yeah," he admits. "I guess I am."

I shrug. "Well, then. Mission accomplished."

"Mission accomplished," Ezra agrees. Pulling his hands out of his pockets, he gives himself a shake, then heads toward the path. "What?" he calls over his shoulder. "Are you going to stand there all night?"

Checking to make sure I've shut the door all the way, I follow him into the weeds. Max and Sarita are standing beneath the sloping eaves of the shaded front steps, their plastic bags swinging idly in their hands.

"It's locked," Max says succinctly, nodding toward the door; a thick rectangular lock loops around the handle, the kind Realtors use, with a numerical keypad.

Ezra reaches out, giving the bottom of the lock an experimental *jiggle*.

He accidentally rips the entire thing free.

For a moment, no one says anything.

"Sick," Max finally comments, pushing the front door open with his shoulder.

Stepping inside, I brace myself for the thick reek of greenish mold, or the stench of dead raccoon lurking in the walls. But no. Depressingly, an abandoned house in the middle of a swamp actually smells better than my motel room.

Sarita tests the light switch, flicking it up and down a few times, then rummages in one of the plastic bags for a flashlight. "I guess breakers and enterers can't be choosers," she says, sweeping the weak beam of light across the living room.

Most of the furniture is long gone, but whispers of Ezra's childhood still cling to the house: threadbare curtains hang from the window rods, and the walls are spotted with faded rectangles where picture frames used to hang. A heavy, old-fashioned console television still stands in one corner, stacks of mildewing cardboard boxes piled haphazardly on top.

"Not bad," Max says, stepping inside. He rummages for another couple of flashlights, handing one to me. I thumb it on, hating how reliant I am on the thin beam of light spilling from the end.

Max and Sarita are already exploring, but as I turn to look at Ezra, he's pulled up short in the doorframe. As the beam of light falls on his face, he flinches, but doesn't look away.

It takes me a second to realize he's worried about coming inside.

"You said the house was owned by a *company,* not a person, right?" I ask quietly. "You should be able to walk right in."

Ezra doesn't seem entirely convinced. Still, he steps forward, his shoulders visibly relaxing as he passes through the doorframe without incident.

"Close it already!" Sarita calls from the kitchen, where she's unloading the snacks onto a rickety folding table in the middle of the room. "You're letting in mosquitoes!"

Ezra obligingly pulls the door shut, scanning the room. "Wow," he says. Reaching one arm up, he brushes his fingers against the low popcorn ceiling of the bungalow. A fine coating of dust drifts down from the ceiling. "It's a lot smaller than I remember."

"You're probably bigger," I point out. "When was the last time you were here?"

Ezra pulls his hand back, brushing his fingers clean on his jeans. "I was nine, I think? Maybe ten. All the summers kind of . . . run together."

"Check it out," Max says from across the room. He's propped his flashlight against the wall and is already digging through one of the boxes on top of the television.

"Max!" I hiss. "You can't rummage around in Ezra's grandma's stuff!"

Max holds up a small rectangular magazine. "It's nothing but old *TV Guide* magazines," he says. "There must be hundreds of them."

Ezra breaks into a grin. "Yeah. She was kind of addicted to soap operas," he says. He reaches up, absently running his finger across the bottom of his tattoo. "Eight-year-old Ezra watched *a lot* of *The Young and the Restless*."

"Dinner's ready!" Sarita calls from the kitchen. "Come get it while it's hot!"

Max looks up at us, his expression flickering along with his flashlight. I'm suddenly aware of how close Ezra and I are standing together.

As if he's realizing the same thing, Ezra subtly shifts away; without him next to me, I can feel the oppressive heat of the room pressing in on me.

"Max," I say haltingly, but he turns away.

"You heard Sarita," he says. "Dinner's ready. Although, if the sandwiches are hot, we have a problem."

Ezra clears his throat, opening another cardboard box. "You guys go ahead," he says. "It's not like I need to eat, anyway."

Reluctantly, I let the conversation drop, following Max into the kitchen. Sarita has laid a small feast out on the dusty table: bottles of soda, bags of chips, and a random assortment of plastic-wrapped sandwiches.

I reach quickly for the ham and cheese, hoping it carries the least risk of food poisoning.

"Egg salad?" Max asks, reading one of the labels aloud. "Really?"

"You're missing out," Sarita informs him, reaching for the sandwich. "Everyone knows that gas station egg salad is a high-risk, high-reward type of situation."

"Yeah," Max says. "I think I'll pass."

Leaning against the chipped linoleum counter, he crosses his arms against his chest, surveying the kitchen.

"So," he says, his voice growing serious. "How long do we think this whole *un-imbuing a mystical bloodstone* thing is going to take? Because I don't know about witches, but this place is *definitely* not vampire-proof," he goes on. "Think about it; Ezra practically waltzed right in here."

Hearing his name, Ezra joins us, an old *TV Guide* clutched in his hand.

I set my uneaten sandwich back down on the table, my appetite suddenly gone.

"It depends," Sarita says. She automatically reaches for her necklace, remembering too late that it's gone; Maya confiscated it, along with our phones. "First, I have to figure out what exactly the coven has done to the bloodstone. I can try scrying, but I'll need something to use as a focus."

"What?" Ezra asks. "Like another necklace?"

"It doesn't *have* to be a necklace," Sarita says, her voice taking on a vaguely witchsplaining tone. "The stone is the important part. Quartz and amethyst to channel your powers, citrine to amplify them, turquoise for protection . . ."

Ezra nods, interrupting her. "Got it," he says. "One sec."

Pushing off from the doorframe, he disappears into the darkened living room, not even bothering to take a flashlight with him. A second later, he reappears, clutching a dusty cardboard box in his hands.

"*TV Guides*?" I ask in confusion.

Ezra grins, dumping the box upside down. A small landslide of old-fashioned costume jewelry spills onto the table: sparkly, gold-plated pins and thick, chunky bracelets; heavy clip-on earrings and ropes of fake pearls . . .

"Whoa," Sarita says, her eyes widening. "It's like 1986 threw up in here."

"I'm sure it's all worthless, or my mom would have taken it, long ago," Ezra says, shoving his hands in his pockets. "But there might be something you can still use?"

Sarita nods, already sifting her way through the pile. "Don't worry," she says. "I've got this."

Max looks at me and Ezra. "What if someone finds us first?" he asks. "I don't want to bring the vibe down, but Cassius is still after us," he points out. "Not to mention Sarita's mom. *And* the rest of her coven."

"Don't forget about the High Priestess," Ezra says grimly. "If she's as bad as Lily says, we're pretty much fucked."

I nod, my fingers curling tightly around the edge of the kitchen counter.

"You're right," I say quietly. "Cassius is looking for me. And the coven is looking for a vampire."

I pause, raising my chin ever so slightly.

"So, let's give them both what they want."

# CHAPTER Twenty-Eight

THREE HOURS LATER, I'M STILL WIDE-AWAKE.

Ezra and I argued for over an hour before he finally gave up, storming angrily into the night without a backward glance.

Sarita disappeared long ago into the bedroom, a piece of Ezra's grandma's jewelry in one hand and the bloodstone clutched determinedly in the other.

And Max, well . . .

Max is stretched out on the living room floor opposite me, staring up into the darkness.

We're only a few feet away from each other, but it may as well be miles.

Through the bedroom door, I can hear a muffled curse, followed by an angry *thump*. The ceiling fan above us vibrates in response.

"I don't think it's going well," Max observes.

Another curse echoes through the darkness, followed by an even louder *thump*. A picture frame vibrates in response.

I prop myself up on my elbows, squinting in Max's direction. "Really?" I ask ironically. "What makes you think that?"

He sits up, as well, clicking his flashlight back on. The narrow beam of light illuminates the dust motes still floating gently through the air around us. I jump a little as a moth flutters past, casting uneven shadows against the wall.

Max leans back, pulling his sticky T-shirt away from his chest. For a long moment, we sit in silence, listening to the soft whine of mosquitoes circling overhead.

"Max," I say, gathering my courage. "Listen, there's something we need to talk about. I, um . . . I . . ."

"I'm not completely clueless, Lily," he says, cutting me off. "I know what's going on."

I tighten my hands around my legs, pulling myself inward.

"I'm sorry," I whisper. "I swear, Ezra and I didn't plan it. It just . . . *happened*."

Max holds himself very still, letting out a long, slow breath.

"But I wasn't talking about Ezra," he says. "I was talking about *you*."

"Oh," I say weakly. "What, um . . . What about me?"

He drops his head back against the wall, looking at me flatly. "Your plan," he says. "I know it's bullshit."

"It's *not*," I say. "I already told you: I need to lead Cassius away from Sunrise Harbor. If I can get the High Priestess and the rest of the coven to follow us, then maybe I can buy enough time for Sarita to—"

"Stop!" Max says, his voice thick with frustration. "I *know* you, Lily. And I know you're not planning on *running*. Not this time."

I look down, tracing the curve of my knees with my thumbs.

Max is right.

For the first time in my life, I'm not running anywhere.

I raise my hands, turning them back and forth in the darkness.

"I'm *dangerous*, Max," I say quietly. "The witch fire . . . it's only the tip of the iceberg. All of the magic I had when I was a vampire, all of the *power* . . . I can still feel it running through me." I pause, swallowing hard. "I'm not like other witches. I'm not constrained by rules or protocols or *natural limits.* At best, I'm an aberration," I finish quietly. "At worst, I'm a threat. Not just to the coven's way of existence . . . but to *everyone.*"

"Lily," Max says, but I don't stop.

"Compared to me, Ezra is *nothing*," I say. "If I turn myself in, I can make a deal with the High Priestess. I can keep him safe. I can keep you *all* safe."

*A promise is a promise.*

"Please, Max," I say, my voice breaking a little. "Let me keep you safe."

In the other room, Sarita lets out another curse, the wall shaking as she kicks it with her boot.

Max ignores her.

"Did you know I got into Dartmouth?" he asks.

I look up at him in surprise, a small jolt of delight running through my veins. "What?" I ask. "No! That's amazing, Max! When did you find out?"

"I've known for a while," Max says with a shrug. "But I didn't want to tell you."

"I don't understand," I say, genuinely confused. "Why not?"

"Because," Max says dully. "I knew you'd be happy for me."

"*Of course* I'm happy for you," I say, still not understanding. "You got into *Dartmouth*."

"And where exactly *is* Dartmouth?" Max asks. "Do you even know?"

"Of course I know," I say, thinking back to my conversation with Sarita. "It's on . . . the coast."

"Do you know the name of the town?" Max presses. "Do you even know the name of the *state*?"

Shit.

Max is right.

I have no idea where Dartmouth is. And I've never even bothered to look.

I can feel sudden tears pricking at the corners of my eyes.

I think of Max spinning me through the air at Mia's party. Looping his arm around me in the hallway, pulling me close. I think of the way he insisted on walking me to my car after our first date, his blond hair lighting up red and blue in the neon lights overhead, and the taste of salt on his lips when I kissed him. Being with Max felt perfect.

But somehow, it never quite felt *real*.

Reaching up, I swipe at my cheeks with the backs of my hands. The heat in the room is suddenly stifling; the stagnant air presses in on me, heavy and damp.

"Max . . ." I say helplessly. "I swear, I never meant to hurt you."

"It's fine," he says. Forcing a smile, he reaches for the flashlight.

"I guess I always knew we had an expiration date. It just . . . got here faster than I thought."

And lying back down on the dusty floor, he faces resolutely away, switching off the light.

I give up on sleep after that.

Grabbing my own flashlight, I tiptoe through the house and slip quietly through the door, sagging against the screen as I gulp lungfuls of warm, muggy air.

It's only marginally cooler outside the bungalow. The night is eerily still, the air thick with humidity and the creeping scent of rot. Most of the frogs have given up for the night, but the low *thrum* of insects fills the air. In the front yard, something rustles through the weeds.

I tense, automatically dropping into a defensive stance. I can feel the heat sparking in my palms, the *gathering* feeling that I've always taken for adrenaline before.

A small opossum scurries across the overgrown path, completely ignoring me as it continues on its way.

Feeling ridiculous, I lower my hands, my heart still clenched in my throat. Turning on my flashlight, I set off into the night.

The stone path leads around the back of the house, overgrown but visible. I walk carefully, ducking low beneath the cypress trees that hang overhead, their branches laden with decaying vines.

The farther I get from the house, the easier it is to breathe.

As the night settles over me, I can feel the tension in my shoulders beginning to ease, the ache behind my temples fading to a dull throb.

The stone path gives way to an uneven dirt track, winding its way lazily through the trees. I keep walking, the flashlight trained on the ground in front of me as I uselessly swat bugs away from my face.

Beads of moisture slide down my forehead, the front of my bra growing damp with sweat. I keep walking, faster and faster, branches slapping against my shoulders as I put more and more distance between me and the house.

Between me and Max.

I guess I *am* still running away, after all.

I dodge beneath another low-hanging branch. But instead of taking another step, I stop dead, staring ahead in surprise.

The cypresses have abruptly opened up overhead, the moonlight pouring through the gap to illuminate the glass-like surface of the water in front of me.

It's a pond.

*No*, I think. This is Florida; *it's a GLADE.*

"Pretty, right?"

I shriek in alarm at the sound of Ezra's voice, stumbling over the nearest tree root. My foot lands with a wet *squelch* in six inches of murky water.

"Aargh!" I look over at the sound of the voice, trailing my flashlight back and forth through the moonlit night until I find Ezra. He's sitting on the ground at the edge of the glade, propped against the back of a gnarled trunk. "Don't sneak up on me like that!"

"Hey, I was already sitting here," Ezra points out. "Technically, you're the one who snuck up on *me*."

Oh, God.

He's right.

What am I even *doing* out here?

Embarrassment pours through my veins, hot and thick and inescapable.

Quickly, I look away from Ezra and turn back to the water, attempting to pull my foot free from the sucking mud.

For some reason, it is . . . much harder than I expected.

I'm about to give up when my foot comes unexpectedly free, the force of my momentum carrying me backward.

My butt hits the mud with an even louder *squelch* than before.

To my surprise, a snort of laughter escapes from the nearby reeds.

Ezra stands up, picking his way easily around the shoreline. Without a word, he plops down in the mud next to me, swatting a bug away from his face. He leaves a smudge of dirt across his forehead.

"For the record, I still think the whole 'using yourself as bait' thing is a *terrible* idea," Ezra says. "But I don't want to argue about it anymore."

"Good," I say, nodding. "Because I don't want to argue about it anymore, either."

For a moment, we simply sit, listening to the whine of mosquitoes.

"Can I ask you something?" Ezra says, waiting for my nod. "Do you really think Sarita can do it? Find a way for me to use the bloodstone without *hurting* anyone?"

"I don't know," I say truthfully, staring out at the glade. "I really hope so."

"Me too," Ezra says. "Because being a vampire kind of sucks."

"What?" I ask, turning to look at him. "Not a fan of the crushing loneliness and ever-present darkness?"

"I was thinking more about the all-consuming bloodlust and never-ending danger," Ezra says. "The dark is actually kind of . . . nice."

Ezra is right.

I'd forgotten how peaceful the darkness can be.

How *comforting.*

How much the moonlight feels like coming home.

"It's not the worst thing in the world," I venture. "Being a vampire."

Ezra side-eyes me. "Uh-oh," he says. "Please say I'm not in for another one of your famous pep talks."

I brush my hair out of my eyes. "The worst thing in the world isn't being a vampire," I repeat softly. "It's *taking someone's life.*"

Ezra's smile fades.

"You're a good person, Ezra," I say. "You *deserve* your life back. But not if it means taking someone else's." I pause, swallowing hard. "It would destroy you," I whisper. "Trust me, I know."

"Lily," he begins, but I shake my head, cutting him off.

We lapse into silence again, peering across the moonlit surface of the glade. Aside from the small water bugs skimming the glassy surface, the water is perfectly still.

Next to me, Ezra is perfectly still, as well. His chest rises and falls at regular intervals, though breathing is more habit than necessity, now.

I'm painfully aware of how close we are, sitting next to each other in the muddy grass. I can feel the faint coolness radiating from his body.

I clear my throat, slapping away an imaginary mosquito.

"Did you know that back in the Middle Ages, they thought vampires couldn't cross running water?" I ask Ezra, just for something to say. "Something about purity, I think. Stagnant water was fine, but an ocean would kill you."

"Seriously?"

I nod. "Apparently. I don't actually know how to swim, so I haven't tested it or anything, but . . ."

I trail off as Ezra leans forward, staring at me in horror. "Wait, *what*?" he asks. *"You don't know how to swim?"*

"Er . . . no?" I admit in a small voice.

"How do you not know how to swim?" Ezra asks, his voice thick with disbelief. "You're a century-and-a-half old!"

I sit up straighter, wiping mud from my leggings.

Well, Sarita's leggings.

"What?" I ask Ezra defensively. "It's not like I didn't *mean* to learn."

Cassius tried to teach me, a few times, but I didn't have the patience for it; halfway through the lesson, I'd grow frustrated and splash away in annoyance, leaving Cassius to make his way to the shore on his own.

If I remember correctly, he once threatened to throw me over the side of the Hoover Dam.

"All right, that's it," Ezra says. "Get up."

I eye him warily as he stands, offering me his hand.

"Er . . ." I say. "Why?"

"Because exactly *one* of your problems is solvable tonight," he answers. "I'm teaching you how to swim."

# CHAPTER Twenty-Nine

AS I WATCH IN DISBELIEF, EZRA STRIPS HIS T-shirt over his head, wincing a little as he tugs the fabric over his shoulder. His burn is still red and angry-looking, the skin only beginning to heal. He kicks his sneakers off, then quickly pulls off his socks and stuffs them inside his shoes for safekeeping. As he reaches for the button of his jeans, a strange, high-pitched gurgling noise escapes my throat.

Ezra looks up, his lean frame silhouetted in the moonlight. "What was that?" he asks.

"Nothing!" I squeak, my voice panicked. Ezra is clearly unaware of the fact that I'm managing to hold myself together by a thread. "I, uh . . . What are you doing?"

"I already told you," Ezra says, unzipping his jeans. "I'm teaching you to swim." He finishes pulling his jeans off, then tosses them into the weeds next to his shirt. His pale skin practically glows in the moonlight, his broad shoulders narrowing to a flat, muscular stomach.

There's a trace of hair below his belly button, trailing its way down to the line of his blue-and-white striped boxers, and *oh my God, I've made the gurgling noise again.*

Ezra grins at me, completely oblivious to my fragile emotional state. "Come on," he says. "Last one in is a rotten egg."

Turning away, he splashes easily into the water, heading for the deeper area in the middle.

I exhale slowly, trying to calm my racing pulse.

This is fine. Everything is fine. It's one friend teaching another friend how to swim.

Alone.

In the moonlight.

Without clothing.

"Would you hurry up, already?" Ezra calls, splashing water in my direction.

I swallow hard.

Then, with clumsy fingers, I reach for my shoelaces, stripping off my shoes and pants as quickly as I can.

As I reach for the bottom of my tank top, I hesitate, glancing in Ezra's direction.

He looks away, pushing his hand through his dark hair.

I quickly strip down to my bra and underwear, splashing noisily into the water before I can second-guess myself.

"What if there are water snakes in here?" I ask, wading cautiously deeper. "Or alligators? Or, like . . . flesh-eating bacteria?"

"Trust me," Ezra says, trailing his hands back and forth through the water as he waits for me to reach him. "You may have traveled the world, but I grew up swimming in this glade. The only thing you have to worry about is leeches."

I stop dead.

"Kidding!" Ezra says.

"Not cool," I say, splashing water in his direction.

Ezra only grins.

I force myself forward, shivering a little despite the humid night air. The water deepens ominously with every step; by the time I reach Ezra, it's almost to my shoulders.

"Okay," Ezra says. "Swimming 101—you ready?"

I nod, bouncing a little on my feet. The bottom of the glade is lined with the same thick mud that rings the shoreline. It's surprisingly cold between my toes.

"The important thing is to relax," Ezra says, pushing a strand of wet hair behind his ear. "You have to . . . trust the process, okay?"

I nod again, momentarily distracted by the beads of water running down the slope of his shoulders.

I look purposefully away.

"Fair warning," I say, clearing my throat again. "If you dunk me, I'm going to punch you in the face."

Ezra solemnly agrees, as if me punching him in the face would feel like anything more than a mosquito bite. "Ready?"

No.

Definitely not.

"Ready," I say aloud.

The water ripples softly as Ezra steps forward, reaching for me. "Okay," he says, his cool hands slipping gently around my waist. "Here we go."

A small gasp escapes from my lips.

Thankfully, Ezra mistakes it for nerves.

"I've got you," he says. "Lean back."

Beneath the water, his hands are steady on my hips. It takes everything I have to concentrate on what Ezra is saying, instead of the feel of his body against mine.

"Hey," he says softly, mistaking my hesitation for fear. "I promise I won't let go, okay?"

Keeping my eyes locked on his, I tip my head back, lowering myself into the water.

It feels wrong, surrendering control like this. I can feel my body tensing, my hands reaching automatically to brace myself.

"Lily, I've got you," Ezra says, a hint of exasperation in his voice. He looks down, his eyes meeting mine. *"Trust me."*

As if trusting someone is that simple.

If my extremely long life has taught me anything, it's that the only person you can trust is *yourself.*

Still, looking up at Ezra, it's hard to remember that fact.

I take a steadying breath and let my body relax.

For a second, it feels like I'm falling. And then Ezra's arms tighten beneath me and suddenly, somehow . . . I'm *floating.*

I can't help the laugh that spills from my lips, the sound drifting lazily across the water.

Ezra grins down at me. "See?" he says. "It's good, right?"

I lean against his hands and peer up at the sky, my hair swirling around me like a halo. Experimentally, I push my arms back and forth, feeling the water trail through my fingers like silk.

Ezra is right.

It's *good*.

Which is how I know it can't last.

We stay in the water until my fingers are wrinkled, and my arms are leaden, and my back is covered with mosquito bites.

Even then, I would have stayed longer; it's Ezra who points out the fact that the sky is beginning to lighten in the east, the almost imperceptible shift between darkness and dawn. Reluctantly, I make my way toward the muddy shoreline, heading for the pile of our discarded clothing. I'm suddenly very aware of the fact that Ezra and I are practically naked.

Let's be honest: I'm mainly aware of the fact that *Ezra* is practically naked.

Forcing myself to look away, I use my tank top to dry myself off as best as I can. Hopping on one foot first, then the other, I manage to pull my leggings on, the fabric sticking unpleasantly to my still-damp flesh.

As Ezra turns, reaching for his shirt, I dart a quick look in his direction while I slip on my shoes. For the first time, I can make out his tattoo: the thin, angular black lines forming a . . .

"Is that . . . your grandmother's *TV*?" I ask, stepping forward despite myself. The boxy old-fashioned television set is unmistakably the same one from inside the house.

Ezra glances down at his arm in surprise, as if he's forgotten the tattoo is there.

"Oh," he says, a hint of embarrassment in his voice. "Yeah. It's kind of ridiculous, right? But I wanted something to remember her by. And you've seen how she was about soap operas, so . . ."

His dark hair is still wet, trickles of water running down his neck, slipping toward his stomach.

"It's not ridiculous," I say, taking another step forward. "It's not ridiculous *at all*."

I'm close enough to Ezra now that I could touch him. I want to.

Hesitantly, I reach out, running my fingers down Ezra's arm as I trace the lines of black ink. He stills beneath my touch, his dark eyes meeting mine.

"Lily . . ."

"Wait," I say breathlessly, cutting him off. "Can I . . . Can I ask you something? About when I first moved to Sunrise Harbor? Sarita thinks you might have . . . um . . . *liked* me?"

Ezra freezes.

My throat goes dry as I remember him sliding into the seat next to mine during study hall, turning to look at me the way he is now.

As if he can actually *see* me.

"Yeah," Ezra whispers. He moves his other hand, his fingers brushing against where mine rests on his bicep. So softly I can barely feel it. "I might have liked you."

"Oh." I pause, swallowing hard. "That's, um . . ."

I lose my concentration as Ezra's fingers graze my bare skin again.

"For the record," I say unevenly. "I might have liked you, too."

Suddenly, Ezra takes a step back. My arms drop to my

sides. "But we can't. Lily, Max and I are best friends. After my grandma died and everything happened with my mom . . . Max has always been there for me. Even when kids at school talked, he always treated me like normal. He's the good guy. He—"

"Max and I broke up," I interrupt. "Officially."

Ezra searches my face.

"Why?" he asks, his voice barely a whisper.

For a moment, neither of us moves.

I'm excruciatingly aware of how close we are. Of the sound of my breath, and the beat of my heart, and the feel of his cool skin beneath my fingers. I've never felt more alive.

I've never *felt* more.

"Because Max is the good guy," I say. "And I don't *want* the good guy, Ezra. I only want *you*."

Ezra reaches up, cupping my face with his palms as he closes the last few inches between us. Pulling me to him, he lowers his head to mine.

I forget how to breathe.

Reaching up, I tangle my hands in his damp hair, pressing myself up on my toes to meet his kiss. There's an urgency inside me that's never been there before, a *need* that leaves me dizzy and breathless.

Trying to steady myself, I slide one hand downward, pressing it against Ezra's chest. For a second, I expect to feel the soft thud of his heartbeat beneath my fingers.

But instead, there's nothing.

Of course there isn't.

Ezra is a vampire.

Dimly, I'm aware of the sky lightening in the background.

It takes everything I have to pull away from him.

"Ezra, wait," I say, nodding toward the sky. "It's almost dawn. We need to get back before—"

Ezra leans forward, cutting me off with another kiss.

I give up, wrapping my arms around his neck and pulling him close.

And then, somewhere in the background, a car door slams.

# CHAPTER *Thirty*

EZRA AND I BOTH STOP DEAD, STARING AT EACH other in the strange, predawn light.

"Sarita and Max," I manage to say, but Ezra is already pulling away with superhuman speed, running ahead of me down the path. His feet are sure beneath him, a childhood full of memories leading his way.

In comparison, I'm painfully slow, stumbling over tree roots and tripping over clods of dirt at every step. By the time I emerge from the woods, panting, it's too late.

At the edge of the driveway, an impossibly frail-looking girl eyes Ezra warningly as she shoves Max toward the open door of a sleek black car; Max's bright blond hair glints as he catches sight of us, his face blank with panic.

"Lil—*aagh*!" he cries, biting my name off with a yelp of pain.

The girl gives Max's arm another vicious twist, his entire body stiffening in agony. Holding him tightly in check, she turns to face Ezra and me, pushing her long dark hair away from her narrow face.

*A dark-haired girl.*

*A rooftop.*

*Blood.*

The world tips dizzily beneath my feet as I look into the face of a ghost, my stomach heaving with sudden nausea.

*No!* I think. *It's not possible.*

But even as my mind is spiraling out of control, my body is kicking into overdrive. When it comes to Max, there's no fight-or-flight.

There's only fight.

Adrenaline floods through me as I surge forward, only to find myself caught in Ezra's iron grip.

Quicker than lightning, the girl's hand is at Max's throat. Another strangled cry escapes his lips as he scrabbles uselessly against her fingers, desperately trying to breathe.

With the slightest squeeze, she could crush Max's windpipe.

I pull up short, Ezra holding me back.

"Wait!" I cry, my voice high and thready. I'm not quite sure who I'm talking to.

Her hand still fastened around Max's throat, the girl looks at me, a triumphant smile spreading slowly across her face.

*I remember lunging.*

*I remember my teeth, ripping into her throat.*

*The light, dimming in her eyes.*

Next to me, Ezra stands taut, his entire body straining from the effort of remaining still. Carefully, he squeezes my arm, silently warning me not to move.

A ray of sunlight breaks through the early morning clouds,

making Ezra flinch. The girl abruptly turns, throwing Max into the car and sliding in after him. Gravel spits beneath the wheels as the engine roars to life.

With a hoarse cry, Ezra lets go of me and dodges patches of sunlight as he sprints after them.

But it's no use; the car is already disappearing around the bend.

A sob rips from my throat as I fall forward, catching myself on the soft earth below. Too late, my hands flood with heat, my fingers convulsing in the dirt. I'm vaguely aware of Sarita stumbling through the doorway, gingerly clutching her temple.

"Lily!" Sarita cries, hurrying toward me. A small trickle of blood escapes from beneath her hand, tracing a thin red line down her cheek. "What happened? *Where's Max?*"

"He's gone," I whisper. "She took him."

Even as my palms burn with unspent heat, I can feel the iciness trickling through my veins.

"Who?" Sarita demands, falling to her knees beside me. "*Who* took him?"

"I don't know," I admit, the shame of my words knotting me in two.

*I never even knew her name.*

I hear the crunch of gravel as Ezra joins us, his face streaked with dust.

"That girl," he says grimly. "She was the one who turned me. Why would some random vampire be following us?" he demands. "Why would she take *Max*?"

"It wasn't a random vampire," I say dully. "It was *her*." I force myself to look up. "The girl on the rooftop. I didn't kill her," I say, the words ripping my throat apart with each syllable. "I . . . *turned* her."

Sarita inhales sharply, sitting back on her heels.

"Oh my God," she whispers, pulling the shard of stone free from her pocket. "*Transference.* That's what the coven has been using the bloodstone for."

Icy realization trickles down my spine.

" 'An insurance policy,' " I say slowly. "That's what Agatha called the bloodstone."

*Not a life for a life*, I think.

*A vampire for a vampire.*

"I still don't get it," Ezra says, looking between us. "What am I missing?"

"Bloodstones cure vampires, right? But witches don't want vampires to be *cured*. The only way a witch gets more magic is if they slay a vampire—and if all the vampires are cured . . ." I face him. "That's why they imbue the bloodstone: to ensure there's always more *magic* for them to drain."

Sarita looks physically ill.

"So when you used the bloodstone, back on the roof . . ." Ezra says slowly.

"I didn't kill anyone," I finish, swallowing hard. "I made a new vampire."

I turned that poor girl on the rooftop.

And then I . . . *left her there* for Cassius to find.

No wonder she's been helping him. No wonder she hates me.

Despite the warmth in the air, I can feel myself shivering.

"But how did she find us?" Ezra asks, pushing his hand through his hair. "We're in the middle of *nowhere*."

I close my eyes, the last piece of the puzzle falling into place.

"The sire bond," I whisper. "The one I had with Cassius is broken. But when the girl turned you . . ." I open my eyes, forcing myself to look at Ezra. "As long as you're a vampire, she'll be able to find you anywhere. I should have seen it sooner, but I thought your attack was random. I . . . I missed it."

"I can't believe this," Sarita says, staring down at the bloodstone in her hand. "I can't believe *any* of this."

"I never should have come to Sunrise Harbor," I say. "I was fooling myself to think I could ever make a *life* here." My breath is tight in my chest, panic radiating through my veins. "I'm sorry," I whisper. "This is all my fault. This is all happening because of *me*."

"Lily, *stop*," Sarita says, her voice sharp. "It's not your fault, okay?"

"Sarita's right," Ezra agrees. He reaches out to touch my shoulder, then jerks away, hissing suddenly in pain.

Shit.

Blinking away my tears, I glance over his shoulder; the sun is cresting the top of the tree line, the pinkish-yellow rays growing brighter with each passing second.

"Everyone in the van," I say, trying to pull myself together. *"Now."*

Ezra doesn't hesitate; he dives for the van, sliding into the back seat as quickly as he can. As Sarita races around the side, I pull open the front door, then stop cold.

A large rectangular box sits on the driver's seat, patiently waiting for me. The gleaming black package is tied with an elegant silk bow.

Cassius.

As Sarita climbs into the passenger seat, I grab the box and climb in, too, slamming the door behind me. In the back seat, Ezra's forehead is drawn with confusion. "What the hell is that?"

I ignore the question, reaching for the silk ribbon.

My fingers tremble slightly as I lift the lid of the box. Folding aside a layer of tissue paper, I reveal a length of silver sequined fabric, shimmering slightly in the early morning light.

Sarita blinks.

"A dress?" she asks. "Why would anyone give you a *dress*?"

Not just any dress: a vintage Versace gown, cut low in the front and even lower in the back. I lift the heavy sequined dress up by the straps, a rush of memory flooding through me. It's been decades since Cassius caught me lingering in front of the window, gazing at the silvery fabric through the glass. We were in Rome that fall, the moonlight spilling through the narrow streets of the Via Condotti and the smell of frying oil drifting up from the food carts. Cassius insisted on buying me the dress, the seamstress staying late to fit it. After, we'd gone dancing at an Italian disco.

I caught him later that night, hunched over the body of an unmoving bartender, the older man's blood drained almost completely.

Cassius had promised it would never happen again.

It was the last time I'd ever worn the dress.

“Look,” Sarita says, pointing toward the box. “There’s a note.”

I set the dress carefully back in the box as Sarita reads out the piece of bright blue paper: “ ‘Lilliana: You still owe me a dance. XOXO, Cassius.’ ”

My stomach sinks as Sarita flips the note over. It’s been written on the back of an all-too-familiar poster: “Sunrise Harbor High Senior Prom: Love Among the Stars.”

“Well,” Ezra says, staring down at the slip of paper. “I hope everyone packed their dancing shoes.”

# CHAPTER Thirty-One

"I STILL DON'T UNDERSTAND WHY WE'RE HERE," Sarita says, glaring at the woman pushing a heavy cart full of lumber down the aisle next to us. She swings the cart awkwardly to the side, giving Sarita as wide of a berth as she can. "I don't like leaving Ezra back at the hotel alone. And besides, we should all be out looking for Max, not shopping for *home goods*."

"We already *know* where Max is going to be," I hiss at her, smiling apologetically at the woman. "I don't like it any more than you do, but we have to face facts: *Max* is the bait now, not me." Even saying the word aloud sends another wave of nauseating anxiety spiraling through me. Sarita opens her mouth as if she's about to protest, but I press on. "And if Max is bait, that means we're walking into a trap tonight," I say. "I don't know about you, but, personally, I'd like to make sure there's at least a *chance* we walk out."

"Fine," Sarita says, not sounding happy about it.

To be fair, it's hard to be happy when one of your best friends has been kidnapped by vampires, and you've recently discovered that everything you thought you knew about yourself is a lie.

Cassius may be our number one problem right now, but Sarita's coven has a lot to answer for, too.

"What about one of these?" Sarita reaches for the nearest wall display, lifting a piece of equipment from the shelf.

"A gun?" I ask. "Seriously?"

Sarita looks down at the heavy plastic compressor in her hand. "It's a *nail* gun. But, yeah," she says. "Point taken."

"Besides, nails are pretty much useless when it comes to vampires," I add as she puts the nail gun back on the shelf. "You might as well be shooting a confetti cannon."

Sarita has already turned down the barbecue aisle. "What about these?" she calls, holding up a pack of bamboo skewers. "We could make vampire shish kebab!"

Her tone is a little too bright, an edge of desperation lurking below the surface. I haven't been a human for long, but it's obvious she's deflecting.

To be honest, I'm probably doing the same thing.

"Maybe," I say, humoring her. "Although bamboo will only slow a vampire down, not actually kill them."

"Really?" Sarita asks, frowning down at the skewers. "What if I stab them in the heart?"

"It needs to be hardwood," I say. "Hawthorn, maybe. Or hickory. Yew wood would be best, but it's hard to find these days. Apparently, people keep building cabinets out of it."

Sarita frowns. "Whatever. I'm still getting these." She tosses the pack of bamboo skewers into the cart before moving on. "So, if we're not looking for, like . . . wooden stakes, what *are* we looking for?" she asks. "I assume you have *some* sort of plan here?"

I look up, scanning the signs overhead.

PLUMBING, FLOORING, PATIO FURNITURE . . .

"Lighting," I say, pushing the heavy cart forward as briskly as I can. "Aisle six."

She trails after me, watching as I make my way through the endless rows of ceiling fans and light fixtures. Finally, I find what I'm looking for.

Sarita blinks up at the row of hydroponic lights in confusion. "Grow lights?" she asks. "*That's* what we're here for? *Grow lights?*"

"Oh, look," I say, pointing toward the price tag. "They're on sale."

I start loading boxes into the cart, grunting a little with the effort.

"I'm sorry," Sarita says. "But *this* is your grand plan to save Max? We're going to *grow a bunch of weed*?"

I load another box onto the cart, my battered body protesting angrily against the movement. The lights are at least three feet long, not to mention awkwardly bulky. "Pro tip," I say, tapping the side of the box. "Always read the fine print."

Sarita leans over the side of the cart, scanning the back of the cardboard box. A second later, understanding dawns on her face.

"Wait," she says. "Will this actually *work*?"

"Of course it'll work," I say confidently, reaching for another box.

What I don't say is that it *has* to work.

Because if it doesn't, we're all screwed.

It's late afternoon by the time Sarita and I finally stumble back to the cheap hotel we checked into this morning, covered in dust and dripping with sweat. Ezra is lying on the bed, the remote balanced on his stomach and the television glowing silently in the background.

At first glance, he could almost be napping.

Well, if you ignore the fact that his eyes are wide open, and every muscle of his body is rigid with tension. I can sense his brittleness from the doorway; if you dropped him, he would shatter like glass.

As we shut the door behind us, Ezra bolts upright, the plastic remote thudding softly to the carpet.

"How'd it go?" he asks. He stands up, his fingers drumming a nervous rhythm against his leg. "Is everything okay?"

"It was fine," I say, sagging against the door in exhaustion. After the hardware store, we made a stop by the high school to put in one last party committee shift. My arms are so tired that I can't even feel them anymore. "Although, Noah kept asking where Max was. Apparently, Sarita and I 'do balloons wrong.' "

Sarita flops dramatically down on the other queen bed, spreading her limbs out like a starfish.

"Question," she says to the ceiling. "Do you think Astrid will be pissed at me *forever* forever? Or until we're old and gray and our feelings don't really matter anymore?"

"Astrid and Sarita . . . talked," I say.

"I take it things didn't go well?" Ezra asks.

Sarita pushes herself up on her elbows, giving him a look.

"I told her that asking her to prom was a mistake. Then she started crying. And then I started crying. And then she literally *ran away from me*. So, no, *Ezra*," she finishes coldly. "Things did *not* go well."

Ezra flinches in sympathy.

"Okay, yeah," he says. "That sucks."

Sarita groans, flopping back against the bed.

"Are you aware of how long I've been waiting to go on a date with Astrid Olson?" she moans. "*Four years.* I've literally spent my *entire high school career* building up to this moment. And now it's ruined, thanks to a fucking *vampire*. No offense," she adds, waving her hand listlessly in Ezra's direction.

"None taken," he says, a slightly dry tone to his voice.

"At least Astrid will be safe," I say, trying to cheer Sarita up. "If she's not at the dance, then she can't get hurt when Cassius shows up. That's the most important thing, right? Even if she, er . . . hates you right now?"

Sarita pushes herself up on her elbows again, narrowing her eyes in my direction.

"Has anyone ever told you that you're *really* bad at pep talks?"

Rolling my eyes, I push myself away from the dresser. "I'm going to shower," I say. "Are you sure you're okay?"

"I'm fine," Sarita says tiredly. "Just mourning the death of my dreams."

The words may be flippant, but I can hear the wobble in her voice.

That's the problem with wearing your heart on your sleeve, like Sarita; it's right out there for everyone to see.

I pause, giving her hand a reassuring squeeze. She squeezes back, managing a half-hearted smile.

Grabbing the box with my dress in it, I make my way into the dingy bathroom, turning the shower to full blast. Which is more of a weak dribble than a blast, actually. Not to mention freezing cold.

Still, it's better than the makeshift sponge baths that Sarita and I took in the bathroom at the high school.

I tip my head upward and close my eyes, letting the icy water sluice over me. I can feel the last few days washing away, as well; clumps of swampy mud and smears of dried blood, layers of sweat and grime and dust and dirt and ash.

Maybe if I stand still long enough, the water will wash away my guilt, too.

No matter what Sarita and Ezra may claim, I know deep down that all of this is my fault.

Sarita is hurting. Who knows if her relationships with Astrid or her mom will ever be the same again?

Max is in danger. He's scared, and alone, and caught up in a war that has nothing to do with him.

Ezra is a *vampire.* Even if we do manage to turn him back, he'll always carry the shadow of these last few days within himself.

And when I think of the girl from the rooftop, well . . .

The shame is almost too much to bear.

When the water slows to a dull trickle, I force myself to step out of the shower, shivering a little in the air-conditioning. In the mirror above the sink, I can chart a course through the past few days, using my injuries as a map: the bruises in the crooks of my elbows, left by the syringes I drew blood with. My scraped palms, still tender from catching myself against the pavement. The lump on the back of my head, the constellations of mosquito bites, the ugly bite mark at my neck . . .

I pause, my fingers still skimming over the edge of the bandage.

I can feel the heat sparking in my palms, sudden anger spiking through my veins.

I may have hurt people by accident, but *Cassius* is doing it on purpose.

Misery follows him like a faithful dog, trotting happily along at his heels.

Cassius deserves to answer for each and every one of these wounds.

And I intend to make sure he does.

Resolutely, I reach for the blow-dryer, awkwardly twisting back and forth beneath the attached cord. When my hair is finally dry enough, I pull it into a simple knot, tucking the loose ends behind my ears.

I remember the elaborately curled updos from my first life; the way my neck would ache from holding still, the dozens of pins scraping tightly against my skull. I'd bobbed my hair short as soon as it became fashionable, laughing in delight as the heavy locks fell to the floor of the barbershop.

If I recall correctly, Cassius hated it.

"Hey, what's taking so long in there?" Sarita calls, tapping impatiently on the bathroom door. "You're not the only one who needs to shower, remember?"

"One second!"

Sighing, I reach for the sleek black garment box; I'm not exactly thrilled to be wearing Cassius's 'gift,' but my actual prom dress is still hanging in my motel closet, and my only other option, currently, is this towel.

But as I lift the lid of the box, my breath catches in surprise.

The dress inside isn't the long silver Versace gown, dripping with sequins and bad memories.

Instead, it's a simple red slip dress.

The same one from Sarita's picture, at the vintage shop on Amaretto.

Blinking back sudden tears, I let the threadbare hotel towel drop to the floor. I carefully lift the dress out of the box and slip it over my head.

It fits like it was made for me, the silky material skimming the length of my body.

"Hello?" Sarita calls, pounding on the door again. "Are you still alive in there?"

I pull my sneakers on and open the door, then tackle Sarita in a massive bear hug.

*"How?"* I ask, barely able to form the word.

Sarita hugs me back, laughing a little. "Call it 'witchy

intuition,'" she says. "Also, I thought we might have time to shop for accessories in St. Augustine. Which in retrospect, was slightly . . . optimistic."

"Thank you," I whisper. *"Seriously."*

She grins, pulling back to survey the results up and down.

"Consider it an advance apology from my mom," she says. "After all, she's *technically* the one who paid for it. Oh, and here. I have another present for you, too." She reaches into her pocket, holding something out for me.

*The bloodstone.*

Hope lurches in my chest.

"Did you . . . Is it . . ."

"It's safe," Sarita says confidently. "Well, as safe as ancient magical crystals can get, at least. I couldn't figure out how to actually *remove* the transference spell," she admits. "But I was able to temporarily bind it. As long as I'm wearing this, the coven's spell should be powerless."

She pulls back her sleeve, showing me her arm.

A length of pure white ribbon has been wrapped around and around her bare wrist, the thin cord cutting painfully into her flesh.

I gasp, reaching for her arm, but Sarita yanks it away.

"I'm *fine*," she says firmly, pulling her sleeve down past her wrist. "It's only for a few hours, right?"

I blink hard, trying not to cry.

"Right," I manage to say. "Only a few hours."

Sarita smiles.

Handing me the bloodstone, she steps into the bathroom, shutting the door with a loud click.

I carefully tuck the stone away in the laces of my sneaker, then smooth my dress, the rough edges of my palms catching the delicate fabric. With a deep breath, I turn back to the main room.

Ezra has already changed into the suit Sarita picked out for him earlier today. It's surprisingly understated for her: classic black and fitted closely to his long, lean body. His white dress shirt is opened enough to reveal a glimpse of collarbone, his dark hair pushed back from his face.

He looks . . . good.

Very good.

I mean.

Yes.

Ezra looks very, *very good* in a suit.

His eyes travel up and down me, from the softly scooped neckline of my dress to the tips of my Vans.

"Nice shoes," he says, the corner of his lips quirking upward.

I pull my eyes away from his open shirt collar. "Thanks," I say, tugging at one of the spaghetti straps of my dress. The hotel room feels somehow smaller than it did a second ago. "Um, you look . . . nice . . . too."

Ezra looks down at his suit. "Thanks," he says. "I guess."

The walls of the hotel room are painfully thin; over the whine of the bathroom pipes, I can hear Sarita singing to herself in the shower.

Ezra tucks his hands into his pockets, rocking back on his heels.

"Sarita gave you the bloodstone?" he asks.

"Yeah. Um, here." I reach for the shard, intending to pass it over, but Ezra stops me with a shake of his head.

"You hang on to it for now," he says. "I don't want to accidentally *crush* it."

"Speaking of which, is that your tie?" I ask, nodding at the length of crumpled material in his hand.

Ezra holds it up, brandishing the knot of black silk in front of me. "I think it's broken."

I can feel a smile tugging at my lip.

"It's not broken," I assure him. "Here, give it to me."

I reach out for the tie, taking it carefully from his outstretched hand, making sure our fingers don't touch. I'm not sure if I can handle it right now. "First things first, you have to button your collar all the way," I say, pulling free his pathetic attempt at a knot and smoothing the fabric.

"It feels like I'm being choked," he complains, reluctantly following my orders.

"Yeah, well, suck it up," I say. "At least it's not a corset."

Pushing up on the tiptoes of my sneakers, I loop the length of silk around his neck, tucking it underneath the collar of his shirt.

Ezra gives a little jerk as, despite my best efforts, my fingers brush against his neck.

"Sorry," he mumbles. "Ticklish."

I concentrate on the tie. "It's fine. Max can't tie one, either," I say. Max's name acts like a talisman; almost imperceptibly, Ezra and I shift slightly farther apart. I clear my throat, not making eye contact with him. "His mom does it for him."

"His mom used to tie mine, too," Ezra mumbles. "For, like, band concerts. Junior high stuff."

I bite down a smile. "You guys were in band?"

"It was mandatory," Ezra says. "I played the trombone. I was awful."

I finish tying Ezra's tie, lingering slightly longer than I need to over the knot.

*Come on, Morris. Get it together.*

"There," I say. "Perfect." I step back quickly, almost tripping over the edge of the bed. Before I can fall, Ezra is there with preternatural speed, his arms sliding around me as he steadies us in midair.

For a long moment, we don't move, his arms secure around my waist and our faces inches from each other. A lock of hair has come untucked, falling over his cheek.

My grip tightens around his neck.

In the bathroom behind us, we hear the metallic screech of Sarita turning off the shower. Slowly, Ezra straightens, pulling away from me.

"We shouldn't . . . Not while Max is . . ." He pauses, pushing his hair back. "Besides, Sarita will be out in a second. We should probably . . ."

"Yes," I say, although I'm not sure what I'm agreeing to. "Definitely."

My pulse is still thudding in my wrists, my heartbeat echoing loudly in my chest. Glancing in the mirror above the dresser, I straighten my dress, checking to make sure my hair is still in place.

"You look beautiful," Ezra says, his voice matter-of-fact.

I blink, the breath catching in my chest.

But before I can say anything, Sarita opens the bathroom door, popping her head into the room.

"Ready?" Ezra asks.

Sarita gives him a withering look. "Do I *seem* ready?" she says, gesturing toward her still-dripping-wet hair. "Speaking of which, get your butt back in here, Morris."

"Why?" I ask nervously. "I'm already dressed."

"You're dressed for a *dance*," Sarita corrects me.

"Right," I say. "Because . . . we're *going* to a dance?"

"Wrong," Sarita says smugly, holding up her makeup bag. "We're going into *battle*."

# CHAPTER Thirty-Two

AS IT TURNS OUT, SARITA'S DEFINITION OF "battle armor" is "enough body glitter to shame the entire cast of *Euphoria*."

I feel like a walking disco ball as we step into the gym, my veins flooding with nervous energy.

"Ezra and I will check around the edges of the room," I murmur to Sarita. "You take the middle. Look for any sign of them."

Sarita nods, stepping briskly forward.

She makes it approximately three steps before one of the theater kids ambushes her, literally *shrieking* in delight at Sarita's outfit. "Oh my God, you look *fantastic*!"

To be fair, Sarita *does* look incredible.

She's dressed in an amazing '50s-style tuxedo that she apparently managed to find at the vintage store earlier this week, her dark hair slicked back behind her ears and the sequined lapels of her jacket catching the light beneath the sparkling sky of tinfoil-covered cardboard stars.

"Come on," the girl says, grabbing Sarita's hand. "We *have* to dance!"

Sarita tries to refuse, but the girl is clearly *not* about to take "no" for an answer.

Giving Ezra and me a martyred look, Sarita allows herself to be pulled deeper onto the dance floor, her head swiveling back and forth as she scans the room.

It's a far cry from the dream dance she'd planned to have with Astrid.

I make a mental note to somehow make things right between them if we manage to get out of this alive.

Maybe I could send them on an all-expenses-paid Caribbean cruise.

Or . . . let them use my employee discount at Burger Queen.

Ezra and I head in opposite directions, each of us making a lap. Ximena Morales is in a bright pink dress, dancing her ass off despite her five-inch heels. Mia Chapman has gone *big*, her giant tulle skirt taking up half the floor. And while Noah's cheeks may be suspiciously flushed, he at least still has his shirt on.

I take a shaky breath, trying not to panic.

Everyone looks so *happy*.

They have no idea that I've put them all in danger.

"Anything?" Ezra asks as we meet on the other side of the gym.

I shake my head. "Not yet. But Cassius always *did* like to make an entrance."

Ezra leans against the wall, surveying the crowd.

"I've never actually been to a school dance before," he admits.

“Me neither,” I say wryly. “Then again, I went to school in the 1800s. Prom wasn’t really a thing.”

My throat tightens as I glance toward the makeshift balloon arch, where a group of the swim kids are posing together for a photo. In a different world, Max and I would have been there, too, dressed up in cheap feathered boas and comically large sunglasses, his arm draped around my shoulder and a cheesy grin plastered on his face.

I swallow hard, looking away.

*Max is all right*, I think. *He has to be.*

Cassius needs a bargaining chip.

And bargaining chips don’t work if they’re dead.

Ezra gives me a sidelong glance, noting the change in my expression. “You really think he’s going to show?” he asks.

“No,” I say grimly. “I *know* he’s going to show.”

Ezra pulls me in front of him, dropping his forehead against mine. “Hey,” he says. “It’s going to be fine.”

I lean into him, letting him steady me. “Promise you’ll try really hard not to die, okay?”

“Not a problem,” he whispers back. “I’m *already dead*, remember?”

My smile fades almost immediately; over Ezra’s shoulder, I can see Cassius walking through the front door of the dance.

He’s dressed in an ostentatious red brocade suit, his black silk shirt unbuttoned halfway down his chest and his hair slicked back at the temples. Next to him, Max looks like a kid playing dress-up, his borrowed suit jacket too tight around his shoulders and his forehead shiny with sweat.

My breath catches as a dark-haired girl walks in behind them, her midnight-blue dress shockingly dark against her pale skin.

Ezra turns, his entire body tensing. Stray pieces of my body glitter cling to his forehead, catching the light of the slowly rotating disco ball overhead.

"Is he glamoured?" Ezra asks tightly, his eyes locked on Max.

"No," I say grimly as Sarita hurries over to join us. "If he was *glamoured*, he wouldn't look so scared."

As we watch, the dark-haired girl leans forward, whispering something in Cassius's ear. He throws his head back and laughs, the carefree sound barely audible above the music.

Almost lazily, Cassius's gaze finds mine, his eyes shining across the dance floor.

He winks.

Hatred pours through my veins. I can feel the heat gathering in my palms, the flames already licking at my fingertips.

"Let's go," I say shortly, already striding across the gym. Is it my imagination, or can I feel the temperature dropping the closer we get to Cassius?

As we near, Max manages a wobbly grin.

It's possibly the least convincing smile I've ever seen.

"Max!" Sarita reaches for him, but the girl in blue steps forward, blocking her path. Despite her frail appearance, the steel in her movements is obvious.

Cassius's gaze runs possessively up and down my body, his eyes flickering in annoyance as he takes in my bright red dress.

*Good.*

"Lily," Cassius says, smiling sardonically. "Fancy meeting you here."

The girl next to him burns with silent intensity.

I shift uncomfortably, the dull heat in my palms becoming a painful throb. "What are we doing here, Cassius?"

"What do you *think* we're doing here?" he asks. "It's the *prom*." He gestures around the gym, his hands sweeping in the cheap paper streamers and tinfoil-covered stars. "The elegance! The grace! The cheap fruit punch spiked with even *cheaper* grain alcohol! Tell me, Lilliana," he adds mockingly. "Is it worth it? Everything you've given up to be here? Everything you've *done*?"

I flinch, my eyes drawn unwillingly to the girl standing next to him.

To the *vampire* that I sired.

"Not so high-and-mighty anymore, are we?" Cassius asks with a smirk.

He leans forward, the warmth of his cedar and clove aftershave at odds with the coolness that clings to the air around him. "You always *did* think you were better than me," he whispers.

Understanding slices through me, the realization twisting like a knife in my gut.

The rest of the gym seems to disappear, the world around us winnowing away into nothing. All that remains is Cassius and me, here, in this moment.

"You knew," I breathe, feeling dizzy with shock. "You *knew* what would happen when I used the bloodstone."

His answering smile says I'm right.

Cassius *knew* the bloodstone was imbued.

He'd been *testing* me.

And I'd failed.

"Why?" I ask, my voice breaking.

"I did it for *us*," Cassius says. "You were so obsessed with finding the cure. Obsessed with the idea of just being *human*." He pauses, shaking his head. "You wouldn't *let it go*. You left me no choice," he adds self-righteously. "You needed to learn your lesson."

Heat sparks in my palms, anger rushing through me like wildfire. "My *lesson*?"

"Don't you see, Lilliana?" Cassius asks patiently. "You're not *just* a human. You were *never* going to be *just* a human."

A fresh wave of fury courses through me.

I can feel the fire licking at my fingertips, the strange purplish flames longing to be set free.

And, just for a moment, I'm no longer standing in a crowded high school gym; I'm cowering in the alleyway outside the factory, my back pressed to the stone arch behind me.

A handsome boy in a top hat stands in front of me, his fangs already dripping with blood.

I watch as Cassius's eyes widen in fascination. He reaches up, wiping his lip with the back of his hand.

His glove comes away red.

I can feel the thin, steady trickle of blood running down my neck, disappearing beneath the high, scratchy collar of my dress.

Cassius leans forward, his handsome face inches from mine. His pupils are flooded with a strange oily blackness that seems to swirl and eddy in the light. As he tips his head down to whisper at me, his breath is cool and sweet on my cheek.

"Who *are* you?" he asks curiously.

I've never been more scared in my life.

Beneath my own gloves, I can feel my palms growing hot, fire licking at the soft material, waiting to be set free.

The sensation is new and strange and terrifying in its strength. But still not nearly as terrifying as the penny dreadful standing in front of me.

Cassius leans forward, trailing one blood-soaked finger down my cheek. His strange button-black eyes are bright with . . . curiosity? Or something darker?

"*What* are you?" he asks this time, capturing my chin in his powerful grip.

Instinctively, I jerk my hands up to push him away.

Instead, the entire alleyway explodes with sudden heat, the strange purplish flames consuming us both in fire.

# CHAPTER *Thirty-Three*

"LILY?" EZRA'S HAND IS ON MY ELBOW, HIS fingers chill against my bare skin. "*Lily!* Are you okay?"

Next to him, Sarita's forehead is creased with concern, her glitter-lined eyes flickering uneasily between me and Cassius. Max goes to take a step toward me, but the dark-haired girl grabs his arm, pulling him up short alongside her.

"There was no fire at the factory, was there?" I ask Cassius, my lips numb. "There was only *me*. I *was* the fire."

Cassius doesn't bother denying the fact that he altered my memories.

"What else was I supposed to do, Lilliana?" he asks. "You were an untrained witch, all alone in the world. You had no idea how to protect yourself. You didn't even realize what you *were*. How much *power* you had . . ."

I stare at him, sickened.

"Do you know what our kind do to witches?" he asks, his voice low and coaxing. "We hunt them down. We *destroy* them.

It was only a matter of time until another vampire found you. Or *worse*, another witch."

He spreads his arms, holding his hands open in front of me.

"Don't you understand?" he asks. "I *saved* you."

All the breath leaves my body in a single *whoosh*.

"Saved me?" I repeat, my voice shaking with disbelief. "You *killed* me, Cassius."

He shoves his hands in his pockets, his smile not quite reaching his eyes. "You always did get hung up on the details," he says.

"Sarita was right," I breathe aloud. "You really are a monster."

"Don't forget," Cassius says, his voice hard, "I'm not the only one with blood on my hands anymore."

The world swims dizzyingly around me as I turn to look at the dark-haired girl beside him.

Despite the deep shadows beneath them, she looks back at me with clear green eyes.

"This is Freya," Cassius says. "I believe you've already met?"

*Freya.*

The heat in my hands is suddenly gone, leaving me weak and reeling.

*The girl I turned, the one I sentenced to a life of unending pain, her name is Freya.*

"Well then," Cassius says briskly. "Now that we're all acquainted, we should celebrate. Who wants punch?"

He makes a show of peering around the crowded dance floor, pretending to search for the refreshment table. Familiar faces swirl past his shoulder: Mr. Markowitz, his arms crossed in perpetual disapproval, the sleeves of his ill-fitting blue blazer straining against his elbows; Shay Wilson, dressed in pale green, scrubbing furiously at a spot on her skirt; Noah Coates, his bow tie already pulled loose, helping himself to a brimming ladleful of punch.

Sarita inches forward, one hand straying toward the hideous amethyst brooch that's pinned to the lapel of her tuxedo jacket.

"You need to leave," she says, her voice almost even. "My coven is already on their way. When they get here—"

"Oh, please," he interrupts. "If your 'coven' wanted anything to do with you, you wouldn't have been hiding out at some godforsaken *shack* in the middle of nowhere." He smiles coldly. "Rumor has it your own *mother* wouldn't even help you."

Sarita flinches.

As Ezra gives an angry hiss, I step in front of him.

It takes all of my courage to look the dark-haired girl in the eye.

To look *Freya* in the eye.

*"Please,"* I say, swallowing hard. "You need to listen to me. Whatever loyalty you may think you owe Cassius, it doesn't matter. The High Priestess is already on her way. If she finds you here, she'll . . . She'll . . ."

"She'll what?" Freya asks in a soft British accent. "*Kill* me?"

I flinch back as though I've been punched.

Cassius's mocking smile stretches even wider.

"You have to admit, Lilliana," he says. "She makes a good point."

Rage spikes through me at the sight of his smug grin, liquid fury racing through my veins.

"For the last time," I say. "It's *Lily*."

And, stepping forward, I slam my hand down on the nearest row of light switches.

# CHAPTER Thirty-Four

FOR ONCE, EZRA IS FASTER THAN CASSIUS.

Grabbing Freya's arm, he ducks for cover, yanking her to safety as $2,798 worth of industrial hydroponic bulbs burst suddenly to light.

It's not like in the movies.

Vampires don't instantly *burst* into flames. There are no flashes of blinding light, no dramatic *poof*s as their bodies turn suddenly to dust.

No, in real life, it's slower; by the time Cassius realizes what's happening, his skin is already blistering, his flesh stripping away beneath the artificial sunrays.

Wresting her arm away from Ezra, Freya starts toward Cassius, an anguished cry ripping from her lips as the lights hit her.

Her hair is already sizzling, the long dark strands fusing with her ruined skin.

I catch a glimpse of Eve Kha as she leans forward to vomit on her date's shoes. A tall red-haired boy I vaguely recognize from gym class crumples to the floor in a dead faint.

"Lights!" Cassius screams in Freya's direction. He's whipped off his jacket, shielding himself from the worst of the glare. *"Break the lights!"* Grabbing a folding chair with one hand, he throws it with preternatural strength, hitting one of the UV bulbs overhead.

The glass shatters into a million pieces, shards of it hurtling through the air like raindrops. I duck, covering my head; my arms take the worst of the impact, tiny, sharp cuts that feel like bee stings.

In the gym around me, all hell breaks loose.

A loud blaring noise sounds above us, cutting through the screams that fill the room; somebody, probably one of the chaperones, has pulled the fire alarm. The sprinklers kick in almost immediately, hissing as they burst to life.

The water is freezing.

Gritting my teeth, I push my way toward Cassius, fighting against the stream of terrified students heading in the opposite direction. My dress sticks to the tops of my legs, tripping me up as I move.

With a loud cry, Max jumps on Cassius's back, tackling him to the floor.

As ideas go, it's equal parts brave and stupid.

Cassius brushes him off impatiently, the careless motion enough to send Max flying backward through the air. He crashes into the refreshment table, knocking it to one side before slamming into the ground.

The gym is emptying out all around us, screams echoing toward the rafters as students stampede through the doors. As Sarita hurries forward, helping Max to his feet, I turn back, eyeing Cassius with single-minded determinedness.

I watch as he rips another grow light down, his skin sizzling angrily in response. He swings the slender bulb in a graceful arc, smashing it against the floor.

*Shit.*

My stomach sinks in realization.

I underestimated Cassius. His age, his strength, his *rage.*

The lights aren't enough to stop him. They're barely even slowing him down.

Fear makes it hard to concentrate, but I force myself to freeze, planting my feet firmly on the floor. I'm tired of running from Cassius. I'm done living in terror. I raise my hands, reaching for the spark of heat inside me, willing my own anger into existence. Purplish flames erupt from my palms, crackling through the air like heat lightning.

Cassius hisses as the flames wash over him, momentarily falling to his knees.

The eerie glow of my witch fire deepens the shadows beneath his eyes, sharpening the hollow planes of his cheeks.

Has he always looked so hard?

Or have I always been too soft?

"Stop it, Lily!" Cassius yells. "You don't know what you're doing!"

"I know *exactly* what I'm doing," I cry back, shouting to be heard over the still-blasting music. "This is who I am, Cassius. Everything you never wanted me to be!"

Footsteps slap across the hardwood floor, distracting me from my momentary triumph. Then Freya slams into me, knocking me to the floor and releasing Cassius from my flames.

She's still weak from turning Ezra; any vampire with an ounce of strength could have finished her off without a second thought.

But I'm not a vampire anymore.

"Please," I choke out as Freya's small hands clamp mercilessly around my neck. "You don't have to do this."

Freya's dark hair falls in a singed curtain across her blistered cheeks. "You're right," she says, tightening her grip. "But I *want* to."

*"Freya."*

She tenses at the sound of Cassius's voice, her bright green eyes burning with hatred for me.

Still, she lets Cassius pry her fingers gently away from my neck.

"Get the rest of the lights," he orders her, his eyes fastened on mine. "Then take care of the other witch."

Wheezing, I try to raise myself onto my elbows. But Cassius is already on top of me, his eyes bright and mocking even through his pain. His skin is healing almost as quickly as it blisters, even faster as Freya follows his orders.

"It didn't have to be this way, Lilliana," Cassius croons, running one finger down the length of my cheek. "You *do* realize that, don't you?"

Tears leak from the corners of my eyes as Cassius's hand closes around my bruised neck. I can feel my trachea grinding against bone as his fingers cut deeper, sinking into my wounded flesh.

"I didn't want this," Cassius says, his face inches away from mine. "I *never* wanted this."

The world is beginning to dim a little.

The sprinklers have finally cut off. I can hear the music again, still spilling from the gym's loudspeakers. The premade playlist has switched to a slow song, something soft and romantic.

At least I won't be dying to the strains of "Y.M.C.A."

"I always knew we were the same, Lilliana," Cassius whispers. "That deep down, you were a *killer*, like me. I just needed the bloodstone to prove it."

The corners of my vision are beginning to dim, the world growing hazy around the edges.

I move my lips, but only a choking noise comes out.

The world is growing darker and darker. My arms no longer beat against Cassius's chest; they've fallen to my sides in defeat.

*This is the way the world ends*, I think, the lines of my favorite T. S. Eliot poem drifting through my head. *This is the way the world ends. This is the way the world ends. Not with a bang but a whimper.*

On the far side of the gym, I can hear the crash of Freya destroying the last of the lights.

"Goodbye, Lilliana," Cassius whispers through the darkness.

Out of the corner of my eye, I catch a glimpse of movement.

And then Ezra is there.

# CHAPTER Thirty-Five

"LILY, RUN!" EZRA YELLS, TACKLING CASSIUS TO the ground. *"Now!"*

Raising his fist, he pummels Cassius into the floor.

I peel myself up, staggering away from them. The world is ringing in my ears, my legs unsteady beneath me.

"Lily!" Max grabs my arm, pulling me toward the door. "Come on, let's *go*!"

"Sarita," I croak, my voice cracked and broken.

*"Go!"* Sarita yells. "I'm right behind you!" Somewhere in the background, I can feel a blast of sudden heat.

Freya snarls in response.

Before I can protest, Max scoops me off my feet, hitching me over his shoulder. Slamming the side door open, he ducks through, heading down the empty hallway.

"Wait," I rasp. "I can walk."

Max doesn't slow.

*"Max,"* I say, digging my elbows into his back. *"Put me down."*

He reluctantly stops, dropping me to the ground with more force than is strictly necessary. My sodden dress tangles around my knees, the fabric sticking to my skin.

"I need to go back," I say, my voice scraping against my throat. "I need to *help* them." I try to concentrate, reaching for a spark of flames in my palms, the anger that can help me set the world on fire.

But there's only exhaustion. It's like trying to light a candle in a windstorm; no matter how hard I try, the heat slips through my fingers, refusing to catch.

I stomp my foot in anger, a wave of helpless frustration washing through me. I'm about to try again when Max suddenly slumps against the wall, lurching violently.

"Max?" I take a step toward him; up close, I can see that his handsome face is drawn in pain, his forehead clammy with sweat. "Are you okay?"

"I'm fine," Max says stoically. "It's only a scratch." He shifts again, trying to hide a wince of pain.

Fear spikes through me.

"No, no, no," I cry. "What happened?" Stepping forward again, I reach out, pushing his jacket lapel to one side. Beneath the heavy fabric of his suit jacket, his thin tuxedo shirt is stained with sticky dark red blood.

I can't help the gasp of horror that escapes from my lips.

Max looks woozily down at his shirt. "Well," he says. "That's not great."

"Come on," I say, looping my arm around Max's waist. "We need to get you somewhere safe." Staggering slightly under his weight, I lead him down the empty hallway. Our footsteps are unsettlingly loud beneath us, the sound of muted music still drifting through the hallways from the gym.

At every classroom we pass, I pause, rattling the doorknob hopefully.

They're all locked.

*"Shit,"* I say, smacking my hand against Mr. Gernecki's door.

As Max slumps beside me, I tighten my grip around his waist, panting a little as I lead him farther down the hall. It's not ideal, but the bathrooms on either side of the corridor aren't locked. "Come on," I say, half pushing, half pulling Max into the girls' room. "In here."

The lights kick on automatically as the door swings shut behind us, but I reach for the switch, quickly flicking them back off. Narrow beams of light spill through the windows from the parking lot outside, casting the bathroom in shadow.

I lead Max into the largest stall, sliding the bolt home behind us.

As if a *bolt* is going to keep him safe from a vampire.

Max slides down the wall, sinking heavily to the floor. I crouch on the linoleum next to him, my dress puddling around my knees.

He gives me a weak smile. "Do yourself a favor and try not to think about the last time they mopped the floor," he grunts.

"Maybe not the time for terrible jokes?" I say, tugging his arms free from his suit jacket. Max hisses in pain.

"You love my jokes," he says, his voice straining with effort.

Biting my lip, I carefully unbutton Max's blood-soaked shirt, trying not to jostle him too much as I peel it away from his chest. "Well, now I *know* you're delirious," I say, trying to distract him from the pain of movement. "*No one* likes your jokes."

Beneath the smears of blood, the wound on his chest is about an inch long, the edges ragged and angry.

"For future reference," Max says, "I'd recommend *not* impaling yourself on a table leg."

"Noted," I say, biting my lip.

Max shifts uncomfortably, the sweat on his forehead growing more pronounced. I place my hand flat on his chest, next to the wound, ignoring the sticky wetness of the blood. "Take a deep breath," I instruct.

He nods, drawing a shallow, rasping breath that turns into a hacking cough.

I can feel his chest hitching beneath my fingers as he coughs again, an oddly dry, painful sound.

*Shit.*

"We need to get you to a hospital," I say, trying not to panic. *"Now."*

"I'm fine," Max protests, biting off the end of the cough. "It's not even bleeding that much."

"It's a *chest wound*," I say. "*Any* amount of blood is too much. Besides, I think you punctured your lung."

Max blinks.

"Well, shit," he says.

"Wait here," I say. Ducking outside the stall, I quietly ransack the paper towel dispenser of its contents. Back in the stall,

I press a stack of them against Max's chest, applying pressure to the wound. "Hold this for a second."

Max reaches up, wincing as he presses down on the paper towels.

With a silent apology to Sarita, I grasp the bottom of my dress, yanking at the seam.

It doesn't rip.

Cursing my lack of vampire strength, I use my teeth, finally managing to make a small split in the seam. I tear a long strip of fabric from the bottom hem of my dress, pulling it tight around Max's ribs.

"Try not to move," I say, tightening the strip of cloth. "It's a miracle your lung hasn't collapsed yet."

Max's face grows pale as he looks down at the makeshift bandage. Blood is already seeping through the cloth, staining the dark red fabric almost black.

"Listen," he says. "If I don't make it out of here, then—"

"Stop it," I say, cutting him off. "You're *making it out* of here, Max Hutchinson. You're going home, and you're hugging your mom, and you're eating that leftover pot roast. You're going to *Dartmouth*, okay? You're going to make your dad proud. You're going to make us *all* proud. Do you hear me?"

Max manages a weak smile.

"For the record," he says, "the pot roast really *was* delicious."

I open my mouth to reply, but Max's eyes have already rolled back in his head.

"Max?" I whisper. "Max?"

His eyelids flicker but don't open.

I lean forward, brushing my lips against his forehead.

"I'm sorry, Max," I whisper, my voice breaking. "I'm so sorry. About *everything.*"

It doesn't take a doctor to realize Max doesn't have much time; he needs to get to a hospital, and soon.

But in the meantime, Cassius wants blood.

And I intend to give it to him.

# CHAPTER Thirty-Six

WITHOUT MAX AT MY SIDE, THE SCHOOL FEELS even more deserted.

I tiptoe through the dark hallway, my shoes squelching wetly with every step. Even to my own ears, my footsteps seem impossibly loud; to a vampire, I may as well be shouting *Here I am!* at the top of my lungs.

My heart thumping, I make my way toward the gymnasium. I'm about to turn the corner when I hear the soft scuff of movement.

I freeze.

"Sarita?" I call softly. "Is that you?"

An unfamiliar laugh floats through the hallway in response, surprisingly low and musical.

*Freya.*

I steel myself as she rounds the corner, barely managing not to gasp.

Freya's long dark hair is burnt away entirely on one side, the remaining strands sticking painfully to her still-blistered neck. A long, angry burn runs the length of her bare arm, the skin livid against her pale flesh as it heals.

"Freya," I say, swallowing hard. "Please. Can we talk?"

She takes a step forward, the hem of her ruined dress dragging softly against the floor. Her eyes flash dangerously.

"I know that you hate me," I say. "And I *get it*, believe me. But Cassius—"

"Cassius *saved* me," Freya interrupts, taking another step forward. "After *you* left me for dead. Or have you already forgotten?"

I swallow hard, my throat suddenly dry.

"I know it looks that way," I say, wetting my lips with my tongue. "But Cassius *knew* about the bloodstone. He knew what it would make me . . ." I trail off, feeling sick. "Cassius isn't a hero, Freya. He sent you to that rooftop to *die*."

"You took *everything* from me," Freya says, as if I haven't even spoken. She takes another step forward, her bright green eyes never leaving mine. "All I wanted was to take something from you."

I suddenly remember Ezra's words.

*It was a girl*, he told me, back at the hospital. *I was waiting for Max to give me a ride home. We started talking.*

Freya must have seen Ezra waiting for a ride next to Max's ridiculous yellow Jeep.

She must have thought . . .

"Ezra," I breathe. "You thought he was my boyfriend."

"But I was wrong," Freya says bitterly. "You couldn't even let me have *that*, could you?"

I can feel the warmth building in my hands as she takes another step forward, my palms burning with unspent heat.

"Freya, *please*," I say, pleading with her. "We don't have to do this."

Freya smiles.

"But I already told you," she says. "I *want* to."

I throw my hands up, but Freya is too fast. Dodging to the side, she spins around me. Pain blossoms like a flower as she slams the side of my head against the wall.

My vision blurs, my stomach heaving in response. When I wipe my arm across my temple, it comes away smeared with blood and glitter.

Freya skips off down the hallway, obviously toying with me.

My head still pounding, I sprint after her, following her toward the gym. Broken glass crunches beneath my shoes, and the dance floor is sticky with spilled punch. The speakers are still piping out music, but it's hard to hear over the sound of my blood whooshing in my ears.

Freya darts from out of nowhere, her fist sinking easily into my stomach.

All the breath leaves my body as I lean forward, dry-heaving in pain.

"Pathetic," Freya taunts, somewhere behind me. "What did Cassius ever even *see* in you?"

I think back to the alleyway, all those years ago. Of the way Cassius looked at me, his pale blue eyes widening with shock. With *recognition.*

*"This,"* I say simply. "He saw *this*."

And, raising my hands, I turn to face Freya.

I'm still easing Freya's limp body to the floor when a flicker of movement catches my eye across the gym. A second later, Ezra is skidding to the ground next to me, nearly knocking us both over in the process.

"Lily!" He looks between Freya and me, taking in her unnatural stillness, my ruined dress, the blood still dripping freely from my temple. "What happened?" he asks swiftly. "Are you hurt?"

"I'm fine," I say. I finish lowering Freya to the ground, then reach up, dabbing uncertainly at my head. "Most of the blood isn't even mine."

Ezra swallows hard, looking away.

"And Freya?" he asks. "Is she . . ."

"I had to do it," I say, my voice breaking. "You have to believe me, Ezra. I swear, I *didn't want to.* But she didn't give me a choice. Freya wasn't going to stop, Ezra," I say, the words tumbling faster and faster from my lips. *"She wasn't ever going to stop."*

Ezra looks down at Freya's motionless body.

"Lily . . ." he breathes. "What did you do?"

Suppressing a sob, I hold my shaking, bloodstained hand out for him to see.

My palm is coated in thick reddish dust.

"The bloodstone," I say. "I *used* it on Freya . . . I *cured* her."

Below us, an unconscious Freya takes a breath, her chest rising and falling softly with the movement.

Ezra reaches out, his cool fingers stilling my trembling hand.

"I'm sorry, I'm sorry," I repeat, sobbing. "I don't know how to save you now." Tears stream down my cheeks.

"Lily," Ezra says softly. "Listen to me, okay? I don't care about the *bloodstone.* I care about *you.*"

I force myself to meet his eyes, wincing at the sight of him; the partially healed gash above his right cheek cuts nearly to the bone, and his left shoulder hangs uselessly at his side, his arm clearly broken.

He needs to feed again soon; without fresh blood, his injuries are healing too slowly.

As if he's reading my mind, Ezra shakes his head.

"I'm fine," he says. "It's worse than it looks."

"And Sarita?" I ask, dread pooling in my stomach. "I thought she was with you."

"No," Ezra says, shaking his head. "I thought Cassius was making a break for it, so I followed him, but he doubled back and surprised me," he adds. "By the time I came to, he and Sarita were both gone."

"We need to find her," I say, trying to ignore the throbbing headache pounding behind my eyes. "But first, we need to get Max. I think his lung is punctured; it's going to collapse soon if we don't get him to a hospital."

Gritting my teeth, I push myself to my feet. Swaying slightly, I stagger toward the door.

I make it about halfway before I trip. Ezra is already at my side, reaching out to steady me. "Lily, wait," he says. "Are you sure you're okay?"

"I'm *fine,*" I insist, pulling away from him. The floor tilts dangerously in response, the gym spinning like a Tilt-A-Whirl.

I sit back down abruptly, bracing myself against the floor.

My hands are smeared with blood: mine, Max's, Freya's . . . *everyone's.*

I wipe them furiously against my dress, as though if I scrub hard enough, I can somehow erase tonight entirely.

But it doesn't work; if anything, I'm smearing the blood around even more.

*I can keep you safe*, I promised, back in Ezra's bedroom. *I can keep* everyone *safe.*

But it was all a lie.

A tiny sob escapes my throat.

"Shit," Ezra says worriedly. "Here." He kneels down in front of me, pulling his jacket off and draping it around my shoulders. "You're shaking."

"It's all my fault," I say raggedly, looking up at him. "I was so sure I was smarter than Cassius. That my plan would work." My words are coming faster and faster now; I can feel the hysteria bubbling in my throat. "But *it didn't.* And now everyone is going to die, and it's *all my fault.*"

"Lily," Ezra says softly. "Hey, look at me." Reaching up, he cradles my face gently in his hands. His fingers are cool against my skin. "Has anyone ever told you that you're kind of a raging narcissist?"

I blink up at him, the unexpectedness of what he's saying yanking me back from the abyss. "What?"

"It's true," Ezra says, his voice grave. "I'm actually worried that you have some sort of complex. Wait, you don't think you're the reason the *Beatles* broke up, do you?"

A half laugh, half sob pulls at my throat.

"I'm being *serious.*"

"I'm being serious, too," he says softly. "You can't take the blame for *everything*, Lily. You *can't.*"

"Max is hurt because of me," I say. "Even if Sarita's safe, her mom will probably never talk to her again. Because of *me.* The cure is gone, and you're still a *vampire*, Ezra. *Because of me.*"

Ezra leans forward, resting his forehead against mine. "Lily Bertha Morris," he whispers. "You're the best thing that's ever happened to me. And if getting to know you meant becoming a vampire all over again, I'd do it in an instant."

For a second, I forget how to breathe.

And then, somehow, my arms find their way around Ezra's neck, pulling him close. I breathe in his scent. My tears soak his shoulder. And I don't let go.

"You *do* know that my middle name isn't Bertha, right?"

I can feel the slow grin spreading across his face.

"I took a shot," he whispers.

And then he's kissing me.

For one endless moment, the world around us disappears. Ezra's arms tighten around me, my body molding instinctively to his.

I shrug out of his jacket, needing to feel his touch against my bare skin. His palm slides down my arm, his thumb stroking the delicate flesh at the base of my wrist.

Need crashes over me, a desperate *wanting* that hits me harder than any punch. I tangle my fingers in Ezra's dark curls.

All this time, I thought that I wanted to be human.

To be a regular teenage girl.

To lead a *normal* life.

But I was wrong.

As it turns out, all I've ever wanted is *Ezra*.

Above us, the loudspeaker crackles suddenly to life.

I pull reluctantly away from Ezra as the unmistakable sound of Cassius's voice floods through the gym.

"Lilliana Morris, please come to the principal's office. I repeat, Lilliana Morris to the principal's office, please."

There's a sharp burst of static, and then Cassius's voice crackles overhead again. "Oh. And did I mention you have three minutes to show before I kill the witch?"

# CHAPTER Thirty-Seven

"LILY, *WAIT*," EZRA SAYS, FOLLOWING BEHIND as I storm down the hall. "It's a trap, okay? You're *obviously* walking into a trap!"

"You think I don't know that?" I ask. "What other choice do I have, Ezra? He's got *Sarita*."

"We don't know that," Ezra argues, pushing his hand through his hair. "Not for sure. He could be lying, trying to draw you out."

"It doesn't matter," I say in frustration. "If there's even a *chance* he has her, I need to go. *Now.* We're wasting time."

Turning away from him, I start to jog down the hall again. My feet are still a little weak beneath me, but the worst of the spinning has gone away, replaced by a dull, throbbing headache.

"Fine," Ezra says, jogging easily beside me. "Then I'm going with you."

I pause again, jabbing my hand at his chest to stop him midstep. "No," I say. "You're not. You're getting Max and Freya, and then you're getting the hell out of here. End of story."

Ezra opens his mouth to protest, but I cut him off. "Max doesn't deserve to *die* here, Ezra. And neither does Freya." I swallow, doing my best to ignore the hard lump in my throat. "*Please*," I add, my voice breaking a little. "Promise me you'll help them."

Ezra's dark brown eyes are unreadable. "Fine," he says at last. "But then I'm coming back for you."

I push myself up on my toes, kissing his cheek. "Has anyone ever told you that you're annoyingly stubborn?"

Ezra slides his arm around my waist, kissing me back for real. "I'm not stubborn," he whispers when he pulls back, grinning. "I'm in love."

I'm still staring after him when he turns the corner, disappearing from sight.

Cassius is waiting for me in the principal's office, his feet propped up on the desk like he owns the place. His suit jacket is long gone, his silk shirt looking decidedly worse for the wear.

There's no sign of Sarita.

"Ah, Miss Morris," Cassius says, making a show of checking his watch. "Welcome. Two minutes late, I see."

His exposed skin looks raw and tender, painfully red and shiny. He's managed to heal the worst of his wounds, but it doesn't look like it's been fun.

"Please," I reply coolly. "We both know you're not wearing a watch."

Cassius smirks. He pushes back the sleeve of his tattered

dress shirt, holding up his bare arm for me to see. His forearm is crosshatched with thin, half-healed scars, the marks glaringly obvious against his marble-white skin. "You always did know me better than anyone, Lilliana," he admits. "It was one of your most endearing qualities."

"Using the past tense already?" I ask sweetly. "You *do* realize that I'm still alive, don't you?"

His mouth tightens. "Believe me," he says, tugging his sleeve back down over his scarred arm. "I am *well* aware of the fact. The UV lights were a nice touch, by the way. It's nice to know that we can still . . . surprise . . . each other."

I fold my arms against my chest, tamping down the fire inside me.

"Where's Sarita?"

"That depends," Cassius says. He leans back in the principal's chair, propping his arms casually behind his head. "Where's Freya?"

"Do you even *care*?" I shoot back.

Cassius shrugs. "Not particularly. I suppose Freya was . . . a means to an end. Though I did appreciate her *loyalty*."

"Sooner or later, she would have seen through you," I say. "She would have grown to *hate* you, Cassius."

I can feel the warmth spreading through me, an almost *electric* heat pulsing at the tips of my fingers.

It feels good.

It feels *right*.

Cassius's smile doesn't touch his eyes. "Maybe," he says. "Maybe not. There's a thin line between love and hate, Lilliana. It certainly took *you* long enough to cross it."

"There's where you're wrong," I whisper softly. "I *never* loved you, Cassius. *Ever.*"

For a second, he looks as though I've knocked the wind out of him.

But of course not.

Cassius hasn't actually drawn breath in centuries.

"You don't mean that," he says, as though he's trying to convince himself.

Somewhere in the distance, I can hear the wail of muffled police sirens; it won't be long before the school is flooded with police.

Fire roils through my palms, the unspent energy reaching a fever pitch.

It's time to end this.

For *good.*

"Trust me," I say, raising my hands in front of me. "I really, *really* do."

But before I can unleash my witch fire, a scuffle echoes through the hallway behind me.

"Sarita! *Sarita!*" I whip my head around at the sound of Maya's voice. "She's here!" Sarita's mom calls. "I found her!"

Another voice floats commandingly down the hallway.

"Spread out," a woman says. "The others can't be far."

Across the room, Cassius snarls.

In a single, terrifyingly graceful movement, he launches himself across the desk. I open my mouth to scream, but it's too late; Cassius's fangs are already buried in my neck.

# CHAPTER Thirty-Eight

IT'S EXCRUCIATING.

Cassius's fangs slice through my throat like tissue paper, ripping my skin to shreds.

Razor-sharp pain cuts through me, my body spiking with panic. I fight uselessly against Cassius's grip, trying desperately to free myself. But every movement only makes the pain worse.

Cassius has begun to drink.

I can feel the blood draining from my veins, the inexorable pull of Cassius's *need*. The floor is cold against my bare shoulders, my still-wet dress clinging soddenly to the linoleum.

Lassitude washes over me as Cassius's fangs cut deeper and deeper.

*So, this is how it ends*, I think vaguely. *Not even with a whimper.*

I let my hands fall to my sides, blinking sluggishly against the overhead lights.

They're not as bright as they were only moments ago.

I can feel myself beginning to slip away when Cassius gives a sudden, rasping *choke.* I gasp as his fangs rip free from my neck, an exciting new wave of pain washing over me. I wrench my hands to my neck, rolling into the fetal position.

Above me, I see a flurry of movement: a crowd of women rushing in from the doorway. I recognize a couple of them from the basement in St. Augustine: Agatha, and the *witchy woman* with long blond hair spilling over her shoulders, Stevie Nicks–style.

*Eleanor?*

*Eloise?*

It doesn't matter.

*Nothing* matters besides the cool-eyed blond woman standing at the front of the group, pinning Cassius in place with a single raised palm.

*The High Priestess.*

Despite the decades that have passed, she looks exactly the same. Even the scent of her Chanel No. 5 hasn't changed.

It shouldn't be possible.

*She* shouldn't be possible.

Witches are *human*, and Montreal was over half a century ago.

And yet . . .

Cassius snarls, blood still dripping from his fangs as he fights against her invisible restraints. She pins him to the wall like a butterfly, then turns in my direction. At the sight of me, bleeding and broken on the floor, her pale pink lips turn smugly upward.

*Like the cat that got the cream*, I think blearily.

There's more commotion near the door, then suddenly Sarita bursts into the office, shaking Maya's grip from her shoulder. "Mom, let me *go*!" Pushing carelessly past the High Priestess, Sarita tumbles to her knees next to me. *"Lily."*

Her eyes widen at the sight of my neck, the panic obvious in her expression. She's covered in a thin layer of grime, sweat and tears cutting rivulets through the coating of blood and dirt on her cheeks.

Beneath it all, I can still catch the sparkle of her body glitter.

*Battle armor*, I try to whisper, but the words come out as a weak gurgle instead.

"You're going to be okay," Sarita says, struggling clumsily out of her tuxedo jacket. With trembling hands, she wads the material into a ball, pressing it to my neck. I notice the angry red marks that weave up her arm as if seared onto the skin by a fiery ribbon. Her binding spell has come undone. I just hope the damage isn't permanent. How many more people can I hurt?

"Do you hear me, Lily?" Sarita asks. "You're going to be *fine*."

There's an unexpected fierceness in her voice, as though if she says the words loud enough, they'll be true.

I want to tell her not to bother with the jacket.

I *want* to tell her that I'm already dead.

But I'm so tired.

The High Priestess spares a glance in Sarita's direction. "And this . . . *dramatic* . . . young woman would be . . ."

"My daughter," Maya says quickly. She steps forward, wringing her hands anxiously in front of her. "Forgive her for interrupting, High Priestess," she says. "But her friend—"

"Is the witch we told you about," Agatha interrupts, bristling with self-importance. "The one with the remarkable powers."

"Remarkable indeed," the High Priestess agrees. She turns back to me, her lips curving into another predatory smile. "No wonder your *vampire* was so desperate to keep you from me."

Cassius snarls again, sending Agatha scuttling backward in alarm. Sarita flinches, but doesn't move, pressing steadily down on my wound.

"Lilliana is off-limits," Cassius growls, his voice full of menace. "We have a *deal*!"

"We *had* a deal," the High Priestess corrects him. "A deal that is now over."

Cassius surges forward, struggling against his bonds like a wild animal caught in a trap. "Lilliana is mine!" he roars. *"Mine!"*

"What is he talking about?" Sarita demands, turning her tearstained face in the High Priestess's direction. "What *deal*?!"

I peer hazily up at Cassius, but I don't need him to say anything. The memories fall slowly into place all on their own.

The innkeeper's wife, back in Lauterbrunnen, the smile fading from her cheeks forever. My silver dress sparkling beneath the disco lights as I stood over Cassius, the slumped body of the bartender lying motionless in front of him.

How many more had there been?

How many had Cassius kept from me?

*Accidents*, he'd said, begging for my forgiveness. *Terrible accidents.*

But what if they hadn't been?

I think back to Montreal, all those years ago: *Cassius, his face drawn, half collapsed against the floor. A white-coated waiter, slumped unmoving on the ground. The cool-eyed blond woman, striding toward me, the air around her already* crackling *with power.*

What if that poor waiter hadn't been caught in the cross fire?

What if Cassius had *turned* him?

*For her?*

"The bloodstone," I whisper, turning toward the High Priestess. "It was just an insurance policy."

Witches are human.

They grow old.

They *die.*

And yet, somehow, the High Priestess looks exactly the same as the day I first saw her.

Whatever she's been doing, it's taken *magic.*

The kind of magic that a witch could only get from draining a vampire.

"You needed *power,*" I rasp. "And you used *Cassius* to get it."

Making a new vampire is almost impossible.

The High Priestess would have needed to find someone old enough, someone *strong* enough to survive the process, again and again and again. Someone who could ensure a near-endless supply of vampires to slay for her own gains.

*Someone like Cassius.*

The High Priestess spares a glance in my direction, smiling thinly.

"The vampire population isn't what it used to be," she says. "Over the years, I've been forced to get . . . *creative*."

She looks at Cassius, who growls, still struggling against her viselike grip.

"I don't understand," Sarita says, her fingers trembling against my neck. "Aren't fewer vampires a *good* thing?"

"*Power* is a good thing," the High Priestess corrects her. She turns back, eyeing me with naked hunger. "It just needs to be properly . . . *harnessed*."

The other night, I'd told Max that my witch fire was only the tip of the iceberg.

*At best, I'm an aberration*, I think. *At worst, I'm a threat.*

At the High Priestess's words, an uneasy ripple runs through the group of women behind her.

Maya steps forward, her expression torn between fear and confusion.

"Surely you don't mean to *take* the girl's power, High Priestess," she ventures. "Lily is one of *us*. She's a witch. She—"

*"Lily!"*

Everyone spins to face the door as Ezra explodes his way into the room, his bruised face blanching at the sight of me and Sarita.

"What happened?" he asks, surging toward us. "What did you *do* to her?"

"Vampire!" Agatha shouts, pointing at Ezra like an old-timey detective fingering the murderer. *"Vampire!"*

The High Priestess gives another *tsk* of annoyance. "Hasn't anyone ever taught these children that it's rude to interrupt?"

With a flick of her wrist, she sends Ezra soaring backward, slamming him into the opposite wall.

Another specimen for her collection.

I reach one hand uselessly in his direction.

"Surely a witch who consorts with *vampires* can be no great loss to the coven," the High Priestess says coolly. "It's best to put her down now. While we still have the chance."

"*You're* the one consorting with vampires!" Sarita says, her voice shaking with rage. "*You're* the one who made a deal with Cassius. *You're* the one who's trying to kill my friend! And for what? More *power*? How many people did you have Cassius turn? How many people have *died* for your greed?"

"We don't have time for this!" Ezra shouts, his shoulders rigid against the wall. "Lily is *hurt*. Someone needs to *help* her!"

"High Priestess, please," Maya pleads. "If we could *talk* about this . . ."

The High Priestess doesn't even bother glancing in her direction. I recognize the manic look in her eyes, can read the greedy twist of her pale pink lips.

The woman standing before me is willing to do anything to get what she wants.

Even if it means killing everyone who gets in her way.

Weakly, I push Sarita's fingers away from my throat. I can feel the fresh wave of blood trickling down my neck as I haul myself unsteadily to my knees.

"You think killing me will be enough to make you immortal once and for all?" I ask the High Priestess. "Then try it. If you want my power, *come take it*."

She steps forward, a moth drawn to my flame.

Her pupils shrink to pinpoints as she stares down at me, her entire existence suddenly narrowing into one razor-sharp emotion: *hunger.*

Her full focus is on me for only a fraction of a second. But a fraction of a second is all that Cassius needs.

Hurling himself free from the High Priestess's invisible hold, he launches himself forward, his fangs ripping into her long, elegant throat.

Someone screams.

It might be me.

Cassius gulps deeply, feeding on the High Priestess's blood. I can see the shock in her expression, the utter *disbelief* as her eyes widen with unfamiliar pain.

With a final, gluttonous swallow, Cassius tosses the High Priestess aside; a rag doll that he's finished playing with.

Blood flows freely down the witch's neck, soaking her ornate collar below. She staggers one step, maybe two. And then, with a small, choked cry, she slumps to the ground, unmoving.

Cassius rolls his head in satisfaction.

"Do you know how long I've been waiting to do that?" he asks, turning to look at me.

I climb to my feet, raising my blood-soaked hands in front of me.

"Cassius," I say, meeting his eyes. "It's not too late to let them go."

"No," he says, his voice sending ice through my all-too-human veins. "You're the one who wanted this, Lilliana. You're the one who chose these weak, pathetic *mortals* over me." He spits the words out quickly, his mouth twisting at the taste of them. "We could have had *forever*, Lilliana," he says. "But instead, you're all going to die."

The witch fire inside me roars like nothing I've ever felt before. I pour everything I am into the blaze: my guilt, and my pain, and my fear, and my longing.

But most of all, my *rage*.

My anger transforms into a towering inferno. "You know nothing about weakness, Cassius." I raise my hand, and I release.

The force of the fire slams Cassius backward, knocking him into the desk, knocking him *through* the desk and into the wall behind it.

I'm already panting with the effort of controlling the blaze, my arms shaking and sweat rolling down my back. Gathering himself, Cassius slices one hand through the swirling flames, cutting them abruptly in half.

I feel the impact as my witch fire flickers once, then twice, a cigarette lighter gasping for its last breath of fuel. I stumble to the side as it extinguishes completely.

But before I can fall, I feel Ezra catch me, his strong, cool hands circling steadily around my waist.

"It's okay," he breathes softly. "I'm here."

"Looks like you're not the only one who learned a few tricks from the witches," Cassius taunts from across the room.

Bracing myself against Ezra, I send another wave of fire in Cassius's direction, bathing the room with searing purple light.

Gritting his teeth against the agony, he fights his way toward me, slowly but inexorably closing the gap between us. Cassius always was the strongest vampire I'd ever met; with my and the High Priestess's blood coursing through his veins, he must be practically invincible.

I send a few more feeble blasts in Cassius's direction, trying in vain to delay him. Dimly, I'm aware of something happening in the room behind me; I catch a flash of blond hair as the *witchy woman* darts forward, dragging the High Priestess toward the door with the help of several other coven members.

"Where are you going?!" Sarita screams, her voice barely audible above the roar of my flames. "We need *help*!"

The heat is growing unbearable, the walls closing in on us as the fire climbs higher and higher. Noxious smoke fills the air, making my eyes water and my throat burn and my lungs cry out with every breath.

But it's still not enough.

As I watch in horror, Cassius takes another step forward, his jaw locked in a silent snarl.

Sarita turns toward Maya, tears streaming from her cheeks. "Mom," she begs. *"Please. Help us."*

This time, Maya doesn't hesitate.

She reaches for Sarita's hand, her mouth tightening with determination. "Lily, listen to me!" she calls. "Sarita and I are going to form a circle! You can focus your power *through us*."

"It's too risky," I say raggedly. "What if I can't control my magic? What if I hurt someone else?"

"Lily, please!" Sarita says. "Just *trust* us."

To my utter astonishment, Agatha steps forward. Looking nearly as surprised as me, she reaches for Maya's hand.

"She's right," Agatha tells me. "Maybe you *used* to be a vampire, but you've *always* been a *witch*. And witches stick together."

Sarita nods, her look of determination mirroring Maya's.

"We're not leaving you, Lily!" she cries. "We're ready!"

Cassius gives another roar, the wordless scream reverberating through the soles of my ruined Vans. His icy blue eyes never leaving mine, he forces his way forward through the flames, one single-minded step after another.

*"Lily,"* Ezra whispers in my ear. *"You've got this."*

Closing my eyes, I let the rest of the world fall away.

I can feel the strength of the circle behind me, the strength that runs through Sarita and Maya and, God help me, even *Agatha*.

Surrendering control, I open myself up to them, letting the circle's magic flow *through* me.

Opening my eyes, I gaze straight at Cassius.

"Don't you understand yet, Lilliana?" He presses another step forward, growing dangerously close now. "You don't belong to *them*. You're mine. *Forever.*"

I glance at Ezra.

Though his eyes are tight with worry, he motions me forward, trusting me completely.

Next to him, Maya smiles reassuringly, squeezing Sarita's hand.

Even *Agatha* manages an awkward nod in my direction.

The warmth that runs through me has nothing to do with my powers.

I turn back to Cassius, lifting my chin.

"You're right," I say. "I *don't* belong to them. I belong *with* them. *Forever.*"

And then, smiling sweetly, I unleash the fire inside me.

# CHAPTER Thirty-Nine

DEATH ISN'T NEARLY AS PEACEFUL AS I THOUGHT it would be.

I can hear the annoying *beep beep beep* of a nearby machine, my temples throbbing along in rhythm.

*Beep.*

*Throb.*

*Beep.*

*Throb.*

I groan, the *throbbing* growing worse in response.

"Lily? Lily? Can you hear me?"

"I think she's waking up."

Blearily, I open my eyes, blinking against the sudden glare of the hospital room. The fluorescent lights spin above me in lazy circles, dancing back and forth like ballerinas onstage. I can practically hear the music that accompanies them: Tchaikovsky's theme from *Swan Lake*.

It's 1877, and I'm at the ballet for the first time in my life.

The dancers whirl gracefully across the stage, their arms fluttering in time to the beat. They bend and dip in perfect rhythm. It's as though they *are* the music, come to life.

*Hum, dee, hmm, hmm, hmm, dee hum . . .*

"Wait," a familiar voice says above me. "Is she *singing*?"

I blink again, trying to clear my vision.

At last, a familiar blond head swims into view.

*"Max?"* I croak, the word scraping painfully against my throat.

Max grins down at me, his smile even brighter than the fluorescent lights. He's wearing an unfamiliar dark blue windbreaker that reads **EMS** down one sleeve; beneath the collar, I can see the edge of a clean white bandage peeking out.

"That's my name," he says. "Don't wear it out."

I nod, gazing up at him in confusion.

Despite his smile, Max isn't looking so hot.

His handsome face is grayish and drawn, every bump making him grimace in pain.

But still.

He's *alive.*

Wait.

If Max is alive . . . does that mean *I'm* alive, too?

*"Lily."* I turn my head, my pulse speeding as Ezra's face swims into view. His dark curls are gleaming in the overhead lights, the bruises on his face almost healed.

For some reason, he looks relieved.

"Hey," he says, a smile breaking across his face. "There you are."

His face is inches away from mine; close enough that I can see the liquid gold swirling in his irises, can count the thick, sooty lashes lining his brown eyes.

Close enough that I can *boop* him on the nose if I want.

I reach up with one unsteady hand, jabbing in the general direction of his face.

*"Boop,"* I whisper.

Ezra smothers another smile, reaching up to pull my hand gently away. "Let's leave the *boop*ing to the professionals for a while," he says. "You're kind of on . . . a *lot* of drugs."

I let my head drop, feeling the thin hospital pillow beneath me. For the first time, I notice that my left arm is strapped to a board, a blood bag running into the IV in the back of my hand.

Ezra is studiously avoiding looking at it.

Slipping my hand from his, I cautiously reach up, touching the side of my neck. I can't help wincing as my fingers graze a thick layer of gauze.

Ezra gently takes my hand again. "Maybe let's try not moving at all."

I lean back against the narrow mattress, closing my eyes.

But a second later, they fly open again.

*"Sarita,"* I say, trying to sit up. "Her mom . . . Agatha . . . We need to . . ."

"Hey, hey, hey," Ezra says, squeezing my hand. "It's okay. Sarita's good, I promise."

"She's on her way to Tallahassee," Max adds, from the other side of the hospital bed. "I guess her mom thought it might be a good idea for Sarita to stay with her dad for a while? At least until they make sure the High Priestess is actually dead. Apparently, there's some . . . confusion . . . on that point." He grimaces, looking appropriately put out by the idea. "Anyway, Sarita says she'll call you soon. And also, to 'keep swimming forward,' whatever that means."

"Wait, Tallahassee?" I repeat, tripping over the syllables. "How . . ."

"Astrid's giving her a ride," Ezra explains, scrubbing his free hand through his curls. "I guess the whole 'Sarita narrowly surviving a gas explosion' thing really sped up the forgiveness process."

"A *gas explosion*? Is *that* what they're saying happened?" I ask.

"They had to tell the police something," Max chimes in. "Not everyone took the vampires-and-witches-are-real explanation quite as well as I did."

"It worked, didn't it?" I ask anxiously. "Cassius is *gone*?"

Ezra nods, his dark eyes never leaving mine. "Yeah," he promises. "He's gone."

Max reaches up to scratch his neck, wincing a little at the movement. "Not to mention about half a city block, as well."

"Was anyone else hurt?" I ask, trying not to puke.

Opening myself up to Maya's circle felt like opening a *floodgate*.

I'm more than happy to close it.

For now, at least.

Max and Ezra exchange a look.

"No," Ezra assures me. "The circle protected you, Agatha, Sarita, and Maya. And seeing as how I can't die . . ." He trails off.

"Honestly, the explosion wasn't even that big," Max says, obviously lying through his teeth.

"And besides," Ezra adds. "The west wing was full of asbestos, anyway."

I close my eyes, mentally filing "that time I magically blew up the school" away for another day.

"Everyone else made it out safe," Ezra says. "Even Freya."

"For the record, that girl does *not* like you," Max says. "I'd stay out of England if I were you."

Oh my God.

*Freya.*

*The bloodstone.*

*EZRA.*

My throat catches as I look up at him.

"I'm sorry," I whisper, hating the hollowness in my voice. "I'm so sorry, Ezra."

He shakes his head, ignoring the dark curls that fall loose against his forehead.

"I already told you," he says softly. "I don't care about the bloodstone, Lily. I care about *you*."

On the other side of the bed, Max awkwardly clears his throat.

"I'm, um . . . I'm going to let one of the doctors know that Lily's awake," he says. "Oh, but before I forget . . . Here." Reaching down, he grabs something from the floor next to him. "These are for you."

I blink as he sets a vase full of daisies down on the bedside table.

"You got me . . . flowers?"

Max grins.

"Yeah, well," he says. "A giant panda seemed weird. Besides, I still owed you a . . . What's it called again?" He holds up one hand, tracing an imaginary line against his wrist.

"Corsage," Ezra says. "It's called a corsage."

"Right," Max says. *"Corsage."*

To my surprise, he bends down, brushing his lips softly against my forehead.

His kiss is warm, and familiar, and safe.

Exactly like Max.

"I'll talk to you soon, okay?" he says.

"Yeah," I say, swallowing the lump in my throat. "Talk to you soon."

As the door swings shut behind him, leaving us alone, I turn to Ezra.

"You need to go, too," I say, struggling to sit up. "You need to leave Sunrise Harbor. *Now.* Maya and Agatha might have helped us back at the school, but the rest of their coven will still be looking for you. And if the High Priestess is alive . . . It's not *safe* for you here, Ezra. It might never be safe here again."

Ezra shrugs.

"Actually," he says, "I've been thinking about taking a gap year. I've heard good things about Paris."

"Paris?" I ask blankly.

"Yeah," he says. "Someone once told me that Disneyland Paris is worth a second chance. And besides, they have lots of other stuff, too. The Catacombs . . . the Musée d'Orsay . . . the third-largest covenstead in all of Europe . . ."

My sluggish brain is having trouble keeping up.

"The . . . the *what*?"

Did Ezra say "covenstead"?

"I know that 'stealing a bunch of bloodstones from an ancient witch stronghold' isn't exactly everyone's dream vacation," Ezra goes on with another shrug. "But still. I was thinking that maybe you'd want to . . . join me? Unless you have other plans."

I can feel a strange sort of warmth flowing through my veins.

And, sure, it might be the blood transfusion.

But also, it might be . . . *happiness*?

"Paris sounds nice," I say. "There's just one condition . . ."

Ezra leans forward, eagerly tucking a lock of curly hair behind his ear. "Anything."

"Promise me," I say. "Under *no* circumstances are we committing a heist."

"Yeah," Ezra whispers, already lowering his mouth to mine. "Sorry to tell you this, but we're *definitely* committing a heist."

# Acknowledgments

Thank you, thank you, thank you to Ellen Goff, Carrie Hannigan, Natalie Sun, and everyone else at HG Literary for continuing to believe in me (and my increasingly unhinged book ideas). There are no words for how lucky I feel to work with you.

Elizabeth Stranahan, I'm beyond grateful for your hard work/brilliant ideas/phenomenal editorial skills. This book is a million times better because of you.

Huge thanks to Trisha Previte for designing the cover of my dreams, and to the amazing Halsey Berryman for bringing it so perfectly to life. Clare Perret, thank you for making me seem smarter than I am. Thanks to Megan Shortt, Rebecca Vitkus, Liz Sutton, Kelly McGauley, Josh Redlich, Caroline Abbey, and everyone else on the Random House team for all their hard work; it is very, very much appreciated.

Ben, thank you for everything, always. Fitz, you're the best writing sidekick in the entire world. And Wyle, someday you'll realize that vampires are cool.

This book was written (and rewritten and rewritten . . .) in three-hour stretches in a study room at the George Culver

Community Library. I'd like to give a heartfelt *thank-you* to everyone who's made me feel so welcome there over the past fifteen years, with a special shout-out to Katelyn, who's been there since the very beginning.

Libraries are awesome.

They're where I learned to love reading, sure, but they're so much more than that. When I was a kid, our local library was where my family went to check out a VCR and watch *Star Wars* together for the very first time. As a teenager, it was where I went to take my driver's test (which, unlike my sister, I passed on the first try). As an adult, living on my own in a tiny apartment with no internet, the library was where I went to check my email and stay connected with my friends and family. It's where I first developed a crush on my husband, aka "Cute Public Library Boy." Weirdly, it's also where I found out I was pregnant with our second child. As a new mom, isolated and overwhelmed, our local library felt like an escape—just a physical *place* to go that was safe and welcoming and *free*. A place where I could talk to other caregivers, and meet new people, and make friends. A place where it was okay for our kids to play for hours and hours on end, or throw a tantrum the minute we walked in, or fall asleep on the story-time rug. A place we could come back the next day, and the next, and the next . . .

I'll say it again; libraries are awesome.

*Support* them.

And they'll support you.

# About the Author

**DARCY MILLER** is the author of several children's books, including *Roll* and *Margot and Mateo Save the World*. Her Strangeville School series has appeared on multiple state awards lists and been praised by *Kirkus Reviews* as "wonderfully weird and extremely entertaining." *I Am Not a Vampire (Anymore)* is Darcy's first novel for teens. She lives in Wisconsin with her two children, her librarian husband, and way too many pets.